DRAGON RAIDER

Sea Dragons Trilogy Book One

AVA RICHARDSON

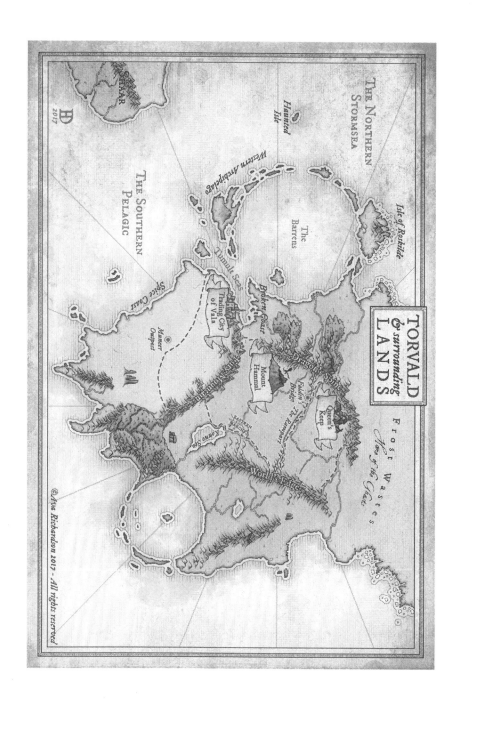

THE NORTHERN STORMSEA

SELLAR

Haunted Isle

Western Archipelago

Isle of Ruslild

THE SOUTHERN PELAGIC

The Barrens

Tumult Sea

Spice Coast

Trading City of Vala

Broken Spear V...

Mamert Outpost

Dragon Spine

Mount Hannal

Valdin's Bridge

Ta'Rampart

Queen's Keep

World's Edge

TORVALD & surrounding LANDS

Frost Wastes Maw of the Glacier

CONTENTS

SEA DRAGONS TRILOGY

Dragon Raider

Dragon Crown

Dragon Prophesy

Cover Design by Joemel Requeza

www.relaypub.com

DRAGON RAIDER

MAILING LIST

Thank you for purchasing 'Dragon Raider'
(Sea Dragons Trilogy Book One)

I would like to thank you for purchasing this book. If you
would like to hear more about what I am up to, or continue to
follow the stories set in this world with these characters—then
please take a look at:

AvaRichardsonBooks.com

You can also find me on me on
www.facebook.com/AvaRichardsonBooks

Or sign up to my mailing list:
AvaRichardsonBooks.com/mailing-list/

BLURB

Will adapting to a changing world make one young woman lose touch with where she came from?

Far from the kingdom of Torvald, on the Western Isles near the coast, Sea Dragons rule the skies. Lila is the daughter of the Raider leader, destined to take his place one day aboard their plundering ships. Her people value only what shiny trinkets they can get their hands on, but she aspires to much more than that: Lila wants the Raiders to become Dragon Mercenaries, dragon riders who help protect merchant fleets and navies from attack. Her father Kasian is skeptical, but a young monk named Danu—with a quest of his own—comes bearing a prophecy claiming that Lila is the lost heir of Roskilde, a born Dragon Rider.

With Danu's guidance, Lila finds the unruly dragon she's

destined to bond with—but the mismatched pair soon learn that much more than just their futures is at stake.

PROLOGUE
THE ROSKILDE PROPHECY

*C*hurning *seas, bright with blood. Fire billowing over the water, and dark skies heavy with thunder...*

"Aii!" The old woman awakes with a start to find herself in her simple round room in her simple round hut. The inner walls are dark, though she knows with the dawn the plaster will gleam white. The floor is yet the solid, deep mahogany planks she has trod for decades. The roof is still the weathered, bone-white but also bone-strong giant supports of giant drift-wood, with heavy, warm thatch over that. Here are not the churning and frothing waters of her dreams. Not the billows of fire, not the dark storm skies.

The old woman sighs deeply, patting her frail chest as if to quiet the night terrors that had so recently fluttered there.

To say that this woman is old is an understatement. Chabon Kaidence is beyond ancient. Her pale skin is deeply lined as if cracked, and her eyes are sunken – but there is still a spark of vitality within their depths, like hidden stars. Even the folds and wrinkles of her skin still glows despite its age.

The Matriarch of the West Witches has been alive for a long time, long enough to know when a dream has stopped being just that, and has instead, become a prophecy.

A pale hand moves unsteadily to the wicker table, where a silver bell sits on piece of rough-woven, colorful fabric. She rings it, once, for the silver chime to cut through the night like a shooting star.

"Mother?" A voice sounds almost immediately at the heavy purple curtains that hang over her door, and, for a moment Chabon blinks from the glare of brighter light outside.

"You fool!" snaps another voice behind the first, and into her room step two women: one is tall and lean, with skin the color of rich, warm earth, and the other is as pale as Chabon lying before them. The first has braids of black hair falling behind her back like tree roots, whereas the pale woman has fields of golden hair streaming behind her like sunshine. It is this fair and pale woman who snaps at her darker colleague.

"Afar, you'll blind the Mother. Turn off that light!" she says angrily, pushing her way into the room to cross the mahogany floor and stand at Chabon's bedside.

Afar scowls for a moment, but she does as she is advised, turning the notches on the lantern until it only emits a dulled, yellowish glow as she steps into the room. Behind her, the

Matriarch catches a glimpse of the wooden walkways that stretch from one hut to the next, crisscrossing the island of Sebol like vines.

"I am blinded by the darkness, Ohotto, not the light," Chabon breathes to her two most-trusted sisters amongst the witches.

"Yes, Mother." Ohotto hangs her pale head in shame, as Afar steps to her bedside bringing with her a pouch of rich and nourishing purple berry juice.

"Are you thirsty, Mother? Do your aches pain you?" Afar says in her heavy voice. She is not a native to these Western Islands, but she has spent many years here, under Chabon's tutelage.

"No time to drink. I will repeat a dream for you, a night-mare – and I want you both to remember it, and to set it down on paper as soon as you can," Chabon says. "It is a nightmare that I have had many times over the years, but now it comes frequently, every moon! Every week!"

"A prophecy." Afar nods her head in awe. This will not be the first such prophecy that has fallen from the oldest witch's lips. Afar Nguoa just hopes that it is also not the last.

"The seas are churning, bright with blood, and atop the waves there are flames," Chabon intones, her voice carrying in the still airs of her hut. "There is a darkness to the skies, a darkness that is more than thunder, but a darkness as if the sun is blocked by great wings…." The old woman wets her lips, remembering the other parts of the nightmare that she has had throughout her life. Like the stationary stars in the sky can suddenly coalesce into a constellation when one squints at them right, so the nightmares fall into place, one after another.

"There is a child, born from the waters. A girl, rising from the north-east sea, under a dragon's angry call and upon her head is a crown made of leaping waves."

"The Sea Crown of Roskilde," the fair-haired Ohotto Zanna states quickly. It is a famous artefact, even out here in the wild and furious lands of the western archipelago.

"Yes, child," Chabon breathes. "I believe it to be so. The royal crown of the island realm of Roskilde, green-gold like leaping waves, fashioned of old to protect the island for all time." Chabon's starry eyes flutter, and she starts to recount her dreams once more. "The Sea Crown will be lost, and then it will be found once more, but the one who finds it will not come from the royal line. A girl will rise from the sea to seize the crown, with a bloody sword in her hand, and in her other she holds fire."

"What does it mean, Mother? Will this girl be a usurper? A tyrant, seeking the Sea Crown?" Ohotto interrupts.

"Wait, sister, let the Matriarch finish…" Afar whispers, as Chabon coughs, looks confused.

"There was something else – what was it? A boy. A boy with a forked tongue… But what part did he play? I cannot remember!" Chabon looks deeply hurt, before her breath eases a little deeper. "The boy and the girl. They will bring with

4

them blood and fury, and before them and behind them there will be the dead..."

The Matriarch sighs, and a shudder runs through her body. Her eyes slowly close, and her hand relaxes.

"Mother!" Afar Nguoa, the dark-skinned witch of Sebol whispers, bending down to touch the old woman's hand.

"Is she....?" Ohotto's breath hitches is the night.

"No, Chabon sleeps, that is all, but I fear that even the Matriarch of the West Witches is coming near her end." Afar frowns deeply as she gently smooths the older woman's long white hair away from her brow, and pulls the blankets a little closer around her sleeping form. "We must write down the prophecy," Afar says. "What shall it be called?"

"The Prophecy of Roskilde – and we can only pray that it will not come true, for it is terrible," Ohotto Zanna states, her eyes searching the darkness for clues and answers that do not come so easily. "If this child rises from the seas to claim the Sea Crown, the delicate peace we have with Havick of Roskilde will fall. Years of our work will be for nothing."

PART I

To Catch a Dragon...

CHAPTER 1

LILA, DRAGON-THIEF!

The claw print in the sand was huge. *Much* larger than even I had expected. *Hang on a minute. I thought that fisherman had told me that this island was inhabited by the sea-greens dragons?* I bit my lip, glad at least that I didn't have my foster-father here to watch my moment of fear. Chief Kasian of Malata was known as a harsh man, even amongst us proud Sea Raiders of the Western Oceans.

The sun was starting to burn off the sea fog that clutched onto this bit of rock where I'd directed my little skiff, revealing that, in all other ways it was just as I had been told: a tiny, rock-topped atoll with a smattering of trees and a golden beach skirting its northern side. This little islet had no name other than a designation, "the last bit of rock before you get to Sebol" the old sea-salt fisherman had told me, and it was on this beach that I had found my first evidence of the dragons.

A track of claw prints, each almost the size of my little boat. Not that the skiff was very big – I had chosen the skiff from my father's flotilla for its speed rather than strength. But still, I calculated quickly – if this foot was that big, then that meant that the leg would be as big as a tree, and the body it connected to… I shuddered. The beast would be, even at the very least, larger than most of the huts and houses on my father's island-rule of Malata.

"You *did* say that this was a bad idea," I murmured at my father, far away and doubtless angry at the fact that I had gone off *again* to try and find the dragons.

And their eggs.

Still, there was little that I could do other than press on. I was Lila of Malata, adopted daughter to the chief of the notorious Sea Raiders of the Western Isles. I did not shirk from a challenge. I *was* the challenge.

The tracks led to the head of the beach and the rocks beyond. The white stone was crisscrossed with lines of black – Bonerock, my people called it. Notoriously hard to shape, it formed the core of many of these little islands that speared the Western Seas. Moving as lightly and as quietly as I could, I passed into the rocks and started climbing, toward the dark cave openings where this dragon must have made its lair.

⁂

It's a long way down from here. I pushed away the thought as I climbed. Why did dragons have to make their dens on the tops of things? Why couldn't they live in nests on the ground? The soft goatskin leather of my gloves was already scuffed and torn, and I could feel the edges of the rock beneath. The heat was making me sweat, and I was glad I had managed to argue my difficult hair into the warrior's braid this morning. *Just a few more feet—*

"Ach!" My foot slipped, and instantly pain tore along my shoulders and arms as I hung from the rocks. *Don't look down. Don't look down...*

I looked down. Beneath me, the rocky walls jagged and snarled out, with the occasional tuft of scrubby sea grass, all the way to the frothing grey-blue ocean below.

Sweet Seas... I breathed, my stomach lurched and my limbs trembled in that way they always did when I was forced to be anywhere up high.

"Don't overthink! Do!" my father would have shouted at me. He had tried to drum this fear of heights out of me ever since he had found it in the child he had rescued after the raid had taken her parents. I closed my eyes, gritting my teeth as I tried to remember the lessons he drilled into me. "You're a Raider, Lila! The most fearsome thing on the four oceans! Nothing stops you. Not a bit of wind under your feet!" And then he would tell me to get up that rigging and tie off that knot, or secure the sail anyway. I had to do it.

"Think of your crewmates waiting for you! What if we had one of that brute's Man-o-Wars on our tail? Your crew are depending on you!" He would shout, which would spur me to get up there and do what I had to do anyway, admittedly with shaking fingers and taking twice as long as any other of the Raider sailors.

Just like I had to do this.

Because if I don't do this, the Raiders are finished. I gritted my teeth, opened my eyes, and pulled. My back screamed in pain, but I managed to bring myself up to the height of the cave opening, my boots kicking on the Bonerock until I found a purchase and – "Ugh!"— I flopped over into the shallow depression before the dragon's lair, panting and wheezing, and waiting for my heart to slowly calm down to just a dull roar, rather than a thunder.

Slowly, the world came back into focus. I was Lila Malata. I was alive. And I was here because my father's Sea Raiders were getting themselves decimated by the self-styled Lord Havick of Roskilde. The Roskildean ships were larger and stronger than ours, and they always seemed to know which shipping routes we were heading for. They would be out there already as if expecting us, ambushing our smaller, faster boats with fire and catapult, and slowly my father's mastery of the seas was being whittled away. I didn't think that we Sea Raiders had another generation in us if this plan didn't work.

The darkness of the cave beckoned. Disturbingly, there was a litter of bones on the front "porch." Small bones as long as my finger, which I guessed were the spines of the marlin fish that the sea green and blue dragons adored so much. I hoped they were that, anyway.

"Lady Dragon... Great Dragon...?" I called out hesitantly, my voice, used to shouting orders from the decks piers as it was, sounding small and hesitant in the darkness. *How are you supposed to talk to dragons, anyway?* I had no idea. We Raiders didn't exactly have a big library, although I had tried to get through the collection of scrolls that my adopted mother Pela of Malata kept. Each one had been stolen from the captain's quarters of some merchant ship or another, and only a few had talked about the great Dragon Academy of Torvald.

And Queen Saffron, I thought, feeling a flush of borrowed courage. The tales said that she was like me, almost. Not a Raider of course, but she was a Western islander who had managed to tame a sea green and blue dragon, and ride on her all the way to the citadel of Torvald, where she defeated the evil King Enric, and there reinstated the Dragon Academy with Lord Bower.

If she can do it, so can I, I thought – and I wasn't even dreaming of flying off to take over a city far from home. I just wanted to raise an egg for my father, and save my adopted people from being wiped out.

Thankfully, however, that old fisherman who had told me that there was a dragon cave here on this atoll had also told me that the dragons go off hunting early in the morning, meaning that their nest would be unprotected. I wasn't *quite* so foolish as to attempt to steal a dragon's egg with an angry mother still sitting on it!

No noise from inside. Good. The footprints I had seen couldn't have been fresh. The last thing I wanted to do was disturb a mother dragon as it sat on its eggs! I crept forward, letting my eyes adjust to the gloom before I could make out the deep piles of dried twigs and grasses making a rough nest. It was warm in here, and made me want to yawn. But what if there was *more* than one dragon in here? What if the old fisherman had been wrong?

Focus, Lila! I told myself. Don't overthink. Do!

Cautiously grabbing onto one edge of the nest, I pulled myself up around the edge and stared inside.

Three eggs. Three, glorious dragons – each the size of my head, fat and round, and heavy with the life that they contained inside. One was blue, one was yellow-orange, and one was a speckled turquoise.

۞

Which one? I hadn't been prepared for this. I had thought through every eventuality on the way here – how I would drag the skiff up to the line of scrub trees and hide it in case any of Havick's scouting vessels were out, how I would race down the beach if I was disturbed... But not which type of dragon I should choose to save the Raiders. In fact, it was faintly baffling *why* there were three completely different eggs here in the first place. I thought dragons might be like the sea birds of the cliffs: one set of parents, one egg – but what if they were more like the sturdy little island goats – all of the nannies and kids together in one warm place? *Could there be multiple dragon mothers laying eggs in one nest?*

The danger had just escalated three-fold, if that was the case. I would need to be quick.

Could I take all three? I patted the canvas sack on my back and knew that it wouldn't hold more than one. I could feasibly put one down my shirt and *maybe* be able to climb back down one handed—

Ugh. No. A sudden wave of vertigo just at the memory of that awful climb swept over me. "Okay then, not three…" I whispered, wondering just *how* angry a mother dragon would get if she lost two of her eggs rather than just one.

Pretty angry, I guessed. An angry mother dragon was the very *last* thing that we Raiders needed on our heads. *But one egg? Surely, she won't miss one out of three, right?*

But which one? I looked at the blue, the orange, the turquoise. The blue dragons were long and thin, right? And the sea-green turquoise where the commonest sorts of dragons we had around here. They flew in flocks, small but fast, sharp beak-like snouts as they dove into the water and out.

But what about the orange? Did they even *have* orange dragons way over in the Dragon Academy? Wouldn't it be something when word reached the court of Queen Saffron that a Raider girl had managed to train a rare orange?

Didn't they have orange dragons down in the southern kingdom? I cursed the fact that, not for the first time, we Raiders had to rely on rumors from passing travelers or stolen bits of knowledge and lore we could get from our plunder. If only I knew more about dragons!

The blue will be quick, but they have notoriously difficult tempers, I thought as my hand hovered over the blue egg. The orange dragons of the deserts haven't even been tamed yet. My hand wavered over that one. It would be a great accolade, but I had no way of knowing if it would be a disaster. At least with the speckled turquoise – which had to turn into our more local sea green and blue, right? – at least with that one I had seen them flying, I knew a little bit about them?

I grabbed the warmth of the egg, and at that exact moment two things happened.

The egg *pulsed* with a beat, as the creature inside hammered on its thick shell. "Huh!" I gasped, and the air about the cave was split with the trumpeting call of a returning mother dragon.

"Skreyar!"

CHAPTER 2

DANU, COMPASS WHISPERS.

The small compass needle that my master Afar Nguoa gave me spun wildly, first this way and then that, and I wondered if maybe the dark-skinned witch of the Southlands had been wrong all along.

Maybe I'm not meant to ever be a mage. Maybe this prophecy is all just some fevered dream and fantasy!

The stars knew that the coven called the Western Witches had been wrong before. The head of our Order, the ancient Chabon Kaidence had been the very one to dream up this little bit of prophecy – that there was a rightful heir to the island realm of Roskilde, one who would overthrow the usurper Havick and restore law and peace to the Western Isles.

"But then again," I said to the no one and nobody that I shared my boat with, "Chabon was also the one to claim that the Dark King Enric would rule for five hundred years – and look what they say happened to him?" The Dark King of Torvald had been overthrown by an upstart boy and a girl from the Western Isles, or so they claimed them to be, and now, almost twenty years later, the Kingdom of Torvald was one of the most powerful realms in the world.

'Prophecies can be turned awry, Danu – just as often as they can come true...' That was what Ohotto Zanna, the other Western Witch I had trained under had counselled me. To me, that sounded a bit like a get-out. If a prophecy could either fail or come to existence equally, then surely that means that some prophecies are just plain old *wrong*?

"But not this one," I whispered. *Please, not this one...*

My personal mentor Afar had been of the opinion that this was one of Chabon's more accurate dreams. It shared the same qualities of other important dreams that Chabon had experienced in the past—it occurred as a nightmare, it kept repeating itself – but it also seemed to match what was happening 'out here' in the Western Isles. The royal line of Roskilde failed some seventeen years ago when their boat was butchered by Sea Raiders, and Havick rose to power. The Sea Crown since then had never sat on its rightful bearer. That not only *was* this going to come to pass, but it also *had* to come to pass. Afar, with her caustic humor, curved ivory staff of office and her dark eyes was more of the opinion that if you wanted magic to work, then you had to get out there and *do something*. Which was partly the reason why I found myself here, on this boat in the middle of the Western Ocean, and about as far from the witches enclave of Sebol as I had ever been.

That, and the fact that if I could prove this prophecy was coming true. I stared hard at the horizon. If I could have a hand in making it happen, then Afar would nominate me to go forward in my training. I would no longer be "Adept Danu" but would instead start the mage training. "Mage Danu of the West." I rolled the title around in my head. It had a nice ring to it, didn't it?

Of course, I would still have many, many years of studying before I graduated with the blessing of Afar and Ohotto and Chabon and all of the other Western Witches on the Isle of Sebol – but I would have done it! I would be the first mage trained in a hundred years! No man had managed to master the arts that came so naturally to the Western Witches. I had to do it. I had to prove that I was right in following this thread of prophecy... That I had the talent for magic in the same way that Afar or Chabon or any other did...

So, once again, I took a deep breath and tried to quiet my excited thoughts. I tried to remember the dream fragments, the very ones that Afar had told me meant that I was deeply connected to this particular prophecy.

A girl. A baby rising from the seas, and the crown of Roskilde on her head.

Suddenly, the compass hand started to slow in its maddened spinning, and pulled slowly, deliberately, north-east. It had to be a sign. It had to be a part of the magic that was in my veins. I looked out into the layer of blue and grey where the sky met the water. Was that a distant shadow of rock there? An outcrop of land, straight in the direction that the needle pointed?

"Come on, please – more…" I tried again, tried to find the pulse of magic inside my heart... But it was no good. The compass returned to its maddened wavering and wobbling once more. "Gah!" I could have thrown it overboard, I was so frustrated. Why was it that my magic could manifest only at certain times – when I was angry or upset or filled with great passion, and the rest of the times it was erratic and unsteady?

Would even Afar believe me if I told her that I had managed to make the compass needle point the way towards the prophecy?

Annoyed and feeling very far from 'Mage Danu of the West' I grabbed the tiller with one hand and pulled on the sail rope, to catch the breeze that would shoot me over the waters, straight to the island I had thought I had seen.

It had to be there. It had to be…

CHAPTER 3
LILA, AND FISH-BOY

"SKRECH!" The roar was deafening as I fell backwards from the nest, the speckled-turquoise egg abandoned next to its siblings, and stumbled backwards onto the ledge of the cave.

"Sweet Mother of the Waves…" I breathed the familiar Raider half-blessing, half-curse as I looked at what was coming for me.

There was a Sinuous Blue dragon, filling the sky like a thunder cloud as it spun around the outcrop, its long, coiling and curling body stretching halfway around to the other side of the small islet.

I didn't know much about dragons, but I knew that it could have killed me in an instant if it had wanted to. *So, it hasn't killed me yet. Maybe it won't fight near its eggs. Maybe it doesn't want to kill me…* But its roar shook the Bonerock, and made me think of the clash of storm lightning or the deep tumult of the hurricane seas. She held her claws tucked up under her body, but I could see that each one was as long as a Raider's sword, and could easily tear me in two.

But Queen Saffron had lived with the dragons, I told myself again, trying to bolster my thin courage. *She had managed to master any fear she had of them – and if she can, I can!* I crouched on the ledge, widening my stance as the Sinuous Blue flew closer in tighter spirals.

"Lady Dragon!" I called out to it, but the words were torn from my lips by a mighty buffet of wind from the dragon's wings as she came in to land.

"Woah!" I staggered on the edge, seeing just what a long way down that it was going to be. I couldn't even climb that fast, without the mother blue picking me off like a crab on the shoreline. My stomach churned, and the ground shook as those great claws seized the rocks of the atoll and the Sinuous Blue curled her body protectively around the rocks, like a snake coming to eat its prey.

"La-lady dragon, I have a request!" I managed to breathe once more as a head the size of my boat swung around the final bend to regard me, her golden eyes flashing. I was terrified. I was in awe. They said the eyes of a dragon had the power to enchant you, if you let them – and I had to say that they were beautiful and awful at the same time, in the same way that a sea storm can also be tremendous when you are tucked safe in your fort, but able to look through the shutters as bolts of lightning tore apart the sky.

Her snout was beak-like, with many rows of needle-sharp teeth that she was showing me. She had the swept-back horns of her breed, and I swore I could see sparks drifting from her nostrils as she focused on me, opened wide her mouth, and *bellowed.*

"Aiii!" I couldn't help myself. I screamed as the bellow of dragon anger pushed me back, almost bowling me over as I was buffeted, one foot losing its footing, and the other reaching out to find solid ground—but there was no solid ground underneath it, only thin air...

۞

Blue and white.

Up and down made no sense, and my limbs were shouting in agony, but I resisted the urge to open my mouth and scream. *'Kick out! Right yourself! Kick up!'* That was the training my father had given me. He had thrown me into the small harbor water myself at seven years old, along with all of the other native-born Raider kids to learn how to swim.

Froth, rock, the buffeting of strong currents.

The water flared from white to dark all around me. No sense using my eyes. Use my feet, my hands, any other sense instead.

The bottom of the atoll's rocky cliffs was a churning crush

of currents, relentlessly battering the Bonerock. My arms and shins stung with scrapes from where I must have already been thrown against the rocks under water, but the action wasn't so violent now. I must be between the wave crashes, or else underneath them. My feet scraped on rock and through silt, and I knew that *up* was the other direction of that.

Luckily for me, if there was anything that we Raiders were good at other than capturing merchant ships, it was swimming. My father's isle of Malata held swimming competitions several times a year, and there was rarely a month that went by without the need to get wet, as we say. It might be working on the hulls of a boat, or hauling up the crab pots, or simply swimming for the joy of it. I wasn't the best swimmer on the island, but I was as good as most – and that made me better than any non-Raider, I was sure of it.

Dive under the waves. Use the pulling-out. Avoid the crash. I fought to keep my mouth closed as I moved, getting away from the rocks and further out along the coastline, knowing that I had to move quickly lest I be taken up by the next wave surge and smashed once more.

My chest burned with the need to take a breath – but not yet. Make sure I wasn't in danger of the waves taking me first…

I kicked again, and then again, before I had to get to the surface. Using the dolphin movements, I angled myself up towards the lighter blues, greys, and finally the bursting whites of the sky as I popped up like a cork, to find that I had drifted a good hundred feet or more from the bottom of the cliffs around the edge of the island.

"Ugh." I coughed, spluttered, bobbing in the water as I checked that the dragon wasn't following me (it wasn't; there were wisps of smoke emerging from the dark opening—it must have retreated into the cave, its ill-tempered residence). Then I tried to get my bearings. Where was the beach from here? My boat? This far out, the waves were slowly pulling me out, dragging me into the Western Ocean more than they were pushing me towards the atoll. I would have to use every bit of strength to fight it to get back, and I was already tired with bleeding legs and arms...

But what else could I do? I couldn't return to father empty-handed, he already thought that this was a crazy scheme. I couldn't allow the Raiders to fail when Havick came to cut them down.

"Ahoy! Ahoy!" Someone was shouting, and, as the sudden swell of the ocean lifted me up, I saw what the hummocks of water had hidden from me before: rounding the atoll's rocks was a tiny sailboat with a figure braced against the tiller and the rope, cutting the prow straight towards me...

Who was he? I wondered, seeing the white crossed-over tunic, the heavy trousers and the waved robe of a stocky figure. Not old though. A bit younger than me, perhaps, but a teenaged boy nonetheless.

I was in no position to refuse this stranger's help, even though I knew that most islanders hated us Raiders, and would sell us out to Havick as soon as look at us… But he pulled alongside me and threw out – quite expertly, I had to admit – a thick rope, attached to buoys of cork wood.

"Grab a hold!" he shouted at me, as if I had never had to do this before in my life. Gratefully, however, I seized the ends of the rope and let my unlikely savior do the hard work of pulling me in.

❦

CHAPTER 4

LILA, THE PRINCESS

"Just what do you think you were doing?" the young man said to me, his eyes wide in a glare of shock. Not the rescue welcome I was expecting, I had to admit as I sat on the bottom of his tiny boat, wringing out my braid of hair over the side. I was, of course, absolutely soaked from head to toe – but at least the sun was high. In that Raider's way, I just shook my head and changed my expectations. If you live at sea, you get wet.

"What do you mean?" I said to the young man irritably. *Who was he to talk to me like that?* He looked only barely old enough to be running a boat on his own, with his soft skin and large, almond-shaped eyes. He had ragged brown hair, edged with bronze gold tips, and wore an over-robe of green to ape the sort that the witches and mystics of the south wore, and he'd said that his name was Danu.

"That's one of the Dragon Isles," Danu said emphatically, as if it were something that *everyone* knew.

"Yeah?" I said. *That was why I was there, dummy!*

"And that particular isle has got a nesting mother on it right now. Brood mothers get *really* twitchy around their eggs – we're lucky that she's not hanging over us right now, trying to cook us to a crisp," he said seriously.

You're telling me? I thought. I had stood right in front of that brood mother, and I had looked down her gullet, straight past her rows of sharp teeth. But still, I wasn't going to tell this guy that, or why I was here. "I'm not scared of a dragon," I lied.

"Well, you should be," the fisherman's son said with a frown as he tugged on the guideline, leaning in and against the wind as he did so to angle our boat away from the atoll.

Away from the atoll, my mind suddenly caught up with what the rest of me was thinking. *Away from my boat.*

"Hey! Wait – I need to go back," I said quickly, half standing easily in the boat and pointing back at the atoll which was now considerably smaller on the horizon.

"What? No!" Danu shook his head. "I think you've had enough sightseeing for one day, don't you think?" He cleared his throat, and said in a high-minded voice, "Dragons are not creatures for our amusement…"

Pig, I thought. Great. I get saved by the most uptight fisherman's boy in the entire Western Ocean. "I wasn't going there to look at dragons," I said fiercely.

"Why where you going to a dragon's island, then?" Danu glared at me. Who did he think he was? Like he owned this stretch of ocean, did he?

"None of your business! Now I need to go back to that island because I have left my boat there, and I need my boat to get back to my homeport," I stated.

"Pffft. It's not worth getting yourself eaten over. *I* can take you home..." He said the last bit awkwardly, like he really would have preferred to be going back to whatever he was doing out there in nowheresville, Western Ocean.

"No," I said flatly. There was no way that I could let this guy sail me back to Malata and the other Raiders. The Sea Raiders had only managed to survive so far by being *very* secretive as to their homeports. Could I trust this kid? "If you won't take me back to the island, I'll just have to swim." I took a breath and prepared to dive overboard—

"No. Wait. Hold on!" The boy turned his little skiff around, catching the wind as he did so. "I don't particularly want to go out of my way anyway. I have important business to the north-east," he said in that high and mighty tone.

Important business catching fish, I thought, but nodded to him all of the same. "Thank you." I nodded. "And I suppose thank you for helping me out of the sea, as well," I said through pursed lips. I didn't say thank you very often to someone who wasn't a Raider. My father had told me that many of the fishermen throughout the Western Isles were loyal to the Roskildeans and their brutish king, Lord Havick.

But a debt owed is a debt owed, I thought. I could at least say thank you for his act of kindness. Just so long as I didn't tell him where I really lived. It turned out, however, that I didn't really need to tell him anything, as the very next words out of his mouth were, "You're a Raider, aren't you?"

Was that a mixture of fear and awe that I heard in his voice?

"No," I said stubbornly, although my light garb, my heavy leather belt with its numerous hooks and hoops (for the many weapons and climbing lines we used on our ships), and my brightly colored headscarf probably made it obvious.

"You are. I can see it." Danu's eyes widened. "What would a Raider girl want with a dragon's nest?"

"None of your business, fish boy," I said, wondering if I really should have jumped into the drink instead.

"What? I'm no fish boy, I'm a mage!" he had the audacity to say. I turned to frown at him, as his lie seemed so obvious as to make even the water laugh. Looking at him again, I saw he had that stocky build and the weather-worn hands of someone who had spent a life on and off the waves. He *looked* like a fisherman's son, but if so, then he was a *long* way out of the normal fishing lanes and he *looked* barely old enough to be out here on the open oceans alone – and besides, there hadn't been a mage since the times of the mad old tyrant Hacon Maddox!

"Are you now, fish boy?" I laughed. The boy was mad, clearly a maddened youth who had stolen his father's boat and probably drunk too much salt water out here on the ocean. Strange how he didn't look dehydrated or sun-seared, but either way – he was either mad or he was a liar.

"I am! I'm training under Afar Nguoa of the West Witches!" He burst out, as if that name meant anything to me, or hadn't just been made up. "Okay, so I may not be an entire mage yet, I'm only an Adept – but I'm training to be one..." he said. "Danu Geidt, Adept of the West Witches," he said his name proudly once more.

"Whatever you say, Danu Geidt." I rolled my eyes. "And I am Lila. Lila of the Dragon Riders of Torvald."

The boy flushed a deeper color. "You are *not* a Dragon Rider," he said in clipped tones. "If I were going to guess, I would say that your people are much *more* comfortable sailing the waves than riding dragons..."

"What do you mean by that?" I returned.

"You dress like a pirate. A Raider," the boy said, and I felt a stab of anxiety. What was he going to do now? Try to threaten me? *Me – a dangerous pirate-Sea Raider?* No, he might be right that I wasn't a Dragon Rider, I thought with a flash of annoyance. But I will be one day. I will tame and train my own dragon, just as the queen herself did!

It must have been the boy's words that made me say, "Go on then, do some magic if you are some great mage-in-training, fish boy." I crossed my hands over my chest. The island was a lot closer now, and luckily, I wouldn't have to spend too much longer in this braggart's company.

I watched Danu squint his eyes, frowning. "It takes years to learn how to perform just one simple spell, Lila-the-Raider. Magic isn't as simple as steering a boat, or using your sword to get what you want," he said sarcastically. "All magic comes with a great price. It could shorten your life, or it could take away your very life force if you are not careful..."

"Okay, right, I thought as much." I nodded, turning back to look at the fast-approaching golden beach. No sign of the mother dragon above us, and pretty soon I would be able to jump overboard and swim through the shallows to the shore-line beyond.

"Alyana, alnana, alyana-Mer..." The boy was making strange chanting words behind me, and I turned to see his eyes were half-closed.

"Are you quite all right back there, fish boy?" I said, before suddenly, every hair on the back of my neck went up.

It was like the first time I had climbed way up high in the crow's nest with my father, and looked out across the sea as the wind rocked the boat from the west, and then from the east. It was a feeling unlike any other that I had ever had before – one of sheer, unadulterated terror.

I had never been good with heights. It was a fact that my father despaired of, and he blamed whomever my real, land-lubbing parents must have been. But that day in the crow's nest, I had felt entirely small, and at the mercy of the entire world. Any meager gust of wind could pick me up and dash me to the deck below. I was helpless before vast and cosmic forces.

Well, now, my skin itched and a prickling creeped all over my body as the boy chanted, over and over. Suddenly the boat beneath our feet *shifted*. We were racing toward the island now, moving faster than we had before, as if the mage-in-training had summoned up our own, personal current. We flew at the beach for a long moment, before the boy's chanting slowed, paused, and finally stopped, and as he did so, the boat also slowed, slowed, and went back to the gentle drifting of before.

"That – that doesn't prove anything…" I said quickly. The boy staggered to one side and sat down, apparently exhausted. "That could have been a freak wind, a strange eddy in the water…" That kind of stuff happened at sea. Lots of people thought that the ocean was simple matter of wind and waves, but it wasn't – there were tides and counter-currents, back-washes, storm surges, and eddies. A lot of very strange things happened at sea.

The boy was too tired to answer straight away, merely shaking his head as he shakily took up a bottle of water.

But still. It had been eerie. Too eerie. I didn't like it.

"You're a long way from home, Raider-Lila," Danu said weakly. "You're closer to the Island of Roskilde than you are to the far islands and the shipping routes that the Raiders usually harass."

I bared my teeth at him. The boy – as strange as he was – already knew too much. Was he going to sell me out?

"And you're young to be out here on your own. No raiding boat nearby…." The boy was frowning as if something had just occurred to him. "In fact, how old *are* you?"

"Seventeen," I said defiantly. "Older than you."

The boy's face grimaced. "Actually, no. I'm *eighteen*, but the magic has a way of making you look younger. It's why magicians and witches lead such long lives."

Oh really? I'd heard enough. We were still a bit out from the shelf of land where the sea washed into the golden beach, but that didn't mean that I had to listen to him. I turned and readied myself to jump over the edge.

"Seventeen years ago…" the boy said out loud. "By the stars!" He hissed, and I looked up, fearful that the mother dragon had come back, and decided that it was now dinner time. But there were no dragons in the sky.

"Seventeen years ago," the fish-boy repeated. "Don't you see? In the north-east, under a dragon's call, rising out of the water with a crown of water around you!" He kept on saying, over and over, his previous exhaustion forgotten as he wobbled to his feet and started laughing and clapping. "I've done it! I've done it!"

"Excuse me?" I raised my eyebrows.

"The prophecy! There's a prophecy you see, and it's why I am here. And I think that it led me to you, Lila-of-the-Raiders.

You are the reason why I am here!" Danu was saying excitedly. "Now, we must get you back to Sebol and…"

"What prophecy?" I said heavily.

"Roskilde!" He clapped again. "You, Lila, must be the one meant to wear the Sea Crown of Roskilde!" He looked so happy and elated – and insane – that I was only too happy to notice the skiff was now skipping over the clear waters of the shoreline, and underneath the gold-white of the sands.

"I'm nobody's queen, fish-boy," I said, diving out of the boat and into the water. Instantly the sounds of the world were muted as I skimmed under the surface, sharing my world with tiny darting fish and the occasional strand of seaweed. When I bobbed up to the surface one more time, it was to still hear the mad fisherman's child shouting.

"You're it, Lila-of-the-Raiders! I've done it!" he was saying, only now realizing that the person he thought was meant to wear the throne of the islands – me, in other words – was swimming away. "Come back! We have to talk!"

I started wading up the beach, around the rocks. I could pull my hidden boat out from where it was and down the small outlet stream to the south side of the island without him seeing me, and I knew that I was the better sailor than him. I could outrun the mad fish-boy, I thought irritably, wondering if this day was going to get *any* worse than it had already.

"Go home, fish-boy!" I shouted. "I'm not interested! And if you come near me again, I'll gut you – and that's a Raider's promise!" I snarled back at him, using my best pirate's glare to show him I meant business.

CHAPTER 5
LILA, OF MALATA

J ust seeing the head of Malata island on the other side of the Spine Rocks made my heart feel a little lighter. A little, I thought wistfully, as I had still failed to do anything that I had set out to do on my quest to the far north of the Western Isles.

Malata was the largest of our isles, and as such, was also the home to the largest of the Raider clans; the Malata clan I had been adopted into. But to get to Malata or any of the Raider isles beyond, you had to get past the Spine Rocks, small spears of Bonerock that stick out at odd places along the reef nearly encircling the Raider islands. Some scholars amongst the Raiders claimed they were actually the body of some great sea beast, come to finally rest here on the edge of the world, but my father is much more pragmatic.

The reef and the rocks formed a complicated maze to

which we have added by hauling out the odd wreck and junked ship, before scuttling them on the reef as further hazards. There sits the *Fist of Flowers*, a large merchant's vessel that forms an excellent wave break, and, sitting farther out is the *Queen Avari*, listed to her side – and one of the Lord Havick's very own galleons that my father captured not six years ago. We could have made a *lot* of money out of that particular galleon, shoring it up and selling it on further south.

"But no!" my father had roared. "We Raiders have to send a message to Havick, to the Roskildeans, and to any other who dares to think that these waters don't belong to us! The Sea Raiders!"

I had been very young back then, wide-eyed and impressionable, I didn't realize then as I did now, that the capture and sinking of the Roskildean ship had been one of the last big triumphs of the Sea Raiders. We had won the ship by chance when the crew had been sickened by bad water and it had been easy pickings for my father and his most trusted fighters to scull over to the galleon in the dead of night in longboats, and to climb up the rigging and seize control.

Even so, having our enemy's wrecked galleon was a very pleasing sight, and always gave my heart a savage leap of joy when I saw it. I picked the route through the reef and the rocks we were supposed to use this season, the route through the ropes, nets of driftwood, and other anchored "wrecks" my father moved around to protect the passage into the islands.

Within just a few hours, my boat was lightly skipping over the waves towards Malata's protected harbor.

Stone walls protected the pier, and the collection of long-boats sat in the wider waters beyond like giant, black-winged sea birds. The smaller shapes of people moved about in the background, fishing or swimming or practicing maneuvers as I changed over to the more tiring work of rowing myself in.

"Hoi! Lila!" shouted one of the men on one of the long-boats—Captain Lasarn of the *Fang,* who appeared to be teaching a younger complement of Raider boys and girls their basic seamanship lessons. He was a big man with dark hair and ruddy features, and only one eye, and at his side were Adair and Senga, two young sailors of an age with me who had become capable enough hands to now work as trainers alongside Lasarn. "You're back!" he called out as I rowed past. "How long has it been this time, two days?"

"Three," I shouted back, allowing myself a grin. The captain was almost of an age with my father—my foster-father —but unlike my father, he was always exhorting me to ever greater 'Raider Adventures.' It had been Captain Lasarn who had first told me that my father was not really my father, though I had never yet let on that I knew the rumors I was not truly blood-kin, not truly a Raider to be true.

"No dragons yet?"

Thanks for reminding me. "No, not yet. But soon, I prom-ise…" I said. *Now that I knew where a nest was, I could go back. If Father allowed me to take a few men with me, I might even be able to bring back all three eggs and be gone before the mother knew...*

I was still dreaming of the dragons as I turned the corner of the stone harbor wall and saw the pride and joy of the Raider fleet; the *Ariel,* my foster-father Kasian's flagship, and beside it the *Fang,* and beside that the *Storm.* All three were technically called caravels in what my foster-mother informed me was "proper sailing speak" which meant that they had three masts and only two upper decks, instead of the Roskilde galleons which had four masts and three upper decks. But these caravels were faster than the heavy galleons, and it was with pride that my father always said that his *Ariel* could outrun any vessel on the sea.

"Daughter!?" It was my father's booming voice, coming from the walled pier as he strode up. "Throw her a rope, some-one! Tie that off!" He barked commands at the Raiders who worked here and there over our three biggest ships. Within moments one of the hands had thrown me a rope and I was pulled into safe harbor, the little skiff already tied off along-side the other small two-person boats and yachts when my father jumped down to the dockside.

My foster-father was a big, barrel-chested man with hair like brilliant silver. He wore the old-style canvas pantaloons under the large waistband leather belt, with its many fixings and hoops, as well as the crossed-over linen shirt. He squinted at me in displeasure—or maybe because he was starting to lose some of his sight.

"Daughter! Three days!" He barked at me, his brow furrowing deeply, before helping me ashore and enfolding me into a tight and fierce bear hug.

"I told you I would be okay," I said as we broke apart.

"Hn." He snorted through his nose angrily. "But it was still a silly thing to do. Silly. When you are leader after me, you cannot be running off here and there and everywhere. You need to keep focused." He slapped one great paw of a hand against his other. "Merchants." Another heavy thud. "Food." *Thud.* "Havick." On the last word his lips curled in a sneer. My father hated the Roskildean lord more than he hated an unseasonable storm or an accident at sea.

"We're close, Father, so close..." I said, pausing before I launched into my tail of coming face-to-face with an angry dragon and mad sailors who may or may not be mages in training. "I know where some are. Some dragon eggs. I can take you to them!" I offered, hoping that at least would pique his interest.

"Dragon eggs," the man shook his great bear-like head. "Three days gone. When you are leader, you may not have three days in a row to spare for such things!" Another grumble. "No. No more. Not this season, anyway. I need you out on the *Ariel* with me, hunting down merchant ships."

"But Father..." I said, annoyed at how petulant and childish I always sounded before him. "These eggs will change everything..."

"No, Lila. I've said it now and it's done. Maybe next

season. But your mother is worried sick about you, so go and see her. And get yourself washed as well, that leather will crack if you don't clean off that salt water."

Gee, thanks, Dad, I thought. Why was it he always ended our talks like this? 'Maybe next season you'll be old enough to chase after dragons' was one phrase I remembered well. 'Maybe next season we'll have *you* captain of the *Ariel!*' The problem was, that my father had just one way of doing things – *his* way. It was the same with how he ran the ships, the equipment, and all of the trappings that made up the Raider lifestyle, everything had to be done just how it had always been done, and not different.

But how everything was always done hasn't got us anywhere! I thought as I trudged back along the walled pier. *We've had no decent raid this season, and now we're down to just three good boats...*

I walked towards the cluster of wooden stilt-houses, huts, and the small fortified mansion with the white walls that was both my home and the seat of power here in the Raiders' territories. As I walked I could feel the eyes of the other Raiders, the hands and the rowers, the sailors and the fighters on me, making me feel even smaller. Why were they so wary of me? Was it because they had seen the argument between me and my father? Was it because they, too, just like my father, thought I was a silly little girl dreaming of dragons?

"He just has no idea how important this is!" I said to Pela, wife of Chief Kasian of Malata, and the only woman who had been mother to me. She was a small woman with dark hair that was always forced back into a warrior's braid like mine was. I'd found her where she spent most of her time, in the small practice courts that she had insisted that my father put in to their walled garden.

The house itself was some old merchant's mansion we think, some private getaway in the bad old years of King Enric of Torvald, when all of those rebellious lords had sought to flee the Dark King's reign, and one of them had set up here, building a small island realm replete with wells, walls on the harbor, and a walled garden for his mansion. The lord hadn't lasted long, as the local island people saw to it that his boat sunk on the reef, and ever since this place had been owned by the Malata people, and finally, the Malata family.

"Your father pretty much told me exactly the same thing this morning about you," my mother said, before letting out a shout. *"Hyugh!"* My mother spun. She wasn't a thin woman, but when she was out with her practice swords on her mounted dummies, she was faster than my father.

Thump. A good, solid hit against the body of one of the stuffed-straw dummies, and then the counterweight bale of hessian-stuffed-with straw swung around –

"Yagh!" My mother barged into it with her shoulder, sending the counterweighted dummy that sat on the other end towards her this time, straight into her sword swing.

Thwack! An explosion of straw and hessian and the creaking sound of the wooden beams, suddenly free of their luggage as my mother stepped back.

"These ones are getting too easy," she complained, but she was still sweating and flushed.

"Why does my father think *I'm* not being serious?" I said, appalled at what my mother had confided in me. "Dragons are a whole lot more important than raiding merchant ships!"

"Oh, Lila…" my mother was already wiping her face with a flannel to get rid of the worst of the straw and dust. "You know that your father won't hear that. For him, being a Raider *is* going after merchant ships. It *is* tending to rigging and re-stitching sails and varnishing hulls. That is what makes us, well, *us.*"

I could have growled in frustration. "I know that, Mother, but I'm not talking about what we *do,* I'm talking about *our future.* A Raider future. One which means we don't have to worry about Havick anymore, ever."

My mother paused to sigh at the oaken cask that served as the water butt. It was a sigh that I had heard many times over the years, and one that would be followed by a brusque acceptance of the way things were. My mother, if anything, was *more* practical than my father. I had seen her digest his tales of woe and ships sunk to the Roskildean fleet. She would always accept my father's command at sea, but back here on land, it was *she* who would have the long, quiet talks with my father

44

about the future of our people. It was my mother who I had to convince of my plan.

"Mother, please, just hear me out," I began.

"Lila, I am sorry, but your father might be right. If we don't manage to get a good take this season..." my mother let the rest of her words drift into silence. We all knew the price for a Raider who couldn't raid. You either died at sea, or you had to bow the knee to the Roskildeans, and become just another client-island for their rule. At the moment, the Sea Raiders were the *only* collection of wild islands left in the Western Isles still free from Havick's rule.

"That is what I am talking about, Mother..." I tried again. "I *know* that Havick is dangerous, I've lost friends on those boats too." My mother's eyes were dark and unreadable. She didn't stop me this time. "I had my hands on them, Mother, the dragon eggs. I touched one, and I came *so* close to taking it, if it hadn't been for the brood mother turning up." *Brood mother,* that was what crazy fish-boy had called the mother dragon. An odd term, and one that I hadn't heard before.

"But what the fishermen's tales say are true, there *is* a brood of eggs on that atoll, and *I* know how to navigate to it. If we can get some of those eggs, tame them, train them, then we don't have to be Sea Raiders anymore, dodging the Roskilde fleet. We can be Dragon *Mercenaries,*" I said, feeling the flush of excitement as I said the words.

"Och, Lila..." my practical mother shook her head.

"Think about it – Torvald has just recovered from a war.

They're in bits. The Northern Clans are still riled up and control the north, and the south – our closest neighbors? They've been involved in infighting between one princeling and some other fat merchant for generations. There's a *lot* of coin about for a mercenary outfit. And who knows raiding better than we do? Just think of the money we could make!" I said.

My mother was silent for a moment longer, before she muttered, "Think of the damage we could inflict on Havick."

"Yes," I grinned fiercely, and saw that grin echo on my mother's face.

"I'll talk to your father, tonight, before dinner. But wait, Lila," she raised her hands to calm down my obvious excitement. "That doesn't mean that I agree with you, or that I am pleased about my daughter running off to steal dragon's eggs. A mother dragon is a very protective beast. You may have to find another way."

Another way? What other way? I thought in dismay, but the discussion was done. She was happy to talk with father about the possibility of stealing dragon eggs, but she also thought that I *couldn't* steal dragon's eggs? I knew that our future – *my* future – hung in the balance of how much faith my parents had in me.

"Now, go get yourself washed and changed for dinner, Lila," she said, not unkindly as she packed up her things and I turned back into the house I had grown up in.

CHAPTER 6
DANU, THE OFFER

I t was an easy thing to track the girl, now that I had met her. Maybe it was just the fact I had more faith that I had followed the prophecy correctly, allowing me to use my magic with more confidence. Or maybe it was as Chabon sometimes mysteriously suggested, that magic works better when you have close contact, and worst over events and people who are far away and unknown to you. The best and strongest of magics occur, or so she had told me, between friends.

The compass this time was able to hold a steady course as I asked it to find the island of Malata, far to the south of the dragon atoll. Even the winds were favorable as I let them catch the boat I had commandeered from the tiny Sebol harbor and flew across the oceans. The only real fear I had was one of running into one of the many patrol boats of the Roskildeans, but, as luck – or fate – would have it, my journey was trouble free.

I arrived at the splintered islands of the Western Archipelago a little after sundown, before stowing the sail and resorting to the oars to pull my way in. It was hard work that made my shoulders and back ache – but it was a good ache. I knew that my mother and father, far away on our little home island of Tamm, would be proud of their son. They were fish-erfolk, going out in the predawn light to tend to their crab pots and near-coast nets before the tithing day, when the patrol boats of Roskilde would come and take a portion of their catch for the royal coffers. Life wasn't bad, under the protection of the Island of Roskilde – they hadn't been raided in their life-time, but it was quiet.

Boring.

Thank goodness I had shown some talent in magic, I thought as I rowed, picking my way between the reef and the hulks that spread out around the parent island like a barricade. My life with the West Witches had been anything if boring. A lot of hard work to be fair, but never dull.

The hull of the boat suddenly made a horrible juddering, scraping sound as it hit some ridge of rock or coral. *Pay more attention, Danu!* I thought, wondering if I might even need to try and summon up a bit of magic to get through the last, torturous bit of the maze. These Raiders had protected their home well, I could see. There was no way a larger boat carrying soldiers would make its way through here.

"If you don't have to, you shouldn't." I repeated Chabon's stern advice to myself over the dark waters. Magic came with a heavy price, even in the short term – aches and nausea, headaches and sickness. Some of the witches claimed that magic itself sucked the life out of you, but still left you strangely alive. The stars alone knew that Chabon looked more like a sea turtle than a living person, and she could barely move from her bed these last few years. But how old was the leader of the West Witches? She said she remembered the time of Hacon Maddox – that was hundreds of years ago, wasn't it?

"Danu! Pay more attention!" My mentor Afar's voice sounded in my head, as if she were here to scold me right now. I bowed my head to the task, alternating between rowing and using the oars to pole in front of me, testing the depths of the rocks. As the light slid from the sky, leaving just the glow of the occasional fish and the strange waters, I slid past the reef and found myself looking at a stone-walled harbor.

There were lights on at the ends of the pier and boats anchored all about. The sounds of loud, joyous singing as sailors did what sailors do when they are not expected anywhere in the morning.

Probably best I don't just sail in there… I thought, angling the boat *around* the back of the harbor to where the land was rockier and broken. I would have to sneak into the Raider island and find the Raider girl by stealth.

This counted as what I have to do, doesn't it? I thought,

letting the currents slowly wash me away from the light and the noise, and pull me towards the rocks behind the small harbor town. It took a long time, but eventually I was rocked towards the large boulders, and I put out an oar to steady myself from the coast. With the slap and crash of the waves everywhere I had no fear of being spotted as I searched for a place I could at least bring the boat up a little way, before starting to scramble and pick my way through the rocks.

The wind was picking up a bit, and on it I could hear brief snatches of song, or the chopping of wood, the crying of a baby as I ghosted towards the buildings and small enclosed farms at the back of the town. A goat snorted her annoyance at my passing, a dog started up savage barking.

I could use magic to mask my presence, I sweated nervously, wishing that I had more training at this. But no one had ever trained a mage before, not the West Witches nor anyone else as far as I knew. Afar had done her best. *But should I use magic now?* Would Afar approve? Would Chabon?

I thought of the way that I had seen the girl burst from the waves of the atoll like a cork released from under water, the water spraying around her in a circle – *like a crown.* I couldn't believe how stupid I had been not to even notice it the first time around! The prophecy that Chabon had dreamed was of the Sea Crown of Roskilde rising from the waves. I had entrusted myself to the power of that prophecy, and allowed myself to be guided straight here, to that island and that fierce, strong Raider girl.

Who was seventeen. And it was seventeen years ago that the island of Roskilde had its most devastating Raider attack, and had lost the royal family *and heir.* I didn't know how it turned out that she had then been taken up by the Raiders as one of their own, but I knew that it had to be so. The prophecy had led me straight to her.

"Who's that? Is that you, Olander?" shouted a voice as a light blared on from one of the smaller wooden houses that I ghosted around.

That was it. I did have to use magic.

Closing my eyes, I crouched down in the dark and tried to find that quiet and calm place in my heart that Afar had showed me was always there.

"The centre of all things. It is always inside of you. Always patient. Always calm. It is in you and in me, and in the rocks and the air…" Afar had said in a reverential voice.

My breathing slowed, deepened. One of the many skills that the witches had tried to drill into me was trances and meditation.

"In that centre-place, you can reach out. With your feelings. Find how you connect to the wind, to the earth beneath your feet. Feel the high winds above you…" My mentor's voice was soothing in my mind as I felt the whisper of wind on my cheek, the snuffle and huffle of a horse in its paddock.

"This isn't magic," I had argued.

"And what do you think magic is, but connection? That which connects us all to each other. That which keeps the fire burning, and the world breathing, in and out..." Afar had laughed. "Reach out, Adept Danu, reach with your heart, not your mind..."

Feeling quieter, I reached out to the soft, huffling night around me. I reached out to the quiet and the hiddenness of those sleepy creatures and plants. I drew to myself a cloak of their natural *don't-see-me, don't-see-me* and stood up.

"Olander? Is that you?" There was a ruddy-skinned, dark haired woman on the other side of the hedge of goat willow, a lantern in one hand, and a wicked-looking scimitar in the other. I gasped a little in shock, and she swung around towards me, hissing like a cat – but her eyes slid off me, protected as I was by the magic that I had summoned.

It's working! It's working! I thought, my heart thumping faster. The Raider woman turned slowly back, pausing in front of me as she squinted at the dark shadows where I was, *almost* seeing something, before shaking her head irritably.

"Bah. Probably just a rat," she scoffed, trudging back to her little house and banging the door behind her. I waited for a few more breaths before taking out the compass, and concentrating on the prophecy. It would lead me to Lila.

৩%৪৩

Lila the Raider, it turned out, had some *very* important parents.

Either that or the Raiders were very relaxed about where teenagers could and couldn't go in their society. I ghosted through the harbor town, following the compass needle as it swung first this way and that at each new avenue. Eventually, however, even I had to admit that it was leading me straight for the grandest and largest house on the rise above the harbor. It was painted white and built of stone like a mayor's or a governor's house, and it even had formal gardens – once, but now long overgrown. I walked past gigantic spreads of lavender and under magnolia trees that needed pruning, to where lights were on and the sound of someone playing a fiddle wafted on the sea breeze.

I wondered at the lack of guards, pausing at the open front doors before I stepped in. But of course, everyone here was a Raider – why would they steal from each other?

The first room from the hallway contained chairs and benches where those I guessed to be captains and senior hands relaxed, playing their small sailor's flutes and one or another of them singing. There was a warm and cheery fire in the hearth, and bowls of stew on the table. I felt a stab of jealousy. I never had this sense of camaraderie growing up.

The compass drew me further into the building, towards the smells of spice and pickles and rich-roasted meat. There was a half-open door, and a long room where a small family ate at a table drawn before a large, roaring hearth-fire.

The youngest of that family was Lila.

"This is our only chance, I know it, Father…" Lila was saying, stabbing at the air with her fork. Gone were the Raiders' leathers and belt hoops, to be replaced with a simple, light green dress with yellow trim. Her hair had been re-braided, and her skin fairly shone in the reflected firelight.

She is the heir to the throne! I thought as soon as I saw her. It was in her bearing, her looks, the shape of her brow. I swear that I had seen similar in the old paintings and books that the West Witches hoarded. I let myself imagine her sitting on the throne. Stern-faced, but still beautiful. She would make a good queen, I thought as she argued with her parents.

"Our only chance to what? Get my daughter killed by a broody dragon?" Kasian, the Chief of the Raiders, said gruffly.

"No, our only chance to survive, as a people!" she pointed out. "Mother? Did you tell him my plan?"

The woman that the girl called mother nodded, but with a shrug, like it was no good.

"She did tell me, and, while I love the idea of Dragon Mercenaries…" a smile flickered and vanished on the chief's face.

So that was what you were up to! I thought, in both awe and alarm. It was a brave, audacious plan – but also a stupid one. Everyone knew that you had to bond with dragons. They couldn't be tamed like a sheepdog.

"But it is crazy. We need to do what my father did, and

what his father did before him, all the way back to when we Raiders were the most feared thing on the seas!" The chief pounded the table with one mighty fist. "We do it by hard work, Lila. By judging the winds right, by getting some salt under our nails…"

"By being chased by much larger, better equipped ships and troops?" Lila said pointedly. "Don't tell me that you're not excited by the idea, Father. What sort of Raiders we would be! Airborne! Able to strike anywhere along the coast, not just the south or the Western Isles. We could even round the southern cape and see what fortunes await to the far east!" Lila had stood up, looking to the far corners of the room as if she could see the future there. "Dragon Mercenaries!" she announced. "The whole world is our oyster. Roaming the seas and the airs, unceasing, for glory and adventure!"

Even the corners of my mouth twitched into a smile at the idea. It was audacious and wild – but it was not the path of the rightful queen. No. I cannot let this happen, I thought as I stepped out from the shadows into the room, and let the magic fall from me.

"I can talk to dragons," I had a chance to say, just as two things happened.

One, Chief Kasian of Malata swore and fell backwards in his chair as his family gasped at my sudden appearance.

Two, a headache erupted in my head like a localized thunderstorm. *"Ach!"* I winced, staggering to one side. All magic has a cost, I remembered. Why didn't I think to take the magical concealment down before I announced myself? Now I must look like an idiot in front of them! I thought as I my hands clutched and clattered to the nearest table for a pitcher of fresh water, to suddenly throw into my mouth.

"Raiders! To me!" the chief shouted as he jumped to his feet and ran to where his scimitar was hanging on the wall. "Stand back, Lila, wife!" He roared–but his wife was quicker, sliding out of her chair and not bothering to wrestle a heavy scimitar from the wall. Instead, she seized one of the butchering knives from their table as she passed her husband to stick it under my nose.

Oh no, I thought, my vision doubling under the pain. I didn't have the skills to fight my way out of here, and I now didn't have the concentration to make any defensive spells.

"I'll show you what we do to spies on Malata!" the chief bellowed as shouts came from behind me, from the room of captains and seniors.

"Who do you work for? Havick?" the chief's wife said fiercely, looking down the blade of the carving knife at me.

"Yes, tell us!" The chief stepped up beside his wife, scimitar raised.

"Mother, Father – no!" Lila shouted. "I know him. Kind of."

"Sire?" Voices came from behind me as I was seized and banged up against the wall. There were suddenly lots and lots of very angry bearded faces being pushed into my own, cutlasses, daggers, and knives in their strong, work-scarred hands.

"Hold him steady, boys," the chief growled, and my handlers stepped aside (but still held my arms and legs) as the chief took his wife's place, drawing back his arm…

"Father – stop! In the name of your firstborn – stop!" Lila shrieked, and I saw the Chief falter in front of me, turning to frown at Lila.

"You would call on Ruck?" the chief said, his face a picture of upset and anger.

"I would." Lila nodded. "I would because I have to. I know this boy. And even though he is mad, and I do not know how much we can trust him – he said that he could talk to dragons. *That* is how we win this war," she said, clearly and directly. *The way a queen would state things. Not challenging, just talking.*

The chief rounded on me again. "Well, can you? You look barely able to walk in a straight line!"

I nodded. "It is the magic, it always has a cost." I found myself looking at Lila as I said this. I had told her that was true, and now, surely, even she could see it. "How did I sneak into your harbor? Get past all of the other Raiders, without magic?" I pointed out as I winced from the headache.

"S'true, sire, none of my men have said anything about someone new coming in. No stranger's boats," said the red-haired, one-eyed Raider who held me.

"Hm." The chief lowered his blade a little, but his upset

look was now replaced with one that I equally feared: disgust. "Speak, witch," he said, his lip curling.

I told them my tale. Of being trained as an adept by the West Witches to be the first ever mage in over a hundred years. I had come to ensure that the prophecy of Roskilde was fulfilled. "And I believe that the prophecy is referring to her." I nodded at Lila.

"My daughter?" said the other woman in the room, a stocky, older woman who stepped up beside the chief, whom I took to be his wife and Pirate Queen. "Then you must be wrong, clearly, *adept*." She was frowning at me.

Could I have got it so wrong? What if Lila really is the natural-born child of these Raiders.

"Seventeen years ago," I began.

"I was born," Lila said quietly, "on Roskilde."

"You knew?" Lila's mother gasped as she looked at her child in shock.

I watched as the young woman shrugged. "You can't keep secrets long in a Raider's community, or on a ship." Her gaze swung to the Raider who was holding me, the red-haired, one-eyed one.

"Captain Lasarn?" the chief barked reproachfully at him, and the man smiled sheepishly.

"I figured it was right that she knew, Chief. That she came from a raid, and that Pela there had just lost her son Ruck, and so..." Lasarn looked sorrowful. "It was better for her to be with us, and to a mother who would care for her, than to be all alone with dead parents, don't you think?" Lasarn asked the room, as if for forgiveness.

For myself, I think what the Raiders had done had probably saved her life, as it wasn't long after that the usurper Havick had taken the throne for himself, and set about exiling or killing all of the old captains and generals loyal to the old Roskilde royal line.

"So yes, Father, I've known for years that I was from Roskilde. That I wasn't your natural child," Lila said with a sad smile. "Although I wish you both *were* my parents."

"Hmph." The chief looked deflated. "I have only ever tried to do right by you, Lila."

"And that is why I must try to tame these dragons. To protect all of us..." the young woman said.

"You cannot tame a dragon, Lila," I said. "Not even in Torvald do they tame dragons..."

The young woman's eyes narrowed as she glared at me. "Then how do they ride them then? Good wishes?"

"Yes," I said. "There is a very old, and very rare thing called a *dragon bond* that happens if both human and dragon give their heart freely to each other. It is a type of magic," I said. *The strongest of magic occurs between friends,* I heard Chabon breathe in my memory. "That bond is forged for life, and with it, you could ride a dragon."

"Then that is what we have to do!" the woman said tartly. "We will travel to the dragon atoll, and you, *adept,* will talk to this brood mother on my behalf, and offer her my bond or whatever it is that you have to do."

"It's not that easy, Lila..." I winced. *And besides, I'm here to restore you to the throne of Roskilde, not create possibly the most dangerous fighting force in the world outside of Torvald!*

"*If* you speak for me with the brood mother, *I* will help you find out more about this ridiculous prophecy of yours," Lila bargained with me. "Trade for trade. That's the Raider way."

The absurdity of using Raider customs to secure her destiny as the eventual enemy of the Raiders was not lost on me. But it was the best offer that I had on front of me.

"Fine." I nodded. "When do we go?"

"No!" The chief stamped his feet, looking hurt and confused. I didn't blame him, as he was watching the breakup of his family if my plan went accordingly. *But the prophecy must be fulfilled,* I gritted my teeth against the wave of sympathy I had for the proud old man.

"No, Lila. I may not be able to stop you running off into the oceans with a boat on your mad schemes – but I can *ask* you this one thing. For me. As the only father that you have known," he said heavily, and I watched as his wife put a gentle hand on the big man's arm tenderly.

"Don't do anything with this young man until we have tested his mettle. My father always told me, never trust someone you haven't sailed with, and I ask you to do the same. Allow me to have one raid with my daughter on the

Ariel, and with this *witch*," the chief snarled – he clearly had no love for the West Witches – "as a hand. *If* he proves himself worthy, then I will wholeheartedly support my daughter in her plan to create the Dragon Raiders."

Beside him his wife nodded. "That is a fair deal, Lila," she said warningly.

"Deal." Lila nodded with a grin.

Now all I had to do was to prove to the second-most-fear-some people on the waves that I was a worthy companion. *Great.*

৩৯৩

CHAPTER 7

LILA AND THE ARIEL

"Hold her steady!" my father shouted from the foredeck, letting Kal, our bald, heavy-set sailing master have the hard work of turning the ship's wheel. My father liked to be out front when we left and entered port, as "there have to be some perks to being captain, right?"

It was a bright day, and a perfect one for sailing. We had a full complement of Raiders, and I would be acting as first mate, second only to Kal and Father. It was a lot of responsibility for me, and I could feel the weight of it in my stomach.

I had to get this right. I had to show Father that I could make a good leader. But it wasn't just my father, of course, that I had to worry about. There was the crew. All fifteen of us altogether, all men and women I had sailed with before – but never in charge of.

A good captain is only as good as her crew, I repeated

another favorite maxim of Father's, and saw just how great a captain my father was. The crew loved him. Even when the seas were calm, and the pickings were low, he had a way to spur them to action or set a fire in their bellies. Did I have that?

I leaned on the rail as the walled harbor of Malata slide past, and with it the cheering and whoops of the other Raiders who had to stay behind. Every excursion out into the Western Seas was an adventure and a challenge, and you never knew how many people come back – if we came back at all.

"First mate Lila!" my father commanded, stalking back down from the foredeck at a jog. "How's the ship?"

I had seen him ask this question of other shipmates before. It was a general all-accounting, that he would expect his first mate to know. "A little low on provisions for a week, fa-captain," I said. "But I expect we'll make that up in fishing. Crew able-bodied and well. Eager for a chance to get out there, sir," I said.

"All shipshape and sail-ready then." I watched my father grin. "Good. Make sure the mates get the fishing nets deployed this evening, and see to it that they pull 'em up before morning."

"Aye-aye, cap'n!" I nodded. It might only be a small over-seeing job, but it was a start. "Where we headed?"

"North," my father grunted, and then lifted his head up to bellow the news at the rest of the crew. "We head north, ladies

64

and gents! Up into the Western Isles. Let's find some fat-bellied merchant!"

There was a rousing chorus of cheers and roars. Those words were music to a Raider's ears. I, however, was a little less enthusiastic. *North?* That will take us straight towards the shipping lanes patrolled by Havick's Roskilde fleet. Was Father trying to do a lightning-fast raid? Or was he itching for a fight against our enemy with only fifteen crew?

Hm. Not that he would see it that way, I knew. 'One pirate is worth ten of Havick's land-loving cabbages!' my father would have declared. I looked at the broad back of my father, and wondering at the way that he could change as soon as he stepped off of dry land. Out here he was no longer simply my father. He was the feared Captain Kasian, Chief of the Raiders, daring and fierce and as slippery as an eel.

As I surveyed the *Ariel*, I saw Danu the "mage-in-training" (or so he claimed) over on the other side of the deck. I narrowed my eyes as I studied him. I didn't *like* him, but he was a necessity to my plans. I didn't like how, from the first moment we had met, he had been trying to tell me what I needed to do, for myself and the grand future of the Western Isles. Like I was just a pawn in his schemes, or like I couldn't make a choice for myself. And the notion that he was a mage at all – a sort of person like the Dark King himself, or like the Dragon Monks of old, I found to be laughable. He looked as though he had grown up around the docks and jetties here at

Malata; a young-looking kid more at home picking cockles than reading scrolls!

I didn't have any intention of believing him or becoming his 'Queen of Roskilde' that he was so certain about. Even if it was true, I *had* a family here, now, with these sailors, and it was the only family that I cared about.

But he doesn't have to know that, I permitted myself to have a small grin.

"But I sure do hope he isn't lying about being able to talk to dragons…" I muttered to myself. All of my plans hinged on it. I would have to corner him when I got the chance to try and see if what he said was really true, or just a boast?

He was coiling a rope at the moment, under the careful eye of one of the other hands – and, I was surprised to see, he wasn't making a complete hash out of it.

We'll see what you're made of, fish-boy.

☙❧

As it turned out, Danu was made of quite good fishing stock. Even Father noted it on the second day, when Kal mentioned that it had been Danu who had told them to light lanterns over the sides of the ship when we dropped nets in the middle of the night.

"You'll get more that way" he said. "The West Witches rely on fish stocks for food, so we do a lot out there…" He shrugged a little self-consciously. "It's not all scrolls and meditation, you know."

Still, I didn't like the fact that the crew were now thanking *him* as he worked to supply them with enough fresh food. That was *my* job, it was my special task given to me by the captain! Danu was just supposed to be proving his sea-worthiness.

I was grumbling to myself as I pulled on the ropes of the mainsail, along with the Brothers as we called them, two hands who had been born on the same ship to the same mother, but were as different as they could be when you talked to each. It was the second day of our voyage, and, with bellies full, the crew were still happy and enthusiastic, despite our direct northwards drive.

"One, two, heave!" I shouted, throwing my weight down at the last moment, and the pole that attached the bottom of the sail climbed up to where another of the sailors – a rigger this time – was ready to lash it down.

"What's going on here?" my father called down as he clambered up from below decks.

"Wind picking up from the north-west, captain," I said proudly. "She would have hit us side on and cut our speed in half, if we didn't raise the mainsail."

"Which will lessen our speed anyway, right, First Mate Lila?" The captain frowned.

"Uh, of course, sir." I bobbed my head. I knew what I had done was right. I had heard and seen my father do exactly the same thing a thousand times before!

"You tied off?" He cast a look above, to receive a wave and a thumb's up from the rigger above.

"Yes, sir." I nodded, feeling stupid.

"Good. Then come with me." He nodded at the brothers that they were dismissed as I fell into step beside him. He walked me slowly up to the foredeck, where we climbed the ladder to the small area of raised platform and rails just above the bowsprit.

"Lila, you need to ask the captain and the sailing master before you start messing about with the mainsail!" my father said urgently but under his breath. He didn't make a big show of saying it, but stood with his hands behind his back as if we were both looking out to sea.

"Of course, I know that, Father – it's just, you said that I was first mate, and you wanted me to take the initiative..." I pointed out.

"It's not for me, Lila." My father sounded annoyed, before nodding over his shoulder. "It's for them. *They* need to see you obeying the chain of command. That means they can trust you, that means they can follow you." He frowned. "I'm trying to give you a future here, Lila," he added.

I was silent for a moment, my eyes scanning the horizon. Maybe I would make a terrible captain. And a terrible queen, if Danu had his way.

"Lila..." My father cleared his throat awkwardly. "Listen to me now. Whatever that boy tells you, whatever he might show you, you need to know one thing: that we love you very much, and that we regard you as family." The big man's voice was gruff and uneven, and he fiddled with the hoops on his wide belt nervously.

"I'm not leaving, Dad," I said in just as awkward a tone.

"But, the adept said that you belonged on the throne..." my father grumbled. "Riches that we Raiders have only ever dreamed of!"

"Well, there's already a man sitting on that throne, as far as I know." I laughed. "And I don't think that Havick is going to give it up any time soon – not that I believe Danu when he says that I'm a queen."

"But your deal with him...?" My father stroked his long beard.

"Just wait, Father. I need him to talk to the dragons. After that?" I shrugged. I hadn't thought the details out entirely. I didn't want to hurt him, but I was sure that we could give him a boat and send him back to the Witches of Sebol. What was he going to do, enchant the entire free islands of the Raiders?

"Ha. Spoken like a true Raider." My father clapped his hands together and laughed. "He's not a bad sailor, mind. He has good instincts, even if he has clearly spent too long behind a writing desk than out on the waves!"

"Hmph." I pulled a face. "He's no Raider though, Dad," I pointed out.

"No. He's not that. We'll just have to wait and see what happens when he sets his eyes on the first Havick war galleon." My father laughed mischievously, and I had a sudden, terrible feeling that this might be something that the slippery and daring Captain Kasian of the Sea Raiders had been planning all along.

"Father?" I asked lightly. "Uh… Why *are* we heading due north, exactly?"

His mustache twitched. His mustache always twitched when he was about to lie. "You know as well as I do that the Western Archipelago is due north. There's a lot of trade going back and forth up there…"

"But that means there are also a lot of Roskilde patrol boats…" I pointed out.

"Are you questioning me as my daughter, or as my first mate, Lila?" My father was suddenly serious as he half turned towards me.

I gambled. "Both?"

"Then I, as your father, would tell you to trust me, and *as* captain, I would remind you that if you have concerns about my leadership of this vessel, you had better take it up with the sailing master." He said the words calmly, but there was no denying the authority that was behind them. It was Captain Kasian who ruled this ship, not my father, and if I planned to question him on any aspect of his rule; from where we were going or when to reef a sail, I had better be prepared to go all the way to get the crew and the sailing master to back me up. In other words, I would have to dare a mutiny.

"Aye-aye, sir." I nodded. "Am I dismissed?"

A perfunctory nod, and I left him on the foredeck to his.

schemes and his plans. I was keenly aware of the stares of the other crew members. *Did they think that we had just argued? What did that mean for the crew if the first mate and the captain* do?

With a worried grimace, I returned to my jobs, but was pleased to notice all the same that, when the north-wester came in, the *Ariel* hardly slowed down at all thanks to my quick work on the mainsail.

⚜

On the third day out, we started to hear the sounds of distant seagulls and the harsh cries of cliff birds. It hadn't taken us long to get this far, almost as if the sea itself had been helping us.

"Rise and shine, boys and girls!" Kal was already banging the ship's bell on deck as I groaned in my hammock. It was a little before first light – and generally, unless there was something the matter, you would let the crew at least wait until sun-up before you got them to work. It was that kind of eager behavior that made the crew grumble and mumble.

My father must be planning something, I thought as I climbed the ladder out of the hold where we had strung out hammocks. As we only had food and water on board – no cargo or booty – we had room to stretch out, and, as everyone knows, a sailor will take every opportunity to rest that comes to them. Sailing was hard, physical, backbreaking, hand-scar-

71

ring, and sun-burning work. I didn't blame the other hands as they grumbled at the early hour, rubbing eyes and yawning.

"Up you get, you swabs!" Kal shouted, doling out bowls of porridge rich with oats, and a hunk of bread on top. I grunted my thanks as I took my breakfast, and retired to a spot under the foredeck with a few of the other hands.

"Huh! What's the old dog got planned for us then, hey?" said one of the Raiders, a small, stocky man with about one whole tooth in his head. He was grinning at me as he said it, clanging his spoon on the side of his bowl. "Because now I *know* he's up to something!"

"It's only porridge, Sam." I shook my head at his theatrics, digging into my own bowl to suddenly realize what he meant. This porridge wasn't the usual watered-down affair that we had to put up with aboard the ship. This had real rich milk, and, I was sure, a small dollop of precious honey in there, too.

Why was the captain waking us up super-early, and being VERY nice to us? I thought, as a shape shuffled over to join us with a sigh.

"Budge up, Sam. It's the fish-whisperer," said one of the other hands, earning a playful groan from Danu as he sat down next to one-tooth Sam. Really? I grimaced. Did I have to wake up to him now as well? It's not that he had been following me around the ship, or that you could ever avoid anyone on a sailing boat, but I had been very aware that Danu had been about a *lot* over the last few days. Even when we were on different shifts, I would find him taking his rest on deck, or else working near me, as if he was trying to keep an eye on me.

"Danu." I nodded, keeping my tone civil at least. A slight from the first mate could be taken as a sign that I was displeased, or that the captain was, by the rest of the crew. I couldn't afford to give the view that there was any friction, if I wanted the crew to come with me to get the dragons.

"Morning Lila, what's going on?" Danu yawned before starting his breakfast. "Wow, delicious!" he said, earning agreement from the other Raiders.

Ugh. He even fits in with them as well, I thought despairingly.

"We're going to be raiding," I said to Danu, trying to keep the ice from my voice.

"Raiding…" Uncertainty flickered in his green eyes, then suddenly his expression shifted as he forced a tight smile on his face. "Well, that's what I'm here for, isn't it?" he said cautiously.

"That is what we do," I said. *Did he look down upon what we do, our way of life?* Before I could think more on that, my father's strong voice bellowed through the predawn dark.

"Right, my crew! There's a reason I got you up and early today – I wouldn't pull you from your bunks without good reason now, would I?" he teased, earning a few wry chuckles from the older hands. Of course he would, but this game of tease and reward, along with rough jokes was a part of what the captain did to win the rest of the crew over. They *liked* him, and they *expected* him to be cunning and daring, perhaps even a bit cruel. *Could I do the same?* I wondered. I had always relied on myself to get things done. It was going to be hard to learn how to encourage and cajole – *and trust* – others.

"I've had word, my hearties, that there is going to be a very important ship running the archipelago today. A nice, fat *merchant* ship straight out of Torvald itself!"

"Hurrah!" The shout went up, and my ears pricked. The Kingdom of Torvald of course traded with the Western Archipelago. Ever since the civil war was won by King Bower, there had been renewed trading links with the place of Queen Saffron's birth. Not that the archipelago had much to trade, but they had rare woods and spices, and of course, Bonerock, if you could find a ship large enough to transport it. But Queen Saffron seemed eager to restore trading links to this part of the world. She hasn't forgotten us, I thought, feeling a flash of something like embarrassment.

Guilt? The Queen Saffron was my hero. A lowly island girl who had risen to become the queen, and more so than that – a dragon friend and rider of the greatest nation in the world. The thought that she was working to make the lives of the islanders out here better made me proud, in an odd way. *And now we are going to steal that trade from them.* I felt nervous at the prospect. *It was what we did. What we had always done. Our way of life,* I reminded myself, setting my qualms aside. *And I knew that we badly were in need of the coin and supplies and food a raid would bring.*

"We don't know where she is, but I reckon she can't have crossed the straits yet. The only sensible route is around the Tumult Seas and straight up the line of the archipelago, which means she has to cross this way before long," Father was saying, as the eastern skies started to crisp with pink and russet clouds.

"We'll find a nice little cove and stay out the way until we spot her – and then…" He clapped his hands together, and the roar of enthusiasm from the crowd was hard to ignore. Even I whooped at the prospect of a successful raid.

⚜

The *Ariel* cut through the waters now grown blue and clear the closer that we drew to the shores. Beyond our sails I could make out the white and jagged cliffs of the Western Archipelago, most of the heights crowned with dripping foliage, and the occasional beach of golden sand hidden in coves.

"It's a fine day!" complimented Adair, one of the younger Raiders, who wore his dark hair held up into a topknot, as was the fashion. He was of an age with me, and, with his sister Senga, were probably my closest friends on board.

"It is." I nodded, keeping an eye on the coasts and the rocks. Adair and I were out by the bowsprit at the front of the vessel, where we could call out warnings of sudden reefs or hidden rocks.

But Kal the Sailing Master and my father had been navigating and raiding these waters all their lives. We passed a large collection of boulders called Giant's Rock and skirted the narrow channel of Eel's Pike, lined with sharp rocks a small ship like the *Ariel* could navigate, if such a risk became necessary. Giant fish leapt and skipped across the water further out to sea, and the cliffs echoed with the sound of nesting birds.

"But still no sign of that Torvald ship." Adair sighed regretfully. Senga was up in the crow's nest with one of the rare spyglasses, likely scanning the distant horizons for sign of our prey.

"Let's hope she's heavy with gold," I said with a worried grin, trying to imitate what my father would say. *And let's hope she hasn't got a Dragon Rider escort, either.* I tapped the railing.

"Sails!" Senga's voice cut through the tension.

"Where? Where?" Father called back. Senga was pointing due east, down the line of the islands, and straight for the edge of the Tumult Seas. "Got an eye on her? What flag is she waving?"

Roskilde, I found myself praying, startling myself that I hadn't prayed for the dragon of Torvald.

"The Red and Purple, captain! She's a Torvald ship all right!" Senga punched the air, and I heard a holler of joy.

"Right! Get that Roskilde flag up, now!" Father ordered as I moved to the kit boxes on the sides of the desk. As first mate, I was expected to be the first to get things done under the captain and the sailing master. If they wanted something tied down, I would be there to do it, or else to organize a crew to get on it. If they wanted us to board an enemy vessel, then I would have to be in the front ranks along with the captain. I motioned Adair to keep an eye on the rocks as I signaled two more hands to join me.

The flag box had a variety of large cloth flags that we could run up on ropes to sit over the sails. Not as big as the entire canvas of course, but would give a picture to a far-away vessel who was in their near waters. We had a city of Vala flag, a whole host of islands local colors, and, then we had the Roskilde flags.

"War or trade, captain?" I shouted back, referring to the two styles of Roskilde flags that we used. One was the sea-crown rising with crossed swords, and the other was just the sea-crown of Roskilde.

"War, first mate!" My father beamed. "Let 'em feel safe that they have one of Havick's very own escorts come to protect 'em!"

I grabbed one edge of the flag and ran to the mainmast, as at my side the crew members took another end, and started threading with ropes. We had to get this flag up quickly, or else the Torvald ship might smell a rat.

Which meant climbing the mast, my stomach lurched. *But I would have to become good at heights if I want to be a Dragon Mercenary.* In fact, and as much as the thought filled me with dread, I would have to become pretty damn *amazing* at heights.

"Sweet seas, give me courage…" I fixed one edge of the sail to my belt hooks, and started climbing, hand over hand, my feet finding the metal stepping rods as I moved. I got about ten feet up when the boat swayed and wobbled as Kal turned us around. The movement made the horizon rise and dip and I clung to the mast fiercely.

"Come on, come on…" I reached out a hand, grabbed the next stepping rod and pulled myself up, looking to see the *miles* of mast above me. Another ten feet when my knees started to shake, and my legs wanted to cramp.

Just keep climbing. Don't look up. Don't look down! I was sweating now, breathing hard. I would do this for my father, and for my crew. I would make them see how great a first mate I was. They would want to follow me on the backs of dragons.

"Lila, here…" I heard a voice say, to find that Danu had already climbed on the other side of the main trunk-like mast to reach out and grab one edge of the false flag. He appeared completely unbothered by the height, even holding on with one hand as he reached out to steady me against the mast.

"Get down! I got this!" I hissed at him, even though my heart was hammering hard in my chest.

"Don't be silly. I'm here to help, not beat you!" he snapped, leaning out to draw up the rope and start to climb up with it, pulling the flag behind him.

"Idiot!" I hissed, angered at his apparent skill at climbing, and at the fact that, unless I wanted the false flag to bunch up awkwardly behind me, I had to climb at pace with him. My anger with the boy broke the fear in my legs and I climbed alongside him. "This is dangerous, what you're doing!" I snapped at him as we both climbed.

"Got you moving, though." Danu smiled, full of self-satisfaction. I swear, if it hadn't meant only holding on with one hand and then plummeting to my certain death, I would have hit him. As it was, I settled for growling at him as we raced together to the yard arm that crossed the sail horizontally, to shuffle our way out, fixing the ropes to the beams. He even knew how to make a double-hitch, it seemed, as he tied his rope off and shuffled back to the main mast.

With a ripple, the flag now displayed the rising sea-crown over the crossed swords. We were a Roskilde navy boat, and we didn't even have to swear those silly oaths of allegiance, or spend years in a naval academy!

"I should tell the captain and have you punished," I said between my teeth as I joined him on the other side of the mainmast. We would have a little bit of time before our boats met, and the climbing had exhausted me as I clutched to the wood and gasped for breath. "What you did was dangerous."

"Lila? You know what that is, right?" Danu was saying, pointing to the Roskilde flag underneath our feet, and underneath *that* (I thought a little giddily) I could see the tops of the heads of the sailors rushing to their places about the boat, surreptitiously putting daggers into belts, and trying to appear nonchalant, lest the other boat could see them.

"Duh, it's a flag." I shook my head, and then immediately regretted it as the world spun.

"It's the 'rising crown' or, more accurately, the Sea Crown of Roskilde. The witches have known about it for years," Danu stated. "It's one of the relics of the old times, or so my Master Afar thinks. A powerful magical object that has kept the island kingdom of Roskilde safe for generations," he stated.

"Great. Good for it." I held onto the mast, wishing that the fish-boy would stop talking now. Down below Adair was again at the prow, but he was fiddling with the grab-lines, I noted. He should only be on lookout duty, I thought, he should know to call up another hand if he spots something else that needs doing!

"Lila, *that* crown should be on your head. It's right now sitting on the head of a usurper. This is a great, great evil in the world, and one which will only create more evil for everyone…" Danu said.

Really? He was going to try to give me a lecture right now? I thought. "I've already agreed with you that I will help you look into this prophecy of yours, adept," I stated. "You don't have to bore me with the details…"

"Lila!" His tone was suddenly hurt, like I had personally insulted him. "It's not *just* the prophecy I'm trying to tell you about – although that is the whole reason why I am here, and why I found you…" He looked appalled and hurt. "It's the fact that a great evil has been done to the islands by Lord Havick. An evil which needs a good person to right it."

"And you think *I'm* that person, right?" I forced my eyes open again to glare at him. "Do I *look* like your amazingly heroic queen?" I muttered, feeling angry at him seeing me like this, scared and clutching the mast. I didn't feel very heroic right now. Maybe I was never going to learn how ride a dragon. I accused myself. *Maybe Father is right. Maybe these are all just useless, fanciful dreams.*

"Yes," Danu said, his almond-green eyes wide with an earnest hope that made me feel ashamed. "But there are many types of queens, or so the histories tell us. There was the Old Queen Delia; some say she was good, others say she was terrible. There is Saffron…"

"Queen Saffron," I corrected defensively. "The only woman to rise from island girl to queen, *and* a dragon friend!" I felt fiercely proud of her.

"And Queen Saffron." Danu nodded, his face quirking into a smile for some reason. Did he find my loyalty funny? "There are good queens and bad ones, and I know that a *good* queen doesn't take money from the poor to fill her coffers."

"What?" I frowned, my anger once again making me forget my fear of heights. *Was he seriously trying to rebuke me for being a Raider, and doing what Raiders do?* "What about if someone takes from the poor to give to other poor people who need it just as much?" I demanded of him. "Because, remember that is what is happening here, Danu – the Raiders need that gold if we are to survive another year. We need the food it can buy, we need the repairs it can pay for, we need the medicine it can bring, just as much as these islanders do!" I snapped, swinging myself to climb down with anger fueling my limbs. I didn't even think of falling at all, until I was jumping down to the deck and shouting for the crew.

"Weapons ready! Stay out of sight until captain's orders!"

CHAPTER 8

DANU, MUTINEER

The Torvald ship cut through the waves towards us, and the Sailing Master Kal kept us to a fast course that would pull us right alongside her. It was just past midday, and it was fine and clear with a brisk wind. An excellent day for raiding.

What under the stars am I doing? I thought in alarm as Lila thumped the leather cuirass jacket into my hands and told me to stay out of the way.

"Lila…" I tried to catch her eye, to impress upon her the importance of what I had been trying to tell her, but she just ignored me, grabbing the next leather jacket to hand to the next Sea Raider. We all were expected to pick up a short-bladed scimitar or a bow, and ready ourselves by the gunwales, out of sight.

So, this is what raiding is, I thought as I crouched beside

the others. Hiding out of sight, and then murdering innocent people? The thought of what Afar might say or think if she could see me now filled me with a deep shame.

But the prophecy had led me here, to that girl! I pleaded with her memory, or with fate itself. How could the prophecy be wrong? Lila was the un-crowned Queen of Roskilde, rising from the waves, I was certain of it – but why would fate want the rightful Queen of the Western Islands to be a bloodthirsty pirate?

I feared not only for my safety, but more than that – I feared what would happen to Lila herself if she carried out her plan to turn her Raiders into Dragon Mercenaries. Would a dragon even agree to such a plan? I thought. The accounts in the library of Sebol had talked about the dragons as a very proud, ancient, and noble species but one that could just as easily be arrogant and cruel. If a dragon went too long without the company of its fellows and brood mates, then they could become wild and evil beings, thinking themselves to be gods.

And the idea of cruel dragons with cruel Riders atop them was something that I couldn't let happen.

"If you don't have to use magic, then you shouldn't," I whispered Chabon's old advice to me. I wondered if that counted for prophecies and the fate of nations as well. If, by my aid, I was just going to introduce a great evil to the world, then maybe I shouldn't. Maybe I should give up this ridiculous prophecy right now, and be content to avert a much greater evil–to stop Lila from managing to create an army of Dragon Mercenaries to harass, murder and steal with impunity.

"What's that, friend?" said one of the Raiders beside me, one of the younger ones called Adair. He looked nervous too, but he also had the gleam of white teeth in his savage, almost manic grin. "You scared? This your first raid?"

I nodded. Both were true, but they weren't the *only* things that I was scared of.

"Look. Most people give up as soon as they see that we're Raiders. Don't worry. I'll look out for ya." Adair gave me a clap on the shoulder.

"You don't even know me," I said, confused.

Adair looked at me with equal bafflement, as if I had asked if the moon was made of blue or white cheese. "Maybe not *well,* but I've sailed with you, Danu." He locked eyes with me. "That's something you never hear about us Raiders. We're *loyal.* If you sail with us, then you're our *family,* see? We look after our family. It's not just us Raider's among the crew, look…" He nodded to the fair-haired brothers. "Their mother and father were from Torvald. Came out here before I was born, took to the seas to escape the Dark King. We took them in, and the brothers were born on this very ship. Look over there." He nodded to the dark-skinned Raider with the shaved head. "He's from the southern lands. Made his way up here escaping the seas-know-what, and we took him in. Half of the hands here are islanders, not from Malata, but from the archipelago."

I looked around and I saw that Adair was right. Where before I had just seen a fierce and disreputable crew, I now looked at them, seeing a motley collection of races, ages, men and women, all working together to protect their free way of life.

"So, I reckon you'll fit right in, especially if you can fish as good as you did on the first few nights!" Adair laughed, earning a stern *'hsssh!'* from the sailing master.

But young Adair had given me something new to think about. *Yes,* these Sea Raiders were a dangerous, blood-thirsty folk. But they were also a loyal folk, who loved their freedom, and were willing to respect others who did the same. I wondered if there was a way that I could use that to make Lila see the better path…?

"Steady now, boys and girls…" the captain said as we drew closer to the merchant's ship. I could peer through the water-run off gaps in the gunwhale, to see that we were close, *very* close.

"Ready the cannon teams…" the captain whispered, and my heart froze in my chest. *We were going to fire on them?* They would drown. Innocent people would drown…

"Roskilde vessel!" A loud voice called over the waves. "We are the Red Dragon's Pride, under Torvald protection, state your intentions!" The voice was loud and fine, not the gruff booming of Captain Kasian.

"Are we close enough to swing across?" Kasian, unable to see, asked the sailing master, who was smiling and waving at the other vessel. The sailing master gave a quick shake of the head at his captain.

"State your intentions!" The same, finely-toned voice called again.

I held my breath, terrified that we would fight, and that we would spill blood. There was only one thing that I could do – what I had to do. I closed my eyes, set my hand on the deck and hunched over as if I were going to be sick, while I tried to find that quiet, inner place and reached out to the magic inside of me.

CHAPTER 9
LILA, DISAPPOINTED

"State your intentions!" The Torvald Captain repeated. I gritted my teeth as I peered at him from where I lay flat on the deck, through a gap in the gunwales. He wouldn't be an easy man to kill, and I was suddenly scared for my father. It's not that the rival captain was large at all – no, he looked more like thin Adair than he did my father – or even stocky Danu! But he had on him a metal helmet and shaped armor, leather scales like a dragon's, with ring mail interspersed. Large gauntlets, and I could see on his deck a phalanx of longbowmen.

They don't look much like traders, I thought, as suddenly, there was a crackle of thunder.

"What?" I thought, looking up to see that there was a knot of dark clouds boiling through the air towards us. They must have been hidden by the near cliffs of the islands, but now they were riding down from the hills, bringing with them wind and rain. The sea got choppy, and the boat started to rock.

"Evasive maneuvers!" the captain snapped to his crew, swinging his vessel further out away from where the wind and waves were threatening to dash us together.

"No!" I heard a low moan as my father leapt to his feet. He hated having to hide before a raid, even though he also loved the surprised shock that he would see in their faces when he revealed himself. We were still too far out to swing across on ropes, and our short bows wouldn't be effective against their armor and helmets.

And they had longbows. "Father!" I hissed. "They've got the longer range!" I warned him. I saw him grunt and nod.

"Bring us about, sailing master. Ready the cannonade!" my father bellowed as the other Raiders started jumping to their feet.

The captain of the *Red Dragon's Pride* had already seen that we were no ordinary Roskilde naval vessel, and was whistling his orders to his crew to put on sails and extend oars. They had the advantage over us with the wind already behind them, but we were the quicker vessel, if the sailing master could cross the gale's path.

"Hyurgh!" Kal the Sailing Master slipped in the sleet, suddenly pelting all of us out of nowhere. Above him the wheel spun, and the *Ariel* started listing out of control.

"No!" I cried out, skidding on the deck to climb up to where the wheel was and seize it's spinning handles—

"Ach!" The fast-rotating handles batted my hands away before I dove at the wheel again, throwing myself bodily against it to slow it down. The pull of the strengthening waves against the rudder was incredible, and I felt the boat slipping out of my grasp, moments before Kal managed to find his footing on the other side of me, and seized the far side of the wheel to add his strength to my own.

"I don't know what happened," Kal muttered. "It felt like someone pushed me!"

Between us, we managed to bring the *Ariel* back under control, but the Torvald ship already well and away, speeding towards the horizon. The storm was all around us, with the waves starting to rise and crash at our hull as the Raiders abandoned their weapons to tend to the sails.

"We can still catch them!" I shouted to my father, storming and grumbling on the deck. "The *Ariel* is the fastest thing on the sea…"

"No, First Mate Lila," my father shouted. "They're ready for us now, and they've got cannons and longbows. I don't want to risk damaging the *Ariel*."

I growled in frustration, even though I knew my father was right. That fat little trading boat had been far better equipped than we had expected. They had armor and seemingly trained soldiers, and we only had three good vessels left thanks to Havick. It was far better to pick on smaller and easier targets than to pick a fight with one we might not be certain to win.

This is why we need dragons, I thought angrily as I manhandled the wheel alongside Kal, and fled the storm.

☙❧

CHAPTER 10
DANU, DRAGON-TONGUE

The next four days aboard my new home proved uneventful, insofar as raiding went. A foul temper bedeviled the crew, emanating from the captain himself, as he stormed this way and that across the deck, picking on minor faults and petty wrongs wherever he could find them.

But no one guessed that it was me who had summoned the storm, I thanked the stars on many occasions. The fact that I was wracked by headaches and nausea for the next three days Adair and the others put down to my "landlubber ways" and, regarded me with amusement, if not a gentle sort of scorn. As for Lila, she was caught up in the same foul mood as the chief was, but I could see her desperately trying to prove herself to the crew. She worked more watches than any other on the boat, often staying up late into the night or through the early hours well past midday, helping with the ropes, hauling in the fishing catch, tightening the sails. I tried to copy her example, but the nausea left by my magic only made me clumsy. I wondered what would come of me after this voyage. Had I already done enough to impress the captain, or would they be putting me on a boat and sending me back to Sebol?

"Sick again, is he?" Was the only remark that I earned from Kal the Sailing Master, as he was more concerned with the mood of the captain.

I was only too glad when the week was up and Kasian agreed, regretfully, that we had to return to homeport. We reached the outskirts of Spine Rocks one nightfall, and the mailing master announced that it would be wiser to anchor at sea than to navigate the crossing in the dark, given how tired and miserable the crew was. The captain agreed, but that night, I was surprised when First Mate Lila summoned all crew to the deck of the *Ariel*.

"What does she want?" said Senga, sitting next to Adair as she always did. The other Raiders didn't know, but everyone was visibly relieved when they saw the captain accompanying the first mate to address us over our simple meal.

"Raiders! Ladies and gents!" the Captain called, his voice loud and commanding, if not especially thunderous. "You may have heard the rumors of what my daughter and first mate here wants to do. Well, those of you who haven't are going to find out now. So, shut up and listen good; for she has my blessing."

Unsure of what their first mate was going to propose, the

crew's ears perked up as Lila took centre stage at the railing of the top deck.

"Brothers and sisters of the seas," she called out, her eyes flashing with passion, and her voice filled with it. "We've had a terrible raid!" she announced. I watched as a ripple of superstitious unease spread through the crew around us. This wasn't usually what a first mate was supposed to say to their crew, I gathered.

"Awful." Lila continued, her eyes shining wet with tears of frustration or anger. "We came close to the best haul we've had in many a year, only to see it slip through our fingers! Now, we're going home to our families, our mothers and fathers and wives and children with nothing to show for our hard work!"

"Ain't that the truth," grumbled Adair, earning a warning elbow from his sister Senga.

"How are we going to feed hungry mouths? How are we going to tend the sick among us? How are we going to survive next winter, with Havick's navy squeezing our territory, every season?" She thumped her fist on the railing.

"Yeah. Disgrace!" one of the more cantankerous Raiders muttered.

"Well, I have the answer, my brave friends," Lila announced to the skies. "Dragons!"

A silence settled over the crew, as I watched something start to happen. Lila was talking to their hearts. She was capturing their imagination. I felt a surge of renewed hope.

She was a queen, all right. She knew how to reach out to people even if she didn't believe that she could.

"You know how strong they are, how powerful, how fast and terrible…" Lila looked into the faces of the crew, holding gazes where they frowned at her, until the crew member was forced to look away. "The western dragons are the Raiders of the sky, going where they want, when they want. Nothing stands in their way – not Havick's ships, for sure!" she laughed, and this time was joined by a savage chuckle from the assembled as they doubtless imagined dragons destroying Roskilde boats.

"There was once a woman from these very islands – you may have heard of her – Queen Saffron Zenema, who managed to raise an army of dragons to retake Torvald from the Dark King. You've all heard that story, haven't you?"

"Aye…" the crew responded.

"She was just like you or me, an island girl, only she rode dragons. And it was those dragons that changed the future of the world. Well – *I* know that my Raiders are brave enough and strong enough to become Dragon Riders. *I* know because isn't that what we do, every season? We fly over the warm seas, through the teeth of storms!"

A few excited cheers rose from the crew.

"If Queen Saffron could do it, then I am sure we can. *I* know where there is a clutch of dragon eggs, and I intend to raise them as our own, so we can become Dragon *Mercenaries!*"

A hushed silence fell over the group.

"Impossible," the cantankerous Raider opined.

"Not impossible. *Necessary,*" Lila countered. "Imagine what power we would have! Imagine how strong we would be! Do you think that fat little merchant ship would have gotten away from us this week if we had a dragon?" I watched as she fell silent, waiting for her crew to imagine what might have happened. I saw slow, cautious smiles spread across the crew, with Adair and Senga being the first.

"So, will you support me in my quest? Will you be ready to take to the skies, and deliver fear and fire to our enemies?" she demanded.

"Aye!" Adair shouted, followed by others. But not all agreed, I could see. Many of the older Sea Raiders appeared wary of this new plan, the crew split fairly evenly, about whether to support Lila's plan or stick to their traditional seafaring ways.

But Lila, I saw, took it as a victory as she nodded and raised her fist into the skies. "To the future! For the Sea Raiders!"

"For the Sea Raiders!" the crowd roared.

☙❧

"You are sure?" Kasian said once again to his daughter before he helped her over the side of the *Ariel* and onto the small boat that the *Ariel* carried. It was a sharp little vessel with a mast, sail and oars, that the Raiders must use for their lightning-fast raids on beach villages. It would work perfectly for our purposes.

"Yes, Father. You know this is the only way," she said softly.

"Then go." Her father nodded gruffly. "You know what I think, but you won *some* support of the crew, and you may be right. It is better that you go and find out now, rather than lose another season."

"And the chance of those eggs." Lila nodded, and gave her farewells.

We were put over the side, and, after using the oars to push ourselves free from the *Ariel,* we were soon picking our way north and west, heading once more out into open waters.

"I hope you really *can* speak to dragons, adept," Lila said a little heavily to me as we worked to unfurl the sail and guide the rudder.

I nodded, not saying anything. And I hope that you find out what being a queen really means, Lila of Roskilde, I thought.

∞

"Are you sure that we're going to need these?" Lila asked me dubiously, patting the heavy oak cask that I insisted that she ask her father to gift to us. The winds favored us, and the spine of the dragon atoll could already be seen on the far horizon.

We made good time, I congratulated myself. *It must be the prophecy, wanting to be fulfilled.*

"Danu? Are you listening to me?" Lila cleared her throat as she said it again. She was stilling acting like the first mate, I thought, even on this, our boat of two people.

"Yes, Lila, I am listening to you. Do you think that we could approach a dragon without gifts?" I said with a smirk. She still had a lot to learn about the ways of dragons.

A frown crossed her features, and I half expected her to argue with me again (it seemed to be one of her favorite hobbies, during the two nights it had taken us to get here).

"Okay then." She nodded, surprising me. Her father had balked at the idea of offering the dragons *anything,* and especially not the *Ariel's* kitty, but, in the end, Lila had pestered him until he had agreed to parcel out a *few* of the gold doubloons, and a *scattering* of the gemstone bracelets and medallions that the Raiders kept on board in case they needed to buy provisions, or bribe officials.

It was a very small offering, I thought with alarm, especially as we were essentially asking a wild brood dragon to give up her eggs to some human that she didn't even know.

"The scrolls are clear," I tried to convince myself as much as her. "That a dragon likes two things above all else: flattery and precious things." Hopefully our blue dragon had simple tastes.

"These scrolls…." Lila tapped her finger on the edge of the boat. "These would be in Sebol, right?"

"The home of the West Witches, where I come from, right." I nodded.

"You were born there?" she asked, trying to distract herself from the task ahead, I reasoned.

"Me? No. They don't usually train children on the island, but I was an exception. My mother and father were fisherfolk from Tamm," I said.

"Hm." Lila nodded. "I know of it. A southern island. Still under Roskilde's Navy, though…"

There wasn't much that *wasn't* under the reach of their powerful, ocean-conquering galleons, I shrugged. "I managed to quell a storm when I was just a child," I said carefully, not wanting to reveal that I had in fact *raised* that storm as well. "They took me to the Isle of the West Witches, fearful that the islanders would probably drown me."

"Mages aren't welcome anywhere," Lila said. "Not after the Dark King."

"No. Not after the Dark King," I agreed. I sometimes wondered if my parents giving me up so early had been because *they* had been scared of me, just as much as others were scared of magicians in general. I knew that even on Sebol, there had been some amongst the wise witches who had counselled caution in training me. *'No one wants another Enric!'* I would hear whispered from behind the shutters. *'What are we bringing into the world?'* And then Chabon's croaking, ancient voice telling them that if they didn't have to kill me, they shouldn't. Those early days had been filled with fear. I remembered waking up in the middle of the night, as scared of these strange women as I was of what they thought I might become. But then Afar took me on. A strict task master perhaps, but kind. "You must learn to trust your heart, little Danu – for I can see that it is a good one," she would say to me.

"We're almost there," I said, eager to change the subject.

"But you learnt about dragons there, on Sebol?" Lila asked, her voice careful, as if she were making complex calculations as she spoke. "They have a lot of scrolls about dragons, do they?"

"Ha. If you think the West Witches are going to help you train the dragons, Lila, then no, they wouldn't," I said, guiding the rudder to take us straight for the golden beach of the atoll. "They are ruled by old Chabon, who thinks the witches shouldn't interfere. It was hard enough for my own Master Afar to convince her to let me go!" I said.

"But can they *all* speak to dragons?" Lila asked fiercely. It seemed important to her. I wondered what to tell her. Would she abandon me to seek their help instead? After I have done so much to get myself here, striking out alone with a boat, offering to help her and her violent people? Would she think *more* kindly of my plan to follow the prophecy and make her the queen if I told her they did?

I didn't want to tell her about the fact that no, only *I* could speak the dragon tongue. It had always been a private thing, a thing that I wasn't sure of myself, and that I didn't want corrupted by telling another soul.

I had been young when I saw my first dragon. It was almost my first memory, I think. Curled up against my mother's chest as we walked the coast, to see a glorious flight of sea-greens and blues diving down the cliffs, straight into the water like thrown spears. My mother had frozen, terrified, but I had heard their voices in my head as they chirruped and talked to each other.

"There, Vasjol! That fish!"

"No, Tiliban, that one is mine!"

"Well, Danu?" Lila pressed me for an answer, her eyes clear and yearning as she bit her lip. She looked so vulnerable right now, so desperate for this plan of hers to go right. She has set herself against everything her people hold dear for this, I thought.

"No," I found myself saying. "Only I can speak to the dragons, that I know of."

CHAPTER 11
LILA, TAUNTING DRAGONS

The boat scraped up the golden sands, and once again I found myself on the dragon atoll where this had all started. But I didn't feel the same, somehow. There was *more* riding on this now. I had the blessing of my father. I had asked the crew for their permission. They were *expecting* me to get this right.

"Help me with this, will you?" I said to Danu, seizing one end of the wooden cask as he seized the other. It was heavy, but most of that I feared was the heavy oak, the iron binding, and the large lock. *If my father hasn't given me enough to make friends with a dragon, I'll brain him,* I thought. Before or after I was eaten, I wasn't quite sure...

We thumped the cask and our small amount of provisions up by the rocks at the edge of the beach, and I set out my cloak to dry in the warm sun. "I want to look my best to approach the dragons," I said.

"They won't care how you look. Maybe how you smell," Danu said in a considering tone, and I couldn't tell if he was making fun of me or not. He had changed, too, over the course of the last week and the two nights it had taken to get here. He was, if anything, quieter and more thoughtful. No longer so urgent and desperate to force me to become the 'Sea-Queen of Roskilde' or whatever it was he believed. For that, at least, I was glad, but I also found him looking at me at odd times, as if he were judging me.

Well, Lila of the Raiders will not be judged by anyone! Let alone Danu, the wannabe mage! I thought haughtily. "I still want to look good," I said, teasing out my braid and using the small metal comb that my mother had given me to brush it through, before retying it back. It didn't take long for my cloak to dry on the warm sands, and I shook it out to fasten it with the gold pin that my father had given me. "So, how do I look?"

"Like a queen," Danu said with a crooked smile, bowing.

"Ugh." I shook my head at his theatrics. "Well, if you want me so desperately to be the queen, you can carry the cask then," I said, turning to head towards the spire of rock where the brood dragon would surely be.

We picked our way through the upland of rocks and scrubby bushes, eventually taking turns to carry the cask of treasures after I had taken pity on the struggling Danu behind me. The sun was heading toward setting when a low, haunting call pierced the air.

"*Skreeee....*" Instantly, the hairs on the back of my neck stood up and a shiver went down my spine.

"Okay, we should stop," Danu said. "She's warning us," he said, heaving the cask onto the floor and stepping back.

"She can't even see us!" I pointed out to the spire of rock, and the dark cave that was already shadowed.

"Don't think she can't. Dragons have senses far better than our own. Eyes like hawks, noses that can smell fish under the waves, ears that can hear the rumbling of frost storms leagues before they come down into the western oceans..." Danu whispered. "She's known all about us ever since we started heading into her territory, I shouldn't wonder."

My mouth went dry. This mother dragon could have killed us at any time she chose then. She could have attacked us when we were out at sea, with no chance of running away. "What do we do?" I whispered.

Danu behind me looked wide-eyed and as nervous as I was. Did he really know as much about dragons as he pretended to? I thought in alarm.

"Ears so good they can hear frost storms?" I checked, to Danu's worried nod. "Fine. It means she can already hear us then." I turned back to the spire ahead of us, clearing my throat, and began.

"Great dragon! We two have come bearing gifts for you. We want to make a peace offering, and have a, uh…" *How do I tell it that I want to take its babies away with me? How would my mother, Pela, feel if someone told her that they wanted to buy me?* "And we want to discuss matters of great importance with you!" I finished with a flourish.

Nothing for a moment, and then a low, answering hiss – but it didn't come from the atoll spire, it seemed to come from the gathering darks. Had the dragon slid out of the cave while I was talking to Danu? Or did it have another secret exit?

"Great dragon?" I tried again, thinking of a different tactic. I would try to impress her. "I am Lila of Malata, successor to the mighty Chief Kasian of the Sea Raiders. First Mate of the *Ariel*, winner of battles, I can…"

"SKREYCH!" The evening was suddenly illuminated by a gout of scarlet flame, and, in that light I could see the sudden shape of a long, blue-scaled body with a pale underbelly. A long, sinuous neck that arched up into the air, atop which was a narrow, pointed head – still able to swallow me whole. Her claws were as long as short swords, and her body as large as the *Ariel,* if not larger.

"*Sweet waters!*" I swore, stumbling back.

"She says that she doesn't care what you call yourself," Danu stuttered beside me. He fell silent, his head bowed as the dragon's head bobbed at him. "She's asking me why I have brought back to her island the egg thief…" Danu was pale and shaking.

We're both going to die tonight, I thought, but what I said was, "I didn't mean any harm!"

"Lady Blue," Danu beside me said. "Strong and wise Lady of this island, you who have seen much in your years, and have seen more than any human could ever hope to – I know that you can see the truth of what my friend Lila here says. She meant you no insult, she merely sought to bond with your newts."

"Schreeeech?" A short, sharper note came this time from the Sinuous Blue dragon.

"Of course!" Danu said, his voice getting firmer as he continued to talk. "Who *couldn't* want to be a dragon friend? To be a dragon friend is truly the greatest accolade that any human can have! No wonder my friend Lila here sought you out, of all the other dragons."

The Blue set her front paws down on the ground with a thump that I could feel through my feet, stalking forward towards us, the tip of her tail lishing and lashing like a disgruntled cat. But I thought that she wasn't going to eat us just yet.

"Offer her the stones, Lila," Danu hissed at me. "Be nice to her!"

He didn't have to ask me twice. I took a hesitant step forward, unlocked the cask, and opened wide the lid. The treasure was pathetically small even to my eyes, but it was also treasure that I knew that the Raiders could ill afford to lose. *I had to make this count.* "Beautiful Lady Blue," I copied Danu's example. "No gem or gold could ever compare to just the gleam of one of your scales, but I would be honored if these found a home with you…"

The dragon's head darted forward to sniff at the treasure, before slowly raising her head back again. I felt a slight pressure behind my eyes, and I thought that I could *almost* hear something, like a soft susurrus of wind in my ears, until Danu spoke.

"She doesn't think much of them."

"I could get more?" I offered.

"No, Sym just doesn't like jewels and gold," Danu said hesitantly.

"Sym?" I asked, and as soon as I said the word, the dragon hissed, and her head darted forward once more to hang over us.

"Uh, I probably shouldn't have told you the dragon's name. She told me because," Danu flickered a finger to his temples, "because I have a touch of the dragon gift, but…"

"Oh." Great. There was no way this dragon was going to like me, because I wasn't a mage, or a witch. My dreams started to crumble before my very eyes, to be replaced by a slow, burning despair.

Again, came that pressure between the dragon Sym and the Adept Danu, but I had my head hung, glaring at my boots.

How could I have gotten this so wrong? After everything I have given to this?

"But Lady Blue, a bond between our peoples would be beneficial to us both! And your children – how strong and brave they are sure to be – they will be known and loved by humans all across the Western Archipelago! Everyone will sing of their exploits!" Danu said, and was answered by the sharp whistles and chirrups of the mother dragon above us. After every exchange, I could tell that the negotiations must be going badly.

"Well, we could 'try our luck' at Torvald, as you so wittily put it, but we would rather make friends with our own wild and free island dragons!" Danu said desperately.

Everything I had dreamed about, I thought miserably. All of the faith and the hope that my father, my mother, and my crew had placed in me to get this right. We Raiders wouldn't last another season if we didn't have a dragon.

"Coward," I spat.

"Lila, no!" Danu gasped.

"Sssssss….!" The Blue dragon–Sym–made a low, threatening hiss like a boiling kettle.

"Lady Blue." I raised my head. *If we Raiders are dead anyway, then we might as well go out in a way worthy of a song.* "I have come here, far, far from my homeport, especially to make friends with you. I did that because I *need* your strength. I *need* your fire, your bravery. *Why* do the Island Dragons live all the way out here, far from the others? Are you all *so tired* of the world that you would rather be forgotten by it?" I said angrily.

"No…no…" Danu had fallen to his knees, aghast.

But I was angry, and nothing was going to stop me now. "I grew up wishing that I was someone else. That I was Saffron Zenema, not when she was Queen Saffron, but Saffron Zenema, the simple island girl." As soon as I said her name, the dragon hissed and reared her head. "You know why? Because of *dragons*. Because Saffron Zenema lived a life full of great adventure, full of bravery, and full of dragons. She did things that no woman has ever done before! She was brave, and so were her dragon friends." I challenged the Blue.

"I thought that all dragons would be as brave as those dragons of the past. You might not like humans much, Lady Blue – and I don't blame you, half the time – but together, I promise, humans and dragons can weave the most powerful stories that will shake the entire world!" I ended fiercely.

"Sckreyar!" The Blue dragon roared, rearing up and pounding her front claws back down again once more on the ground. But I stood, defiant, and I stared at her. *If you're going to kill me, then do it now, while I've still got the courage to stand and take it…* I glared at her.

But, amazingly, she didn't kill me. She didn't pour her dragon flame over us. Instead, she very gradually lowered her head to my level, to sniff at me. Her large, scaled nostrils flared once, twice, before she *huffed* heavily, blowing sooty air all around us. And then, wondrously, she withdrew, stepping back into the darkness until all I could see were her glowing eyes, growing smaller and smaller, until they too winked out.

"You idiot." Danu breathed. "You amazing, incredible, idiot."

"What?" Suddenly I had to sit down as my knees started to shake and I gasped for air as I realized that I had challenged a dragon with nothing more than my words, and won.

"It seems that as well as shiny things and praise, dragons like a challenge." Danu was grinning at me wildly. "She says that she likes you. You have guts. She said you have some of the same fire that Saffron of Zenema had, and that is why she will let you stay on her island until the hatching, tomorrow night. The newts will choose for themselves if they want to bond with you, and she will not interfere." I watched the mage gulp in amazement. "This… This is astonishing. I've read some of the histories of Torvald, they talk about a Choosing Ceremony, a Testing, nothing like this…" He was tapping his lips, deep in thought. "Don't you see? This could be the first dragon-initiated bonding!"

I didn't know what that meant, but, right now, all I cared about was the fact that I had done it. I had dared the dragon into helping me, and it seemed to have worked.

Kinda.

CHAPTER 12
DANU, AND THE HATCHING

To be honest, I half expected to see the blue dragon charging down at our camp when I awoke the next morning, certain that what had happened last night had been a dream.

It wasn't, though, of course. Somehow, miraculously, that crazy girl had managed to convince a dragon into allowing her hatchlings to bond with her. It still made my stomach turn over when I thought of the sight of it: the brave Lila standing with her chin struck out, defiant, as the Sinuous Blue had lowered her snout and snuffed her. Her front fangs had been clearly visible, almost as big as the girl's chest. It was like something from the old books.

I grumbled as I got up, to find that the fire had already been stoked, and a new mat of tide-wood had been laid across it. Our camp was simple, beside the keel of our small boat on the beach, with just a blanket each to call our beds. Not like the huts of Sebol, I grimaced. The West Witches lived simply, but their long years of serving the Western Archipelago meant they had also become rich, of a sort. Not Roskilde rich, but enough to be able to afford fine bedding, rare incenses, well-made furniture.

The Raiders, on the other hand, seemed to be *much* more industrious, I thought as I saw Lila already returning with a brace of silver sea fish on the end of a thread-line.

"We'll roast them over the fire, and have a decent meal before the hatching tonight, at least," she said with a grin.

Gone was the surly, annoyed chief's daughter of the last few days, and instead of her fierce braid, I saw that she had let her hair hang wild as she fished. There was a lot of it, and it softened her features.

"You should smile more often," I said, not stopping to think about it. It was something that Chabon had said to me once, scolding me that I was always too serious. The smile on Lila's face transformed her from a blood thirsty Raider into a young, wild princess of the sea.

"Should I now? Why?" Lila's grin turned into a frown in an instant. "Because it pleases *you?*"

"I uh, no, I just mean…"

"From what I remember, it wasn't any *smiling* that I did last night that made that dragon respect me." She dumped the fish onto the just starting to smolder driftwood. "Cook that, will you? Or don't they teach adepts how to cook fish out there on the Haunted Isle?"

The Haunted Isle. That is what the more superstitious of the Western islanders called Sebol. We witches weren't *universally* respected across the islands, I had to remember.

But, I knew well how to cook fish. The West Witches might receive lots of gifts from their allies, but that didn't mean we also didn't support ourselves. I brushed down one of the large rocks by the side of the fire, took out my knife, and started to skin and gut the medium-sized fish, throwing the bits to the gulls that were even now gathering for the scraps.

I could almost get used to this, I thought, as I worked and Lila combed the beach around us.

"She didn't like the jewels and gold," Lila said distractedly. "When we offered it to her, she wouldn't take it."

I shook my head. "I read that dragons love riches, but not all do. She must be the odd one out."

"Maybe we didn't offer her enough..." Lila rehearsed out loud greeting the hatchlings. "Welcome to the world, brave little friends!" she said with a very wide, and very fake smile.

"They'll see through that a mile off," I pointed out. If there was anything that the scrolls and books *had* made clear, it was that dragons could tell when someone was lying to them or trying to trick them. They were cunning creatures themselves.

There was a crack like a branch snapping in half, followed by a splash and I looked up suddenly to see a high plume of water slowly falling back to the sea. It must have been a whale or a jumping fish, I thought, before suddenly another shape descended out of the heavens, and entered the water like a dart.

They were dragons. Not as large as Sym in her birthing cave, but still *very* large compared to us. Another, circling above us, folded its wings and shot straight down like a thrown dart, plunging into the water and disappearing. It had been a turquoise blue, with the reflected light of the sun highlighting green along it's back.

"Sea Dragons!" I called out in joy. They were just the sort I had seen when I was young, when I had first realized that I could hear dragons.

Closing my eyes and sitting up, I tried to find that quiet place inside that connected me with all things, and then, to the three creatures that were even now diving under the waves.

"Ha! There – that one!"

"No! That one is mine!"

They were young Sea Dragons, playing as they chased and caught fish. The sheer joy and passion they had for the activity spread through my mind and I found myself grinning like a lunatic.

"Dragons! Will they harm the eggs?" Lila was saying to me urgently, kicking sand at me.

"Ah, what? No – I, uh, I don't sense any malice from them at all, not towards us or the Sinuous Blue…" To be honest, I had no idea what the normal behaviors between dragons were.

I knew they were clever, intelligent, and could be highly social animals – but these dragons didn't live in large broods, so...?

"We will have to be ready to defend the eggs," Lila said, as the fish started to char on one side.

With a joyful roar, the three Sea Dragons burst from the water, swooped around the atoll once, before one peeled off and swooped lower around us.

"Fish!" The thought pushed its way into my mind. I didn't think the dragon was *talking* to me, but rather that it was just being careless how it 'thought-talked.'

"What does it want?" Lila had crouched into a defensive stance, one hand edging towards her short bow.

As if that would do any good whatsoever.

"Come on, Talamand! We must return!" One of the other Sea Dragons was joyously shrieking, as 'our' dragon flicked its tail irritably, and swept back to its fellows, heading eastwards.

"I think it wanted fish..." I looked over to the now smoking fish on the fire. I knew that the Sea Dragons ate fish, and that they clearly enjoyed diving and hunting them through the waves.

"Do *all* dragons like fish?" Lila asked pensively.

"I don't know," I replied honestly. "I have never thought to ask them."

"*Roasted* fish." Lila nodded, gingerly picking up our breakfast and juggling the fish between her hands before laying them on a broad pad of leaves. "The dragons have their own fire, right? Well – I bet that is hard to control, compared to delicate human hands, and small human cookfires and stoves." She nodded, picking up the plate of leaves and disappearing up the beach with them.

"Hey! That's breakfast!" I shouted after her.

"It is. But not for us!" she said with a laugh. "If you want some more, you'll have to catch it yourself!" Lila walked up the beach to where the rockier upland began, and I saw her pick her way across the boulders and past the scrubby trees until she could ascend the Bonerock spire.

৩১৫৩

"Did she like it?" I asked my companion when she made her way back down again, hands empty of fish or plate.

"She wouldn't come out to try, but I heard a low grumble when I reached the cave, so I just put the food down outside and backed away," Lila said, a small frown before shrugging.

"You're lucky she didn't eat you after last night," I pointed out.

"No, I think that we're onto a good idea. Dragons like fish, right? And what's better than roasted fish? If only we had a bit of olive oil and seasoning." She sighed, crouching down to where I was already cooking the one large sea-trout that I had caught.

"That is a good catch," she said with a wry smile. "We'll make a Raider out of you yet."

"And *I'll* make a princess out of you," I countered, earning a frown, and the time of smiles was over.

"I don't *want* to be a queen, you know." Her voice was heavy and awkward, as if she were admitting to stealing a last bit of cake.

"I know that, but that already makes you pretty a good candidate," I pointed out.

"Roskilde is my sworn enemy," Lila said exasperatedly as I flipped the slab of trout over.

I remembered what Adair had showed me on the deck of the *Ariel.* All of the different races and nationalities, all of the different beginnings that people had. "Think of the Western Archipelago as a *family*, Lila," I said. "We all share the same waters, we all fish for food, we all trade. A big storm that comes through is likely to hit most of us as any..." I said. *Everyone on a ship was a family,* I remembered the young pirate saying.

"But my family doesn't try to kill me, and blow me out of the water!" Lila almost laughed. Almost, for her humor was tinged with sadness and worry.

"You should read some of the histories that *I've* read where it's *usually* the family who are trying to kill each other," I muttered. "But anyway. Families don't have to like each other. They don't even have to get on. But they're all connected. Just think about that for a moment," I said. "If the Western Isles could work together, could help each other, could stop fighting each other – then just imagine what we could achieve!"

"But Roskilde wants all of the Sea Raiders wiped out," Lila said.

"No, *Havick* wants that. Remember, half of your own crew comes from Roskilde, even probably have family still up there?"

Lila nodded and fell silent. It was true, and at last I thought I might have hit upon a crack in her armor. After all, *she* had been found during a raid, and during that raid *her* parents had died. How many of her crew members *didn't* want to raid the Roskildean or island villages where they might have uncles, nephews, or nieces?

I was about to point this out to her, when another shadow crossed the island, this one immense. We looked up to see the wings of a Great White dragon flaring over us, majestically moving around the atoll to descend to the far side of the island.

"A White dragon?" I stood up in awe. They were the largest of the dragons. Truly immense in scale, and could probably destroy entire towns alone.

"Saffron's den had a White dragon as their mother," Lila said breathlessly. "It was Saffron's closest friend other than her dragon."

"She died." I didn't want to break the girl's heart, but she had to know…

"I know. Everyone knows that story, *adept.*" Lila frowned

at me. "But she was the only White to live out here in the wilds, unless *another* one does now."

The chances of seeing four dragons in the same place, one after the other, was slim indeed. *No, not slim,* I thought. *Absolutely unheard of.* "What are they doing here?" I muttered.

We didn't see anything of the White as we practiced and rehearsed Lila's 'greeting the dragons' but the next set of dragons to arrive was a duo of Sea Dragons, flying low over the waves and landing on the far side of the island.

"This is too much of a coincidence," Lila said, keeping an eye on the boat. I could see her judging how long it would take her to get it out to sea in case any of the dragons decided to attack. Too long, I think the answer was clear, especially when another Sinuous Blue arrived, and shortly afterwards, two Stocky Greens.

"What do we do?" Lila asked me.

"I don't know! I've never been invited to a conference of dragons!" I pointed out, half in awe, and half in terror.

"But we *have* been invited to a hatching," Lila said. "And I'm guessing that's what all these dragons are here for too."

She was right, it had to be the only answer, I thought as a flight of the smaller Messenger dragons, some only as big as a forearm, swirled and chattered over the atoll before landing on the rocks. Then came another Sinuous Blue, two more Greens, and a flight of Vicious Oranges. More dragons arrived from every corner of the canvas, until the sky was filled with the sound of their shrieks and calls.

"Skreayach!"

"A new one!"

"Sym is having newts!"

Their voices were too much for my dragon sense, and so I had to use the restricting meditations that Afar had taught me, imagining a wall around my mind with windows that I could open when I needed to hear what the dragons were saying. Dragon-thought was like being filled with a rush of poetry and emotion all at the same time, because dragons do not think in the way that humans do. They do not have separate thoughts, words, and memories. Instead, their feelings *are* their thoughts, and their memories *are* their feelings. To have such a loud cacophony of dragoness, even if it is overwhelmingly joyful and happy, was too much for small human senses.

"You are right, Lila, they have come for the hatching," I gasped, as the day slid towards evening, and the sun started to lower itself towards the Western Seas.

Evening. When the dragon Sym had predicted that the eggs would hatch.

◈◈◈

The early evening airs were alive with screeches and whistles, peeps and roars. The dragons occasionally snapped at each other if one settled too close, or stood on another's tail but I was amazed at how peaceable they were. As the sun burnt the sea, and the sky turned orange-pink, a loud, mournful howl started from Sym's cave and was taken up from the dragons.

It seemed to last for ages, a long, wavering note that seemed mournful and defiant at the same time, finally holding a clear, sonorous tone that seemed to echo over the waters – before silence.

All of the dragons around us in the gathering gloom, their eyes bright and the last of the sun glinting from their scales, eerily raised their heads at the exact same time to look expectant at the cave.

"Can you feel it?" Lila asked me, the whites of her teeth showing as she grinned at me, excited.

I could, I nodded. It was like waking up on a spring morning after a long winter, when something in the air that promised more of everything, even though you didn't know what it could be. More light, more warmth, more *life*. "Yes. The eggs have hatched."

CHAPTER 13
LILA, AND THE HATCHING

As the last notes of the dying sun faded, the sky came alive with stars over our heads. The dragons had quieted, expectant, and I held my breath.

"Skrip?"

"Skree-ip!"

There were cooing chirrups and the soft sounds of the mother dragon coming closer to the beach, toward *us*.

"Now's our chance," I whispered to Danu, standing up to walk towards the noise. I tried to remember the words I had composed to greet them. '*Oh, noble dragons, born of fire and wind...*' I tried, before a spike of worry. Should I re-introduce myself to the mother dragon first? Shouldn't I ask her, formally, once again, if her hatchlings will bond with me? Danu, it seemed, didn't know the etiquette required to greet new baby dragons – and neither did I.

So much for all his training at mage-school, or whatever they call it, I thought with a heavy huff as I chose a spot that seemed to be right in the path of the encroaching dragons.

"Hsss!" A slithering hiss came from the rocks further up the beach, and I saw that the massive White dragon had pulled itself to the edge, looking first at me, and then out into the darkness. An answering rasp of a croak, and on the far side there emerged a Stocky Green, and another, then a Sinuous Blue.

All of the dragons were congregating on the beach, I realized. To watch what happens next.

There was a whooshing sensation of wind above me, as a large shape swept across the beach to land on the island, visible in the stars and the dying embers of our fire. A Red. A fantastic-sized, Crimson Red.

"Skreyar!" It crowed a joyous greeting at the others, and they hissed and chirruped, as if welcoming it. I had never seen a Crimson Red dragon. They were broad of limb and strong of body, larger than the Stocky Greens, not as long as the Sinuous Blues. This one seemed tired as its wings drooped; it was clear that it had flown a long way.

A series of whistles and chirrups emerged from the darkness, as the hatchlings emerged. All of the eggs had hatched, and hatched well. Each dragonet the size of a large dog, they tottered, tentative at first, into the soft light snuffing and pawing at the soft sand.

I gasped. They were beautiful, one a sea-turquoise green,

one a long blue, and the third a yellowing-orange, all with short, stubby tails, large, staring eyes, and snouts that ended in a dull point – an egg tooth?

The turquoise one made a long, mewling peep into the night, and suddenly all of the assembled dragons were cooing and chirruping at it. Even surrounded by these giant, deadly beasts, I did not feel any threat from them. The dragons appeared to be encouraging, singing to the younglings.

"Human." A voice rang in my head, and I looked up, surprised to see that the darkness above the beach head had now morphed into the proud head of the mother Blue. She was standing a little behind and over her creations, daring me to greet them too.

Just looking at them, I felt that my heart would burst. "Little friends!" I called out to them, earning a curious look from the sea-green and turquoise one *(the noisy one,* I thought proudly). "Look at you! Look how strong you are!" I said, all of my previous words and poetry forgotten as I reveled in their stubby limbs, their shining scales, their sharp little fangs, perfectly white.

"Meeeep!" The sea-green and turquoise took a few hesitant steps down the beach, looked back at its siblings, and then charged towards me.

Yes! I had done it! I had done it! I went down on one knee as hot tears of gratitude spilled down my cheeks— only for the little Sea Dragon to race past me, and launch itself to attack the receding surf.

"My friend?" I said a little uncertainly. "I am Lila. Lila of Malata, I would like to be your friend..."

The baby dragon completely ignored me. Well, there are still two more, I thought, my cheeks burning with embarrassment as I turned to the other two hatchlings.

"Noble dragons! Borne of fire and wind..." I began, as the small blue took one look at me and raced back up under the pillars of its mother's legs.

"What adventure I can offer you..." I said to the last remaining yellow-orange dragon, who hissed at me, revealing its sharp fangs, before immediately jumping past me, scampering up the rocks to swipe at the snout of the Crimson Red, who playfully bared its own fangs, before nudging it with a nose back down into the soft sand.

"I come bearing gifts..." My voice trailed off, as each of the three baby hatchlings resolutely ignored me.

"You have your answer, Lila of Malata." The words of the mother Blue rang in my head like a struck bell.

I had failed. None of the dragons wanted anything to do with me at all.

৩౩৩

"How could this be? But... But I did everything right?" I said, trying to sound indignant to Danu, although my voice wavered and I feared I might suddenly break into sobs. Danu had called me back to the embers of the fire, his face aglow with excitement as he watched the hatchlings and the other dragons recede up the beach.

"But Lila, there *isn't* a right way to do this. No one else has ever attempted it, as far as I know…" Danu was whispering, trying to cheer me up. He was just happy to be in the presence of the dragons, I saw, and could hardly stop his fool grin from spreading over his face.

But he doesn't know just what is at stake… I kicked the sand with my feet. My father had vouched for me with the rest of the crew. The crew had placed their trust in me to provide them with a future. I was trying to save them, and their way of life – but I had failed. I wasn't good enough for the dragons, or dragons didn't want anything to do with us humans any more.

"What do I do now?" I said to myself, but it was Danu who answered.

"You reclaim the throne, Lila! Don't you see–this *must* be the prophecy, coming to fruition! You couldn't deny it, just as much as I had to see you rising from those waters, that day! You were meant to unite the peoples of the Western Isles, for good!" He was bursting with pride.

"You're only saying that because it's something *you* want," I snapped. I didn't want to be anyone's queen. I didn't want to give up my dreams of flying dragons, just like Saffron of Zenema did.

And I didn't want to see the look on my father's face when I returned with nothing to show for my efforts.

"No, it's not just that," Danu argued, but I groaned and turned away from him.

"Enough for one night, Danu. I've failed at the only thing that I've ever really wanted to do with my life. Let me have one night's sleep, at least, before I have to decide what to do next."

The fish-boy, much to my surprise, obeyed my wishes and kept his own counsel. I tugged the blankets over me and curled up into a ball, even though I didn't feel cold in these warm waters. The joyous chirrups and calls of the dragons followed me to my dreams, where I was forever stuck in a room, and unable to get out to be with them.

❦

"Lila."

The voice spoke into my dreams, and I tried to push it away. Don't wake me up yet, Danu, I thought groggily. I knew that it must be getting late, and even though I had a terrible night of nightmares and anxiety dreams, I felt so crushed and defeated that I didn't want to face my life just now.

What was I to tell Father? Mother? The crew?

"Lila, wave-rider," the voice repeated, and I realized this voice *wasn't* Danu.

I was still sleepy, even though my body was warm with the early sun, but I could tell that the voice wasn't a human one. It was inside my head, for starters.

A dragon. I froze, awake now and with my heart hammering in my chest. There was the sound of crunching sand from somewhere nearby. Somewhere *very* nearby. Had I offended them by spending the night here on the beach? Had the mother Blue wanted me to leave then and there when her new-hatched dragons had rejected me so profoundly? I had no way of knowing what was the correct thing to do.

Maybe now she will eat me, I thought miserably. What a fitting end to a very short tale. 'Stupid dragon-girl fantasizes about dragons and then gets eaten by one' sounded like just the sort of tale that Captain Lasarn or Sam or Kal would spend many years spinning. Just not in front of my father, probably.

Well, I wasn't going to get eaten without a fight. But where was my knife? My bow?

Packed into the boat, because Danu said that it would be 'very bad form' for me to suddenly walk around the newly hatched dragons with weapons bared. Not that he knew anything about dragons, I decided.

"Lila wave-rider, arise!" The voice sounded in my head once again. It was undoubtedly draconian, I thought. *But I can't hear dragons,* I thought. Only this one, I *could!* There was a sensation of *size* to that voice, the way that my father had a booming voice even when he was talking normally. And there was a feeling of soot and claws and strength behind it as well. Definitely a dragon.

Tensing my muscles, I waited for the crunch of sand to begin once more, letting the dragon get as close as I dared. I

128

felt a wave of hot, sooty breath wash over me as I moved. The dragons of this island had already shown they didn't want to bond with me. It was only a matter of time before one of them decided to try and eat me. *Lasarn and the others had been right. I am the girl dreaming of dragons who ends up getting eaten.*

Only I wouldn't be.

I rolled. Hand grabbing the sand and turning, flinging it into the air meaning to blind the beast—

"Skreyar!" The roar of the dragon standing over me was deafening as it hopped lightly back, shaking its snout with a sneeze. I froze at the size of the beast. It was almost as large as a Crimson Red, much smaller than the mother Blue – and it was multi-colored. It had deep black scales along the ridge of its back, turning a delicate midnight blue, purple, and plum color in blotchy stripes towards its middle, where a line of turquoise green rippled along the edge of a paler creamy underbelly. I had never seen a multi-colored dragon, before, and it looked at me with shining, gold-green eyes.

"Crux."

I heard the word as clear in my head as if Danu had whispered it into my ear, and with it, came a wave of mirth. The sides of its great maw appeared curled, and a fork tongue flicked into the air, as if it were making fun of me.

"Let's see how you like it, Lila of the waves!" The multi-colored dragon made a quick, pouncing charge, shoving its

feet onto the sands between us and enveloping me in a plume of beach dust.

"Ugh! Ack!" I coughed and hacked, brushing the film of sand from my face as I realized the dragon was playing with me. I didn't sense any malice from its voice Instead, I felt a strong impression of laughter. *It wasn't trying to eat me,* I thought. Then what *was* it doing? Just making fun of me?

"Are you laughing at me?" I demanded of it, standing up to wave my finger at its snout.

"Yes," the dragon announced. *"You are very small. I am big."*

"Rargh!" I kicked sand at it, causing it to pounce back again, holding its head up and ears forward just like a cat does when it is excited. It made a churring, pleased warble of a sound as it then pounced forward again, showering me in sand.

"Hey! Stop that!" I shouted, coughing and floundering in the sudden sandstorm before I fell over.

"Now you look like a sea turtle," the dragon chirruped, opening its mouth to hiss loudly, and I saw myself in my own imagination how the dragon was seeing me. On my back, covered in sand, limbs waving in the sand as if I was indeed an overturned turtle. I started to laugh. It was ridiculous. *Is this dragon trying to...be my friend?*

My laughter was met by the sound of whistling peeps and hisses from the multi-colored dragon above me, as it trampled and stamped its feet in the sand some more, sending up plumes of sand over both it and me.

"You idiot," I said to it, still grinning.

"Not as much as you, trying to bond with newts," the words in my head said, laced with dragon mirth. *"All they care about is chasing fluff and sniffing for rats."*

"Huh." I found myself grinning at the dragon's words, even though they broke my heart. Yes. I had been wrong. It wasn't the first time, but I wondered if it would be my last. After this, I would have to become the First Mate to the Ariel for good, and abandon my dragon dreams.

"I am Crux," the dragon repeated, the humor fading from its voice as it arched its neck to reach down and gently breathed in the air above me with its snout. But I felt no fear in front of the large dragon, none at all.

Something hit my heart like a wave; *no,* something *inside* my heart moved like a wave. As I looked up towards the dragon, into it's green-gold eyes, I felt an answering connection. Another misfit, renegade soul like mine, and it was reaching out to me.

A dragon bond? I felt both scared and jittery with excitement.

But this Crux was older than the newts. He sounded young in my mind, but perhaps of a dragon-age to me, a youth ready for adulthood. Not a baby. How will I train you? I thought, suddenly realizing that this alternative could even be worse than not having returned with a dragon at all. There was so much to learn. How to ride a dragon, how to handle the harness and saddle. Where to even *get* such equipment. How to attack Havick's ships when called…. *I know nothing about training adult dragons.*

"Lila of the waters. I am Crux, and I like you, I think."

He thinks?

"If you do not wish to be a dragon friend then I will not blame you – not many would stand by a dragon, through thick and thin, when we have so many enemies." Crux started to raise its head a little, and Lila had the feeling that she must have insulted it. She sensed a wariness coming from Crux. Was it that he was multi-colored? The only multi-colored dragon that she had ever heard about? Why was he not with the other dragons?

"I have flown a long way to bear greetings to Sym's brood. There are so few of us Phoenix dragons left…"

"Phoenix Dragons?" I murmured.

"That is what we call ourselves. The multi-colored. The dragons of many shades." Crux was proud, defiant even. *"We have no natural home, and all the other breeds are cautious around us. But no matter. I know what I am: a dragon, borne of fire, raised to be strong."*

Crux was an oddball out here, just like me. That, I think, was when it happened.

I reached out with my heart, completely unable to stop it from answering the Phoenix dragon's call.

"Crux? I am Lila wave-rider, Lila of Malata, Lila of

Roskilde. Please forgive me—I would be honored to call you my friend," I said, and found that Crux had already lowered his snout, crisscrossed with the scars of some old battle, and our skin and scales touched.

A bolt of electricity between us, a sense of exhilaration as the contours of our souls met. It felt to me then, that I had been waiting all my life f0r such a true friend. I saw him and what he was; mischievous, a little proud, a little guarded around the other dragons, and he saw me for what I was; alone, always-vigilant, trying to be bigger and tougher than I felt.

And both of us accepted each other just for what we were.

"Come, Lila wave-rider. You shall be Lila air-rider, now!" Crux drew back from my touch to scoop my upturned-turtle body in his mighty claws and hop towards the open beach.

"What are you doing?" I managed to say as there was a sudden crack as of mighty sails unfurling. His wings, dark on top and lighter beneath, had unfurled and blotted out my skies as he took another hop, and then, with all the strength of a firing cannon, he threw himself up into the air with a joyous roar.

"Skreayar!"

PART II

Air-Riders

CHAPTER 14

LILA AND CRUX

We flew. Crux was faster than any boat I had ever sailed upon, and his wings boomed with the sound of thunder as he made his sharp turns.

"Skeyarch!" The bright sun was high above us, the sky was a deep blue, and the dragon above me called out a fierce challenge to the world.

"Whooot!" I myself howled at the thrill of it. The dark waters of the western seas blurred below me, the wave tops becoming just white lines, and then the edges of gigantic ripples making their way across the ocean.

I'm not scared, even though I am high up, and being held by his front claws that could rip me apart easily, I am not scared, I thought. I laughed at the wonder of it. Was some magic of the dragon's holding me, or was it that something had clicked in my heart, that meant that I was no longer scared of falling and failing.

"Wave-rider, air-rider. This is what you were meant to be, Lila." Crux's words, again filled my head as he swooped low over the oceans, so low that I could see the curves and curls of the waves, the leaping fish.

With a sudden clicking noise, a trio of grey and blue dolphins leapt into the air, spinning and corkscrewing underneath us as they kept pace with the Phoenix dragon's flight. I could reach out and touch the water behind them, before Crux once again cracked his great leathery wings, and we swooped up into the heavens.

"Let me ride, brother dragon!" I called up. I didn't want to be held anymore. I wanted to feel what it was like to ride a dragon just as Saffron rode a dragon. *How all of the Sea Raiders will eventually ride dragons...*

Crux checked his speed, moving his claws up to his shoulder. *"Careful, Lila,"* his thought-voice came with his emotions, his care and thirst for adventure. I had spent my life on a boat, I could climb – even if I hadn't liked it too much before. I set my hands to the scale-plates around his neck, and drew myself up, finding that there was a depression at the base of his neck and just ahead of the vast slabs of shoulder and wing muscle. Behind that, the tines of his back jutted out, looking wickedly sharp, while ahead, the nubs of his neck horns were smaller and rounded. With a grunt of effort, I managed to scrabble into this space, finding that my knees could slide over each side of his neck, a bit like I imagined what riding a horse must be like.

"Ready?" Crux's voice in my mind was full of amusement.

Before I had a chance to agree, Crux had taken a breath and snapped his wings, powering himself forward as he tucked his claws in under his body. I shouted, half out of fright and half out of joy as I seized the horn ahead of me, and felt my back press against the base of the thicker tine behind me. *What about Danu, back on the island...?* I had a moment to think, wondering if I should have said anything about my friend back there – but before I could, Crux was launching himself through the air at lightning speed. If I had thought that we were going fast before, then I clearly had no idea just how fast he could go!

Crux shot over the oceans like a released arrow, heading out and up, until I could see the far impressions of other lands on the horizon. Was that... Roskilde? Had we really flown that far?

Roskilde. It was a darker landmass, lifting its head into a haze of clouds. I had only ever seen the land of my supposed parents from afar, never up close – but I had no intention to see it now, either. That's the place that Danu wants me to rule, I thought. That dark island was large, far, far larger than Malata and the rest of the Free Islands of the Sea Raiders all put together – but that made it appear heavy and stolid. *Crux calls me wave-rider, air-rider – not throne-sitter!* I thought, wondering if there was a way to turn the multi-colored creature.

"I don't want to go there, Crux!" I called out, knowing that he would hear me. On a boat there would be a rudder, or you could reef one sail and open another, or even use oars to turn. Not so with a dragon.

Our flight slowed, but we still raced towards it. Crux cocked his great head up towards me, one giant gold-green eye spinning.

"But I have so many things to show you, Lila. The southern part of that island has a lot of little men with painful darts, and many more smelly men who live in stone houses – but the northern part has frozen icefalls and snow fields that you can swim like the oceans!" Crux reveled in my ignorance – not mocking me, I knew instinctively, but rather he was like Adair was to his sister Senga whenever he discovered something new about an island or caught a fish that she had never seen before. The dragon was eager to show off the world that he had flown through.

"And beyond that? I have never travelled to the far north, but east of here are mountains that scrape the heavens, and green lands where no human has trod for a hundred years! Deep forests and still lakes, river fish and canyons that howl with the winds..." Crux was making a twittering, almost singing sort of sound as he thought of all the marvels and wonders that he could show me.

"No, please, Crux. Take me back," I said, laughing. "I shall have to get a harness if we are to ride together."

"Never!" A ripple of unease shivered through the Phoenix dragon. *"I have heard the tales of what the north used to do to the wild dragons—chains and harnesses, old mutton and rangy goat. I will never be tamed so!"*

The strength of his unease shocked me, I had to admit. His emotions were fiery as they rippled through me, as fast as thought. "Okay, okay – no harness and reins for you, ever – but *I* might need a saddle if this is to be comfortable!" I said.

"You may have a saddle, since you are only very small." Crux let out a hot breath of soot, before flaring his wing, one pointed skyward and the other down, and we turned in a wide circle, back in the direction that we had come from.

CHAPTER 15

DANU, DRAGON FRIENDS, DRAGON MAGES, AND ADEPTS

"Lila? Lila – where are you!" I called for what must be the seventeenth time this morning. Our camp was a mess, with sand everywhere, our fire completely put out, our blankets thrown aside. But the boat was still here, as was the small chest of jewels from her father. She hadn't left, as I had at first been scared that she might have done.

I had returned to our camp after watching the newts greet what I gathered was Sym's previous clutch–dragons named Kim and Thiel. The two took to their little brothers and sister with great interest. After that, I was overcome by a sort of warm glow of happiness that everything was as it should be with the world – Lila could no longer turn the Sea Raiders into murderous Dragon Raiders, and that meant that she could follow her rightful path to the queenship – I had caught a brace of sea fish, returning up the beach to find our camp destroyed, and Lila gone, her things all still there. She hadn't run away. *Had she been attacked?* But no human – not even a Raider – would surely sneak an attack on this island right now, with all of the dragons it had in the air.

The dragons, I thought in a sort of petrified horror. Lila had managed, by the skin of her teeth it seemed, to impress Sym into attempting a bond, but that didn't mean she had any idea of how to approach a dragon. Had a dragon challenged her? Had she offended it?

I searched around the camp, for any clue, even as my heart felt like a block of ice, slowly being chipped into fragments. If a dragon had turned on the fierce Raider girl, then there was nothing that I or anyone else could do to try and stop it – or save her.

But I had to, I thought, as my despair turned into a cold sort of fury. One that wasn't fast and passionate as the Chief Kasian's was, but the sort of anger that made all sound disappear from the world, and my jaw clench. *I had come so close to fulfilling the prophecy, and I have faced the wrath and the mockery of the West Witches. Stupid Ohotto telling me that I was a fool for believing it. And Lila didn't deserve to die, not like this. Not as some dragon's play-meat.* I looked up the beach, wondering how I would find the dragon responsible, and what magic I could summon once I did...

"Skreyaar!" A cry split the sky.

"Danu!" To my amazement, it was Lila – she was coming towards me, riding on the back of a type of dragon I had never seen before. She was laughing and whooping as she flew low over the shallow waters, the dark and red tail of the noble creature sending up sprays behind it.

The dragon was a little like the native dragons of the Western Isles – in that its wings were more arrow-shaped, making it fast and light. But it was stockier and bigger, with larger limbs – and, of course, the black top scales that could almost look blue under the right reflection of light. These dark scales gave way gradually to blotches of purple and plum around the dragon's sides, before a trim-line of viridian green snaked from just under the eyes to the tail tip. I had never seen the like of it – and I had spent a long time studying every scroll that the West Witches had on the different types of dragons there were in the world!

"Lila? Are you all right?" I shouted, bending into what Afar had called her 'attack crouch.' One hand in front to cast any cantrips, one hand in the dirt to draw strength from the earth beneath me.

"Ha! Yes!" she hollered, and the multi-colored dragon turned on an arrowhead to suddenly flare up above the beach, dropping into a crouch that shook the ground and sending a plume of sand in all directions as they landed.

When I had finally finished coughing and rubbing the sand from my eyes, I saw that Lila had already stepped down and was hurrying past me to the boat. "I'm going to pack every-thing up. We're going, Danu – we won't be needing the boat anymore!"

"Uh… okay?" I said, aware of how feeble I sounded as the stocky and fast, multi-colored dragon stood over me, looking at me quizzically.

"Danu Geidt, dragon-friend, adept." The dragon spoke in my mind, cocking its head to one side, and running its tongue along its jaws.

"How do you know my name?" I swallowed.

"Skreych!" It chirruped in amusement. *"Most humans live in their minds like they live in their stone houses: closed doors, closed windows. But there are some like you, Danu Geidt, who live with all the doors and windows open."*

"The dragon-friends?" I whispered. Wasn't that something that Ohotto and Afar had tried to warn me about? Ohotto was one of the senior witches on Sebol under Chabon. They had both been responsible for my training, although it was Afar who was my personal mentor. *And Ohotto had viewed both my magic and my dragon ability as dangerous.*

"Yes. Dragon-friends, witches, mages. They are all the same." The dragon made the mental equivalent of a shrug, which made me laugh, as I couldn't *see* the dragon make any such movement, but I *knew*, just by the power of the voice in my head alone, that was what was happening.

"Then, then I am pleased to meet you, sir dragon," I coughed, standing up and feeling more than a little awkward. *You can't exactly shake a claw, can you?*

The multi-colored dragon was silent for a long time, long enough to make me sweat, before he lowered his head to the sand, and then the rest of his body as well. *"I think that you will do. I was warned by my den mother to beware of magicians and witches and humans with strange powers. There are legends that they come from strange and foul practices."*

"Not so!" I found myself bursting out. "Although, I cannot speak for any other than myself and the witches that I know, obviously..." I stammered. Where did the magic gift come from? I wondered. Was it the same as my ability to talk to dragons? Afar had said they were tied – but she had never claimed any ability to understand these noble creatures. "Hearing dragons came to me naturally, when I was a babe. I didn't do anything to get it."

"Yes. I can smell that on you." The large eyes were a deep green, and I could tell just how easily someone could fall entranced by a dragon. They were fascinating and hypnotic. *"You are one of the true dragon-friends, Danu Geidt. I am Crux, a Phoenix of the East."*

A Phoenix dragon? I had never heard of their kind before. "Of the East? You mean, Torvald? The Dragon Academy?"

"Skree-ip!" Crux made a hissing sort of trill, its great maw open and its tongue hanging from the side, and I realized that he was sniggering at me. *"A whole LOT farther east then that, human. There are whole lands out there that you here in the west have never even dreamed of!"*

Suddenly, a rush of images swam into my mind. White-walled towers. Forests that sparkled and glowed at night, as if they were the stars, and the heavens had been reversed. Ziggurats in the sands. An inland lake so vast as to have its own islands, where people moved on small canoes. Mountains so high that the sky grew black near the top. A cave whose every surface shone with solid crystal. Perpetual storms that churned and raged around a vast bay, whose eye was a smoking volcano…

"Stop!" I cried out, as the images and sensations were too much. I had thought that I knew what the world was, but I had been wrong. Very, very wrong.

"We will explore them one day, human. You, Lila, and Crux," the Phoenix dragon promised, even though it almost sounded like a threat.

"Danu, Crux? You two getting along?" Lila said as she jogged back excitedly, with both of our packs tied and rolled up with our blankets and few scant belongings. "Give me a hand with the gems, will you Danu?" she said nonchalantly.

She appeared transformed, I thought. Strong-limbed, with hair teasing out from her braid in a ragtaggle way from the flight. She panted a little, and her skin glowed with health. But more than that, she seemed *happy.*

It was a shame that the mother Sinuous Blue dragon Sym, and territorial head of this island, had to come and ruin it then.

"Skreckh!" Sym roared at Crux as she appeared over the rocky scrubs, angry and fierce. *"What is the meaning of this new thing I smell? You have bonded with the human girl? On MY island? Who came to ask MY favor?"*

CHAPTER 16
LILA, A BOND IS A BOND IS A BOND

"*Mine!*" Crux shouted, his voice loud and terrible in my head, the strength and venom that he put into it forcing me to my knees amidst the sands.

"Danu – are you all right?" I managed to say, as the witches' adept scrabbled back to where I crouched.

"I'm fine, Lila – but the dragons…" he was saying, slowly helping me to my feet as, before us, the much larger mother Blue reared over the stocky but smaller Phoenix. Her hisses split the sky and drowned out the sound of the surf, and her tail lashed behind her, shattering the scrubby trees and sending boulders flying.

"Are they going to fight?" I said, terrified I was going to lose the first dragon I had met straight after meeting him!

What have I done? I thought in alarm.

"They might. We had better get out the way, Lila," Danu said, his hand finding mine and trying to pull me to one side.

No. I felt a flare of anger rise through me, twinned with the savage anger that I could feel from Crux *inside my own head.*

Mine. That was what the dragon had called me. The recognition came with a surge of pride and, somehow, sadness too. Even though I knew that my foster-mother Pela and my foster-father Kasian loved me, even though I knew that they had done what they could to feed me and protect me – I could no longer say the same of them as I could of Crux. The dragon didn't claim me because it had lost a child, or because I might be a princess, or because I was small and needed protecting. The Phoenix dragon claimed me because he had *seen* me, right into my very soul, just as I had seen his. We had seen in each other a fierce, rebellious spirit that we both appreciated.

I felt that when a dragon said *"Mine"* about a human, it meant not just for now, or for a season. It meant forever – and I felt the same.

"Mine!" I shouted up at the mother Blue, angrily. "Mine!" I repeated, shaking off Danu's hand to stand beside Crux's stocky legs as the great Blue weaved and turned in front of us in her fury.

"A silly human, and a more foolish dragon!" The mother Blue spat a gobbet of solid fire, bursting one of the shrubs into instant cinders. *"You both either have no knowledge, or do not care of the insult that you have given me! This is MY island.*

And you, Lila of Malata, came here to give your heart to MY children. Are you so faithless to choose another?"

No. That wasn't what it was like, I could have shouted at her, but suddenly I felt as if I really *were* stupid and faithless. *Is this how the dragons see me?* It was a very far cry from what I had imagined of Queen Saffron and her island dragon. The tales told of a meeting of minds, a joining of hearts, a shared goal... How did 'faithless Lila, eager to bond with any dragon that turns up' compare to that?

"Do not think so, Lila. Sym is just jealous." Crux bared his teeth at the larger dragon. *"Very few humans even come to ask this great gift of dragon kind anymore, and fewer still have the bravery and heart to match a dragon. Mother Sym is jealous that a dragon friend has been found and her hatchlings are not interested!"*

There was a sudden hiss and a swipe of the Blue's tail, narrowly missing both of us.

"This is *her* island," I said – not that I meant that we shouldn't have bonded so strongly and so deeply as we had, but perhaps we should leave, right now...

"Lady Blue!" A human shout surprised me. It was young-looking Danu, Danu the fish-boy, striding up the beach towards the larger dragon. Was he coming to my aid?

"You dare speak to me, little dragon mage?" the Blue roared at him. I saw him flinch, and Crux beside me tensed, ready to attack.

"There is no law or custom that humans cannot converse

with dragons," he cried out. He was angry, too. "But there *is* a custom surrounding the bonds between humans and dragons. You know as well as I do that they are sacred things. A bond is a bond is a bond. It cannot be broken – not by you, or by the king, or by anyone else!"

"Hsss!" the Blue lashed her tail again, sending up another plume of sand, but she did not strike out at Danu, or us.

"The little one speaks truth," another dragon voice said— once again in my mind – but it was neither Sym nor Crux. I was shocked, as I thought that only either a 'queen' dragon or a bonded dragon could share thoughts. Now I started to wonder if it were *all* dragons who could share thoughts, should they wish to.

Rising over the headland of rocks came the Crimson Red, one of the rarer breeds of dragon. Not as rare as my beloved Phoenix, of course, but never seen out here in the Western Isles. Crimson Reds were only seen in central Torvald, and Mount Hammal itself. It was the old emblem of the ruling house of Torvald, because of the ruling family's long associa- tion with red dragons. It had arrived last night for the birth, and must have flown a long way to get here.

"You!" the mother Blue hissed, but she did not screech or snarl as she had before.

"Yes. I come from the sacred Dragon Mountain. I know of what I speak. A bond is a bond is a bond as the boy says. It cannot be broken by mortal or dragon will alone," the Crimson Red said in a tired voice.

Another loud hiss came from the mother Blue, and I feared she might ignore the other dragon and Danu completely, but instead, she just turned with a snap of her wings and leapt into the air, barreling back to her atoll and her cave.

I panted as I laid a hand on the scales of Crux's leg, surprised to feel it warm, as if radiating heat from an internal fire. Crux had turned his head towards the Crimson Red, who just regarded us all on the beach with its wise golden eyes. It nodded slowly to Crux, as if content, before rising into the air on powerful leathery wings and turning eastwards.

"I still think that we had better leave this island," I muttered, and received an indignant growl from Crux beside me. I could feel the shape of him in my mind, as if there was a part of me that looked out into him, and vice versa, and I could tell that he was upset and riled up, but that he wasn't so mad as to not agree with me.

"Come on, my brave friend," I murmured at him, and he made a purring, chittering noise as he was mollified somewhat.

"Well, I think that you're right about that," Danu groaned, as I helped him with the chest of jewels, and showed him how to climb a dragon's leg. "What about your boat?" Danu nodded back to the top of the beach where the boat still sat, shoved in a tangle of boulders and scrubby bushes. "Won't your father be mad if you lose it?"

"It's just a small-boat," I said pragmatically. "Besides, we now have a dragon! A good trade, don't you think?"

Even as apparently worried as he was about the flying, Danu smiled through his anxiety. "I guess it is. And maybe it's not a bad idea to leave a spare boat on Sym's island as well, just in case anyone has to escape playful hatchlings any time soon!"

Before the sun was halfway across the sky – we had already started our journey back to Malata, there to introduce my fierce Crux to the Raiders.

๛

The islands that we had left became smaller and smaller as we soared, Crux slicing through the air as fast as a kittiwake – no, faster.

"It's amazing!" I shouted back at Danu, who sat behind me, his face caught in a rictus of a grin that was half terror, half joy, one arm clutching the awkward small chest, and the other holding onto my side in a fierce grip.

"That's one way of putting it," I heard him shout back, the wind ripping at his words. This high up, the wind was fiercely cold, and I realized that if this was to become my regular mode of transport, then there would have to be changes in the simple linens and breeches that I wore.

"What do the Dragon Riders of Torvald wear?" I shouted back to Danu, as much to take his mind off how fast we were flying than anything else.

"Padded leather harnesses that they attach to the saddles

and lines," Danu shouted into my ear. "There are some draw-ings of them back in Sebol."

Sebol. The Haunted Isle, the home of the West Witches. I would have to go there if I were to discover more secrets of how to ride and train a dragon.

"Crux will never be trained, silly Lila!" The Phoenix laughed into my mind, tucking his wings to his side to shoot forwards and down, his speed increasing so that it tore at my stomach and made me feel weightless.

"Aiii!" Danu shouted. At first I thought that it had to be a scream – before it changed into a loud howl of joy as Crux bottomed-out of his dive, raising his wings to scoop along the waves as he had done with me before. I joined his shout of excitement, and, for a moment, it felt like all three of us had become one larger creature – a deadly predator that was made of wind and wings, of fire and teeth.

But before I could pause to think about Danu Geidt and his Haunted Isle, I had to think of the Raiders. *And my father.* What would they think of Crux? They would be overjoyed, wouldn't they? How could they *not* be?

We flew for the better part of the day, covering the distance it had taken me and Danu to sail this way in a fraction of the time. As the sun turned over the mast (as my father would have said, meaning it was well past midday) Crux once again swooped to the sea to skim the surface, catching great sea cod as large as my chest, which he brought to his maw to crunch and swallow with one loud snap. *And paniers,* I thought. *I'm going to need something to hold food, and equipment – and weapons.*

Crux kept flying, seeming to know where I wanted to go before I could even raise the thought in my mind. It was a little like riding a ship – in those rare moments when the entire crew and every plank of wood was working in unison to beat towards their goal on the horizon, and you felt like you were flying *over* the waves, with one heart and will.

We saw other denizens of the oceans on our flight. A pod of whales, their flesh a milky blue and white, larger even than Crux was, breaking the waves with mighty flumes of water before crashing back down again.

"Old brothers and sisters, that is our name for them," Crux informed me, and I wondered at how much the dragons knew of the world beyond my ken. There were also the small specks of ships – the radiating circles of fishing boats that trawled and plied the waves out from their own islands, and then – the larger galleons of Havick.

"The enemy!" I gasped, and felt an answering surge of pride from Crux below. Three of them, with the flags of the Roskilde Sea Crown over crossed swords.

"Shall we attack them?" Crux roared, but I shook my head. Each of the war galleons were larger that Crux was – not that I doubted he might bring one down – but they would also have cannon and ballista, and lots of naval soldiers with bows, I thought bitterly.

"No, my brother." I patted his warm scales at my side.

"Not yet. I want my people to see how strong and fierce you are. I want my father to be amazed at your scaled hide, and your sharp teeth!" It was true, I did want these things – but I was also very aware of the fact that this was only the second time that I had ridden a dragon, and the first for Danu. The Sea Raiders would prepare as much as they could and send out all three of their smaller warships against just one of Havick's galleons. *I will not have you hurt so soon in my service,* I thought as my heart twanged in sympathy. If Crux had heard my private thoughts at all, or had any thought about my worry, he said nothing to me in my mind, but we continued south.

By the time that late afternoon came upon us, we had crossed the tall, mountainous islands of the archipelago and beyond, heading for the smaller, fractured landmasses of the Free Islands. The seas became choppier and wilder, and the winds that were treacherous even to our Raider boats picked up. The currents were tricky down in the south of the world, and that was one of the reasons why my father had made his home here.

"There! That – beyond the reef, and the ruined ship!" I pointed at the small, semi-circular island of Malata, with its ornaments of rock and shipwreck sitting around it.

"Skrech!" Crux roared and started his long glide down towards my homeport, straight over the reef and over the small scattering of Raider's longboats, as shouts and alarm bells were sounded.

"No, it's all right, it's me!" I shouted; but it was no good –

they couldn't hear me over the sound of their own fright and the clashing of Crux's wings.

The boats in our stone harbor rocked as Crux hung in the skies before them, beating his massive wings. He lowered towards the nearest place that he could see to land – the deck of the *Ariel* itself, where Father must have been practicing drills, as there was already a full complement of sailors on board!

"Cannon ready!"

"Ware dragon!"

"Archers!"

I heard the shouts of the crew and the Raiders running up the stone dock as I tried to stand up on Crux's back. The crew of the *Ariel* had run to the sides of the railings, some of the bravest readying large hooks and spikes, their fear apparent in their faces as Crux's talons bit wood, and the I felt the *Ariel*, my father's pride and joy, bob lower in the water.

"Dragon!" There was a shouting voice – my father's voice – as he emerged from his cabin, a long sword in hand and face fierce, as he came face to face with his adopted girl, standing on a multi-colored dragon.

"Lila?" His look of astonishment was priceless.

CHAPTER 17
DANU, A DRAGON RECEPTION

My knees shook, and my stomach felt queasy after our flight – but I also felt a sense of elation. *I had actually flown on a dragon! Me, Danu Geidt!* The boy with the dragon tongue – after all of those years of reading what I could in the scroll rooms of the West Witches about my gift (they didn't have a lot, to be fair) and anything else that I could find out about dragons – *I had finally done it!*

But now Lila was a step closer to her dream of creating the Dragon Mercenaries. That thought crept into the back of my mind to ruin my appreciation of the flight. Fire raining down on ships, sailors, *people.* How could I stop her from her goal, but still help her?

But even with that thought tainting my exhilaration about having flown, it was also true that riding a dragon hadn't been how the pictures had looked. They had featured proud, stiff-backed people in fine armor and leathers slicing through the air, holding swords and lances in their hands. The *old* Dragon Riders of Torvald, of the sort before the Dark King came to the throne.

No, my flight hadn't been like that. If anything, it felt as though I could do with a hot bath and sitting on a soft cushion for a month!

"Is that you?" I heard the Chief of the Sea Raiders say, as there was a clang on the deck. Chief Kasian had dropped his sword in amazement at the sight of his daughter sitting atop the back of a dragon on his ship.

"It is, Father – look at the friend I made!" She laughed, climbing down, with much greater grace and skill than I managed, to throw herself into her father's stunned arms in a hug.

I hit the deck wishing that my knees weren't made of jelly, but even with my complaints, I could still see the look of worry that crossed the chief's face. Maybe he never expected his foster daughter to ever *truly* do what she had intended. Maybe he had wanted her to return, even defeated and spirit broken, to her homeport so that he could convince her of her rightful place amongst the Raiders. *Or what he wanted to believe was Lila's rightful place,* I corrected.

"She's... She's so *big!*" Kasian said faintly.

"*He,* father. Crux is a *he,*" Lila said enthusiastically, making me wince as she gave away Crux's name freely. *A dragon's name should be given by the dragon alone,* I thought

– before I remembered that I, too, had given away Sym's name to Lila before the mother Blue could introduce herself to the princess.

"Hss." There was a bad-tempered lash of a tail from the multi-colored dragon, and sudden twang as ropes snapped and a set of casks were sent spinning over the side. The Raiders nearby jumped back, their hands clutching at their weapons – as small as they looked compared to the dragon! Crux must be annoyed at his name-giving, and I was about to step forward, but it appeared that the dragon had already communicated that fact to Lila through their mental connection.

"Oh, I am sorry, brother – you must forgive my clumsiness, and help me learn," Lila said. "This is my foster-father, the Chief Kasian of Malata, the Chief of the Sea Raiders!" She inclined her head to Crux, seeking to rectify the situation, not even noticing how Kasian stiffened at Lila's introduction, a shadow passing over his eyes. To him, he *is* Lila's father, I thought, suddenly aware of how complicated the situation was between them.

Crux gingerly leaned forward to sniff at the man with his great snout, before huffing a large cloud of sooty smoke, making the man cough and flap it away.

"He says that he's pleased to meet you, and that any father to Lila can be a father to him. His name is Crux," Lila interpreted.

"Oh. I see." The chief was still astonished, peering behind the dragon to see the damage his tail had already done to the

Ariel. "I thought you said that you were bringing eggs, Lila? Or *smaller* dragons?" he said hesitantly.

❦

As soon as the Raiders had realized that Crux was not intending to eat them (just yet), they relaxed only slightly, with Senga and Adair being the first to hurry to Lila's side. I hung back, watching the exchange, suddenly feeling out of place.

They look so happy, I thought as I watched Lila hug Adair fiercely, and then take him to be introduced to Crux. I had to admit that I felt more than a little stab of jealousy at that. Didn't Lila want *me* to be there too, when she introduced Crux?

Enough, Danu, I scolded myself. I should be pleased that Crux was being taken to so well by the two younger Raiders, and that we had managed to successfully negotiate with an angry mother dragon! Besides, I had other things to worry about – such as the future of the Western Isles, and Princess Lila.

The princess-to-be, I thought as I watched Lila scramble back atop Crux's back with ease now, her laughter infecting the two young Raiders with her confidence. Adair approached cautiously, and his sister Senga not at all, at first, but slowly, Adair took a few hesitant steps forward to be snuffed by the Phoenix dragon, to loudly exclaim, "He's like a hot spring –

only not so wet!" He laughed, finally beckoning his sister over to the same experience.

It was the dragon's internal fires, I could have told them, if they had bothered to ask me. Dragons are ancient beings, so old as to have always been. They were creatures born with fire inside of them as snow is born of water.

Lila *did* have it, I thought as I watched her. She had a way of reaching people – but not by her shouts or scowls or her commands, it was instead when she was at her most joyful that others responded to her. Now, if only I could get her to use that for the good of all of the people of the islands – not just the Raiders.

"You dream big, little dragon friend," Crux's voice shone in my head, and I looked up to see that he had turned his head lazily, bathing in the affection the way that a cat bathes in sunlight. His great green and gold eyes were half-closed, and he was making a pleased, *churring* sound.

"I do," I whispered back to him, but he only closed his eyes as if nothing had been said between us at all.

"Father? There is more news!" Lila called to the chief, who was trying to minimize the damage that a full-grown dragon was wreaking on his boat. There was already a mess of lines that had been brought down, and one of the aft sails was in danger of losing its rigging.

"More?" Kasian said faintly. I don't think that the old Raider could handle this much change, this fast.

"Yes. On our flight south we saw three of Havick's war

galleons, heading south across the Barrens," she crowed joyously. "Too much for our three boats to take on alone, but, with Crux here…"

The chief's stance shifted, his back straightening in the same breath as his frown deepened. "No, foster-daughter. We couldn't. Even with this marvelous beast," (I noted that he added the last part a little quickly) "that would be one ship each, and the *Ariel* and the others could never outgun one of those galleons."

"But Father," Lila said.

Don't let her do it! I thought desperately, before instantly feeling a little ashamed. I wanted Lila to succeed – I really did, but, to further divide the people of the Isles? She needed to be taking the dragon to the others, to encourage us all to stand up to Havick… That was her destiny, I thought – or at least, that is what the prophesy told me. *But a queen doesn't threaten and bully people, a queen doesn't need mercenaries…*Or *shouldn't* need mercenaries, I added. Some monarchs were worse than others; *Dark Enric for one*, I shivered.

"How far off were they?" the chief called out.

"A day or more from the Free Isles," Lila responded, this time a little more somberly.

"They could be heading this way, or on routine patrol." The chief was growling. "At least that is a very fine way to use a dragon!" He called up at her, trying to ameliorate the tension between them. "We have advance warning of the ships. We should scatter the pirate fleet so if he does decide to attack we can harry him!" The big man looked happier now that he had a purpose again. A purpose as a Raider, not as a mercenary. I wondered if Lila noticed this distinction, or whether she was too caught up in the flush of her new bond to pay it heed. As the chief started barking orders to the other Raiders, they, too, seemed to take heart at the prospect of sailing rather than flying.

The princess will have her work cut out for her, if she wants to turn them all to the ways of dragons rather than boats, I thought, as I joined behind Adair, Senga, and Lila as they readied to go ashore.

"I will fish, and then I will find a spot in the cliffs to sleep," Crux announced to Lila, clearly audible through my own dragon connection.

"I will come with you to select a nest," Lila immediately turned and said.

"Lila – you must see your mother," her foster-father said, a look of worry passing over his face. I wondered what the big man must be thinking, now that his daughter had a new mentor and best friend in the form of a dragon. Was he scared of losing her?

"I can find my own nest, Lila wave-rider. But I will return tonight." Crux yawned, blowing hot breath down the length of the *Ariel*. I saw several crew members make the sign to avert the evil across their chest, before hurrying on with their work.

No, this really doesn't bode well, I thought.

With Lila off with her father, and Senga and Adair going back to their families in the huts and buildings of Malata, I was left standing on the docks amidst the tides of bustling Raiders. The docks were always busy, it seemed. A constant buzz of activity filled my ears as the crew replaced the broken lines of the *Ariel*, and retrieved the cargo that had tumbled over the deck. The other two of the largest boats were cleaned and repaired, with bits of cargo and kit carried off and others put on as the Raiders prepared to follow the chief's wishes. It was nighttime now, and lanterns were lit up and down the length of the dock. My steps ghosted into town, where already there were loud voices and singing rising from some of the larger of the open meeting places.

I didn't need any spell of *no-see-me* here, as I walked. I was ignored just as completely anyway, as all of the Raiders who weren't working had plenty to discuss and talk about.

I am Danu Geidt, adept and dragon-friend, and I am alone, I thought a little miserably as I sat on the edge of the stone seawall. Looking out across the small harbor, out between the boats that bobbed there, I saw the first glimmer of stars over the western horizon, where somewhere very far away the Haunted Isle, or the Isle of Sebol, would also be lighting its lanterns.

"Oh, Afar," I breathed to my distant mentor. "What am I to do now?" Why did it seem that once I had actually supposedly "helped" Lila, I now felt like I had failed? Maybe my mission wasn't just to help Lila get her dragon, but to help Lila realize who she truly is…

❧

CHAPTER 18
LILA, UNSURE AND ADRIFT

"Mother?" I said to the woman who was gathering and stacking leather training hauberks. It was evening and the lights on the house had been lit, but still my mother was working in the sheds out the back.

"Oh Lila, thank the waters." She looked harried, older than she had when I left only X days ago. *Had she always had that grey hair at her temples?*

"I did it, Mother," I said with exhausted relief. I hadn't imagined just how tiring riding a dragon could be! "Although I think that I will have to get a saddle made."

"Word came to me that a dragon was landing on the *Ariel*." Mother shook her head as if it were a disgrace, but she was smiling at the same time. "Your father will not be pleased, no doubt," she added.

"Wood can be mended. Ropes can be re-spliced." I

shrugged it off. "But *I did it!* I got a dragon to bond with me…" I still didn't quite know *how* I had done it – or even if I had done anything at all. I explained the events of the last couple of days, as much to prove to myself that what I had gone through was actually real.

Maybe I hadn't done anything at all, I thought. It had seemed like Crux had chosen *me,* after all, because of whatever he had seen about me that he liked – not the other way around.

"Just like all friendships. We never deserve them, but they happen anyway," Pela intoned sagely. "And the mother Blue? She just let you go?" There was a twinge of worry to my mothers' voice, a bit of steel in her eyes as I knew that she was assessing how worried she would have to be. Was she about to have an angry den mother dragon descend on top of her island, seeking vengeance?

"She did. Thanks to Danu, and a Crimson Red who spoke for us," I told her.

"Ah. Danu the wizard's boy…" My mother looked across the practice yard for a moment, before turning her eyes back to me, quizzically.

"What?" I said, feeling a little flustered, and I didn't know why.

"Nothing, Lila. So, are you going to go with him to find out about the prophecy now, or…?" My mother still looked at me with skeptical eyes.

"Good heavens no!" I laughed. "I was hoping that he

might return to the Haunted Isle all on his own!" I laughed, but something clutched at my heart as I said it. I was being unfair. *And Crux wanted Danu to fly with us,* I remembered. *Whatever this bond was between me and Crux – Danu was a part of it now. But he wants me to be a princess – and I don't want to!* I knew I was also lying to my mother, wasn't I? *No. I did want Danu to get out of my hair and stop going on about that silly prophecy of his.* I had a dragon now, after all – why did I need to go off to find out about the history of long-dead kings and queens and the prophecies made about them.

"You made a promise, Lila, to help him investigate the prophecy," my mother said seriously. "You know the way of it. A Raider has to rely on those around them. We're family. And our promise to our own is our bond."

"But he's not one of our own!" I burst out, hot and bothered and feeling *very* annoyed – but in that same instant I regretted saying it. He had stood up for me against the Blue dragon. He had even tried to cover my fear of heights from the rest of the crew back on board the boat.

"Lila! You sailed with him. That makes him family," my mother said crossly, readjusting the training hauberks on the stack even though they were fine. "Believe me, daughter, it pains me to have to agree with him – but your word is a bond."

A bond is a bond, the way that my mother's words echoed both Danu's and the Crimson Red's was uncanny. It made me feel small-hearted, and now that I had bonded with Crux –

with a being who accepted me just as I was, tomboy, Raider, fierce, stubborn and all – I didn't want to be that person.

"You're right, as always, Mother," I said, hanging my head. "I will talk to him."

"Good. I'm *not* telling you to run away to be a princess, but I *am* telling you to honor your promises," my mother said, before she sighed. "And anyway – there is something that I have been talking about with your father, I mean – your foster-father."

Hearing my mother call him that out loud shocked me, somehow. *Why? It is what he is,* I argued with myself. But for some reason, it made my heart ache to think that *they* might be pulling away from me. *Just as I have from them, insisting on going after dragons.*

"What?"

"This." She turned to the basket that she had been working from, reached into the bottom to pull out a bolt of cloth – one of my old linen shirts from when I was a child.

"A shirt?" I raised my eyebrows at her.

"It's inside. I should have shown it to you a long time ago, I guess – but there was just never the time." My mother huffed and fussed with the hauberks, not looking at me as I carefully unwrapped my old shirt to see a smaller square of cloth. White linen, of a finer sort than I had seen the Raider's make. It even had a delicate lace edge all around it in scallop shapes, and in the corner, was an embroidered moniker.

"Lila," it read in flowing script, whilst underneath was the

unmistakable green Sea-Crown of Roskilde. The scrap of cloth was old, but still strong. It smelled very faintly of my mother's – my foster-mother's – lavender and mint cloth-saves. I realized that it must have been bundled away at the bottom of a chest for years.

"Is that…" my hands started to tremble all on their own.

"Yes. It's you, Lila. Your name, over the crown. It was with you when the Raiding party found you and brought you to me. It was swaddled in with the blankets – I don't think anyone had thought to search the blankets of a child for anything of value – but yet there was."

"But that could just be the crest of Roskilde." I tried to ignore the fact that my heart was telling me. Why I was a little fairer than the other Raiders. Why I was a little longer limbed. "Any babe in Roskilde could have this…"

"No, Lila. A mother doesn't furnish her child with the country's crest, but with that of their own family. A mother doesn't just attach a flag to a child that someone else dreamed up, a mother wants her child to have her own name, her own home," my foster-mother said sadly, and I knew that she was talking about herself. "That is *your* crest, the Sea Crown. You *are* the Princess of Roskilde."

I had always known I was the product of a raid. But, in the way that we Raiders have, I thought that it was just happenstance that the story of my life matched the prophesy so. I had never taken Danu's tale seriously. That I really *could* be the Princess of Roskilde.

"You knew?" I said in a low voice. "All this time, and you knew?"

My foster-mother shook her head. "I guessed. I never knew. Or I didn't let myself guess. It was a fine ship you were found on, but your parents were already dead. I was so sad from the loss of my own son Ruck," she said with dark eyes.

The words 'my own son' tore through me like a gale through an unprotected port.

"I reasoned maybe you were some lady's daughter, one of the ones who had stood against Havick as he rose to power back then. Those were crazy times, Lila, and I am glad that you were not able to see them." My mother gave off her stacking and sat down heavily on the edge of a cask in the evening gloom. "I was half-mad with grief over Ruck, I think – but even out here in the Free Isles, we caught some of the news. Roskilde collapsed over a winter, and the counsellor Havick rose in power. There were murders. Ships mysteriously sunk, courtiers poisoned. No one knew who it was at first, until the royal family themselves disappeared, and the Raiders were paid to attack the villages with increased force."

I didn't want to hear what my mother had to tell me. I didn't even want to empathize with the people of those times. So, what if they had been raided? That was life out here on the islands. Raiding was raiding!

But the look on my foster-mother's face only broke my heart a little more. She looked scared and even ashamed – even though she had nothing to be ashamed of, at all.

"We attacked the splintering Roskilde, seeking out their ships wherever we could find them," she said sorrowfully. "It was not an honorable time for us, Lila – I admit that now. We didn't question the money paid us to make the raids…and that was when we found you, and when I found that cloth with you. I told myself you must belong to the nobles, but I didn't dare ask or think further. Now with that wizard's boy here…"

"Mother. I will never leave you. I will never *not* be your daughter," I promised her, suddenly angry.

I wasn't really a Raider. That was a fact that I had always known, of course, ever since Lasarn told me so many years ago – but that fact didn't seem to make a difference before, and now, to find out that Danu had been right, that entire wars and battles had been fought around my birth – that was something else entirely. *I need time to think.* I shoved the cloth into my shirt. *But I also need my mother to know that I will be here for her.*

"Mother," I said, putting a hand to her shoulder.

"Ah, Lila." The woman smiled sadly and patted my hand. "You are a good girl. Brave and fast. You take after Kasian in that." She raised her head. "But even my old bones can see when there is a sea change coming. You will call me Pela from now on, and you will call your father Chief Kasian."

I opened and closed my mouth, stunned. "But…"

"It doesn't mean that I don't love you, Lila, it means that I am letting you be your own person," my mother – *Pela* – said. "I am righting the wrong which has been done to you a long time ago. A Raider keeps her word, and a Raider honors her debts."

At that, the woman stood up, a tear running down one cheek as she turned and walked stiffly back into the house. *Oh, mother.* I felt ashamed at causing this sadness in her. She had only ever sought to protect me…

But my shame warred with a new feeling of joy in my heart. *I could be my own person.*

🙖🙖🙗

The usual carousing of the Raiders seemed odd to me as I walked down past the huts to the dock. Their voices were no longer the friendly voices of family, but instead, they were the voices of people who had stolen me.

No, given me a life, I corrected. I felt a knot of anger in my chest, but I couldn't say who was better deserving of the blame for keeping me from the life I was born to for so many years. Was it to my father and mother – my *foster*-father and mother— who better deserved the blame? Or was it to Havick who had killed my parents and left me to die as the Raider attacked? That was what Pela—her given name still awkward even to think—had said – that my parents had already been dead when they had found me, so it was no crime Pela and Kasian had committed in taking and raising an orphaned, abandoned child. Still, I felt angry at the Raiders for *not* being my family, somehow, for taking me from them – even though I knew that it wasn't their fault.

"I am your family, Lila," the warm voice of Crux against my mind, and with a fierce rush of belonging. My steps followed that warmth out, parallel to the harbor where I heard the rising sound of voices, and smelled fire.

Above the harbor, a small path rose to the low hill that served as a lookout across the reef beyond. To my surprise, I saw that it was busy, and that a bonfire had been lit. There was a crowd of Raiders – mostly the younger ones, but also some older, sea-grizzled sailors standing to the edges of the firelight.

And then there was Crux. He sat on hunched legs with wings folded, regarding the humans around the fire. Every now and again, one of the younger ones would dare to approach him, throwing a hank of mutton or fish at the dragon, for him to catch in the air with a quick dart of his head.

"What's going on here?" I found myself smiling at the sight, despite my difficult emotions.

"It was Danu's idea, Lila." It was fierce Senga who said it, her hair braided into knots as she passed me a flagon of watered-down ale. "He said that the Raiders should welcome the dragon, get to know him a little."

"Oh, he did, did he?" I felt a flash of annoyance. Why did the fish-boy think that he had a right to tell me what to do with my own dragon?

"Not yours, Lila. A dragon isn't anyone's but himself's," the dragon croaked in my mind. *"But the boy was right."*

Oh, was he now? I thought a little glumly. It seemed that I have even managed to get being a dragon-friend wrong. I narrowed my gaze at Danu near the bonfire, trying to encourage some of the younger Raiders to approach Crux.

"No, I don't think so," one of the Raider mothers said, calling the little black-haired child closer and away from the adept.

"Danu?" I strode up to him. "Care to explain what you are doing?"

He looked at me with a nervous grin. "Lila! Thank goodness you are here. Maybe the others will see that Crux isn't a threat now. You can show them how you ride him?"

"Excuse me?" I said in alarm. *Who viewed Crux as a threat?*

"I AM a threat, Lila wave-rider." Crux yawned behind me, stretching out his head to lay on the grass at my side, his dark and bright scales shining in the firelight.

"You are great and powerful," I said, leaning over to sit with my back against his neck. There was an appreciative gasp of wonder from the crowd at the sight, although to me, it just felt like a natural thing to do. Danu joined me, sitting facing me rather than against the dragon itself. Maybe he was the one who was scared of the dragon, I thought wryly.

"While you were gone," the young-looking adept said in a hushed tone, "I was at the docks. Your father has been re-provisioning the ships, and I had a chance to walk around. Some of the older sailors say that they were unhappy about having a dragon make a home on their island." Danu kept his voice low, and between the crackle of the fire at his back, and the soft murmuring breath of the dragon behind me, I don't think anyone could hear.

"Who said that?" I asked quickly. "Couldn't they see that Crux wasn't a danger to us?"

"I am always a danger. To everyone," Crux said in his lazy snooze, sending a slight tremor down my spine. *Even to me?* I wondered for a moment, before discarding that thought.

"I don't know. But it was the older Raiders. They said it was unnatural. And that Raiders weren't meant to be friends with dragons," Danu explained, his eyes wide and serious. "So, I tried my best. I remembered from the scrolls that they used to use bonfires to call dragons in the ancient times. I thought that perhaps we could have a celebration of the dragon rather than fearing it."

Damn. It was a good idea, I had to concede to him. "Thank you," I said, even though Danu's words had only made me feel even more at odds with the rest of the Raiders than before. How could they *not* look on Crux with the same wonder and admiration that I did?

"The younger ones get it. They're still scared, but they're not"—Danu scrunched his features as he tried to find a kind way to say what he had to say.

"Spit it out, Danu," I said.

"The older ones are *mean* to Crux. They call him monster, brute, terror," Danu said in an even lower voice, but one of

178

Crux's ears twitched all the same. Given what the Phoenix dragon had been telling me, I rather thought that he might have *enjoyed* being called those things!

"Okay. I thank you again, Danu," I said, suddenly aware of how much work we still had to do. I thought 'we' but then I realized I hadn't actually intended to include Danu in this Dragon Mercenary scheme at all. And yet he had used what he had learnt on the Haunted Isle anyway, to try and bring the people and the dragon together. Pela was right. I owed him, and more than that, I needed his expertise.

"Okay, fish-boy," I said heavily, not altogether happy with what I had to ask him. "You seem to know more about dragons than anyone else. Did you find all of this out on the Haunted Isle?"

"Sebol. It's called Sebol," Danu frowned momentarily, but he nodded. "Yes. They have the biggest collection of scrolls outside of the Dragon Academy itself. It is said that they were a part of a chain once, of Dragon Monks fleeing the time of the Dark King, spreading out across the islands. They reached the Dragon Isle where—"

"Where Queen Saffron was born," I said. As if *I* didn't know the tale by heart.

"No, not born there. She was born of a Torvald family, but was smuggled there," Danu said, his face suddenly lighting up. "Hey, in fact, her story is a bit like yours, don't you think? A missing girl, hidden in the islands, growing up to recover her birthright…"

179

Not like mine! I was about to say angrily, but I couldn't. Because it *was* like my story, a little. I was a baby who had been left for dead, and raised by those who weren't her parents. So was Saffron, kind of. Maybe I had more in common with her than I thought. She was still an islands' girl, just as I was, and she still raised the Western Dragons to her side...

Just like Crux had rallied to mine.

"Of course." Crux thumped his heavy tail in the darkness, as if this was something that I should have realized already, and shouldn't question.

"Thank you," I said in a quieter tone to the dragon and Danu both. I felt a very tentative sort of hope. Even though my previous life had been shattered, and my mother – Pela now – had told me the truth of my birth. There was still hope for me. I could walk the path that Saffron had walked.

"You walk your own path, Lila wave-rider, air-rider. Never anyone else's!" Crux raised his snout to look at me with his great gold-green eyes, and I nodded.

"Yes, Crux. You are right." I patted his scales, finding them radiating warmth. I wondered for a moment what all of this must look like to the other raiders beyond us, whether they would think that I was bewitched, or whether they would take this as a sign that the Raiders had friends in draconian form.

"Well, anyway, the fleeing monks reached out to the mystics and witches that already lived here. The Witches'

School of Sebol has been around for centuries you see, and Chabon agreed to guard what knowledge she could of theirs, as the Dark King destroyed all that was left in the Empire of Torvald. *That* is how come I know so much about dragons," he said, although his eyes slid aside as he said that last part.

"And the prophecy?" I swallowed nervously. A Raider keeps her word.

"A girl will rise from the waters, with the Sea Crown on her head..." Danu intoned, as if he had memorized it by heart. "That's you, Lila."

I didn't doubt it anymore. Pela had told me that I had come from the sacked ship, and I had the scrap of royal cloth to prove it. "So, does that mean I have to get the Sea Crown? That I *will* get the Sea Crown? That I *should*?" I asked.

Danu opened and closed his mouth, and his eyes did that thing where they slid away once again, before returning to mine. Is he hiding something? I thought.

"The heir to the throne of Roskilde was lost, presumed killed at sea by a group of Raiders some seventeen years ago, and Havick rose to power," he said, placing his words carefully.

"My father," I said. "He was paid to perform many raids at that time."

Danu frowned. "Really? By who?"

I shrugged uselessly. "Pela doesn't know, exactly, and I don't think Kasian does either. Money is money, as they say." I thought about my father's often harsh humor about the

Roskildeans. "The Sea Raiders have always been on the receiving end of Roskilde 'justice' even though we don't recognize their sovereignty. I'm not sure that, back then anyway, they cared where the money to capture and raid Roskilde ships came from."

"But it makes sense. If Havick sent someone with money to give to Kasian for raids, Havick could pretend that it was the Raiders who had killed you and your real mother and father." Danu nodded. "But what matters to us is that somehow, despite the fact that Havick told everyone that Raiders killed your real parents – *he* still emerged with the Sea Crown on his head! *Why* did he have it, after their deaths? Why didn't Chief Kasian take it if he was supposed to have killed the king of Roskilde?"

"You're right," I said. "And I think that even Father would've remembered killing a king. It would be a story worthy to sing for generations, don't you think?" I smiled sadly.

Danu nodded as I carried on.

"So Havick has the Sea Crown, but the prophecy says that *I* rise from the waters with it?" I said, cautious. "Is that it?"

"Well, there is more as well..." Danu said, a touch indignantly.

"Go on."

"We need to tread carefully, Lila. Prophecies are dangerous things. If I tell you a bit that you're not supposed to know, it might not come true, or the wrong part might come true, or something else might happen altogether!" Danu said with wide eyes.

"How do you know you haven't already told me a bit I'm not supposed to know? And besides, forewarned is forearmed, as my foster-father says." *Why was he hiding the rest of the prophecy from me? What good would that do?*

"Not in the case of prophecies. You'll just have to trust me, Lila, *I* am the adept here," he said.

"Uh-huh," I grumbled. He *had* been right about trying to get the rest of the Raiders to like Crux, I reminded myself. Maybe he was right about this as well. "Well, for now I think I am going to bed," I said to Danu, gathering my cloak around me. "Have you got somewhere to sleep?"

"Oh, I uh… No." Danu looked suddenly small and self-conscious. "I was thinking of staying out here, with Crux. Aren't you heading back to your house?" he asked.

"No." I tried to keep the resentment from my voice. I knew that I would still be welcome there, obviously, but I didn't feel like sleeping in my old bed again. "I will stay here with Crux too. After all, *I* am the one who is bonded with him!" I added in a proud tone, hiding the hurt that I still felt at what my mother had said.

"Oh. Okay. Most of the other Raiders have gone now, anyway," Danu said, and, when I raised my head over Crux's neck I saw what he said was true. The lights of the harbor still glittered, and the sounds of the Raiders still singing or telling loud stories rippled over the water. Just like any other night in the Free Isles.

"Well, good night, Danu Geidt." I inclined my head, curling up in my cloak under the crook of Crux's chin.

"Good night, princess," I heard him say in a softer tone, as I fell into a warm and deep sleep.

CHAPTER 19
DANU, LESSONS

Over the next few days, Malata was a hive of activity. It was different from my time at Sebol. Never before had I seen half sozzled men leap into a harbor with joyous whoops first thing to drive the sleep from their minds. Never had I experienced so many voices rising in shouts and arguments as when the night catch was brought up onto the harbor and divvied out between the various Raider families.

But all island life–whether on a pirates' island or a witches'—had some similarities, it seemed. There was the business of fishing, the cleaning and beating of linens, the rekindling of cook fires. These were tasks that everyone knew and turned to as a matter of course – although the Raiders often did it with louder voices and laughter, whereas the witches usually regarded every task in solemn silence.

I found that, just like Sebol as well, there was no such

thing as a useless body. After having a breakfast of rolls, cheese, and cured goat, I was quickly commandeered by one or another loud Raider to help haul in a net, hold a line, or lift boxes. On Sebol, most of the time everyone was busy studying or meditating, and so those of us who might be younger or more able bodied were often sent to perform the necessary tasks that kept the community running: cleaning, cooking, minor repairs.

I found a pleasing sort of numbness to this physical work. I didn't have to worry about the prophecy *all* the time, but instead could laugh with the other Raiders at their workman-like jokes, or groan when a line snapped, or a catch was poor.

I had discovered that the chief's plan was to get the *Ariel* back in a shipshape state, and to send her out to scout for the three Havick galleons, and to tow the other Raider warships to just inside the reef, ready to move if danger was announced. There was an argument between he and Lila, right on the docks, when he also announced that *he* would be captaining the *Ariel,* and that *she* had to stay behind here on Malata – and not even serve as his first mate. I watched as the chief and his foster-daughter argued, feeling frozen. Should I say anything? Intervene in some way – and if I did – would that help or harm the prophecy? Would it set Lila on her rightful path, or encourage her against it?

I wondered why her father had made this sudden move. Was it because he feared what damage Crux might do to his beloved boat? Or that he just wanted her to be safe? I could tell from the way that Lila heard the news, that she had taken it as a personal rebuke as her father sailed off without her.

But we had our own problems, I reminded myself. The more time that we had to get the Raiders used to the dragon – perhaps to even *learn* how to ride a dragon – was better, in my opinion. *And the longer I had to convince Lila to abandon her Dragon Raider schemes and take up the quest for the Sea Crown, the better*, I thought. I was already pleased that she had started at least asking about it – and she had made the connection with Queen Saffron and her own story. Maybe I really could convince her that this was a nobler path than being a mercenary and dragon-born Raider!

⚶

With no ship to sail or mission to command, however, Lila threw herself into dragon lessons. We started in the late afternoon, as a lull in the work of the harbor gave both Lila and me some time to return up the path to the lookout hill, where Crux was making his home. "If we get enough people interested in Crux – *and* they can prove themselves not too stupid or careless around him," Lila told me on the first morning, as we waited for the potential Dragon Mercenaries to arrive, "then we have a real shot at going back to the atoll and requesting that Sym allow her newts to train with us. I won't just be asking her to trust *me*, a lone human, but *the Sea Raiders*."

I could see how Lila wanted to impress the dragons with

her dedication to their bond, but I wasn't sure that the dragons would care what group or nation we called ourselves.

"Is this it?" I saw Lila's crestfallen consideration of the others who had joined with us to learn the ways of dragons. There was Senga and Adair, and one other – a chubby boy named Tung. They were the only ones of the Sea Raiders who had taken any interest at all in learning more about dragons.

"But at least there are three, huh?" I saw Lila square her shoulders. "Three potential mercenaries, and three eggs..."

Above us rose a little cloud, thin and high, meaning strong winds but no threat of rain – yet. Below us was the harbor village of Malata, the tall governor's house of Pela and Kasian, and the small speck of the *Ariel* as it headed north and west beyond the reefs. As I turned, I saw that Lila's eyes lingered aboard the ship that she had been promised, with a look of fierce concentration.

"Anyway," she shook her head to herself, fixing her face into a tight smile. "From small beginnings, mighty things grow," she said to the three youths there, and Senga and Adair whooped. "If the Phoenix agrees, then you will all take turns riding on his shoulders for a short turn around the island, to come back here and report to the rest of us how it was. Remember that this is something we have never done before, so we are all learning here. Anything you think helps – tell the rest!"

As I saw her take the other Raiders into her confidence, I was again reminded how naturally good she *could* be at leading, and at being a princess. Just like back on the boat – it wasn't when she was commanding or *thought* that she should be leading, but rather when she was engaged, body, mind, and heart in something, that others warmed to her enthusiasm.

Not like Havick, I thought, watching as Lila approached Crux with the stack of blankets and rope that she wanted to fashion into some sort of saddle. Crux turned and sniffed at the material, one scaled lip curling a little, but he still laid his long neck low on the ground to accept her offering. He only growled once, when the rope that slipped around and under his forelegs to loop back to the blanket ties were tight.

"I'm sorry, my friend!" Lila immediately rushed to loosen where a rope had caught between muscle and shoulder blade, re-tightening over a slab of the dragon's thick muscle.

No, I don't think that Havick would ever say sorry. I had never met the usurper of Roskilde, of course, but I had heard the tales. Every now and again a boat from a poor family would dare approach the shores of the Haunted Isle, begging for aid from the witches. Although the West Witches always tied to remain impartial, they would allow the fisherfolk to land and take food and water, and heal any physical complaint they had. They would tell of high tithes and taxes, or cruel prison terms and harsh guards roaming the main island in search of any who broke Havick's decrees. The island realm of Roskilde was suffocating under his rule.

"Tung? You want to try with me first?" Lila said to the

portly boy, dark hair, with purple sashed shirt. He was a little shy, but he smiled and nodded.

"Hello...?" I watched Tung say to Crux, and the dragon turned his great head to regard him steadily. A gentle huff of Crux's nose, and the acceptance was granted – *so long as Lila comes as well,* I thought.

Lila climbed Crux's foreleg to ruck up the blankets and create a more comfortable saddle for herself, before reaching down to help up Tung. Crux didn't appear to mind his boot-scraping and clumsy climb, or his shifting about as he settled in behind Lila.

"Okay, are you ready? Remember to hold on to-*owoooh!*" Before Lila had a chance to say anything, Crux had stood up and shaken his neck, causing Tung to screech a little and seize a back tine as Lila flattened herself toward Crux's neck.

Tung's going to fall off! I thought as Crux bounded to the lip of the hill, wings snapping open as he jumped into the air and *soared.*

"Skreyar!" The dragon roared as he swept over the harbor – sending burly Raiders leaping into the drink in fright – before flapping his wings to pull up and up into a circle around the island.

"Look at him go!" I heard Adair say, and I couldn't help but grin, too. How could anyone not instantly fall in love with dragons?

The dragon grew smaller around the back of the island,

before turning, sweeping his wings once more to return, this time low and fast over the land.

"Hit the deck!" Adair shouted, as the dragon shot over us to turn in mid-air, chittering in reptilian laughter before daintily landing on the ground once more.

"Tung? Tung, you lucky beast – how was it?" Adair was running forward, shouting, with his sister Senga only a few steps behind him.

"Urk." The youth managed to slide down the scales to the floor, looking distinctly pale. "Great," he managed to say, before collapsing to his knees.

Oh dear. I thought, as Adair and Senga started to laugh. "Us next! Us!" The siblings were shouting, but Lila shook her head.

"One each, with me… Neither of you have ridden a horse before, let alone a dragon," she said.

"No, we fly together!" Senga said fiercely, earning a turn of the head from Crux, and a narrowing of his eyes. "I'm not going to fly with you anyway, Lila. When I get *my* dragon, I'll be flying with my brother – or alone!" she said haughtily, before adding in a mutter. "It doesn't look that hard anyway… Just sitting and holding on…"

"Let them try," Crux whispered into my mind and I guess Lila's mind as well, as she looked suddenly distraught at being overruled. I felt a tremor of fear as I looked over the large Phoenix dragon, his strong claws, his ripples of muscle. *Was this safe?*

"Okay. The Phoenix says you both can ride together – but be careful. Don't get overexcited. Let *him* do the flying..." Lila was saying as she clambered down.

Adair and Senga couldn't wait to scramble up the forelegs of the dragon. Both being good climbers they swung from scales and elbow horns to the spine tines in no time, with Crux this time shifting his weight a little in response to their urgent grabbing.

"Settle, settle you two. On the saddle..." Lila was saying, but once again, Crux was impatient to get into the air. He stood up with a shake (Adair tumbled backwards, before clinging onto the tines), bounding forward and once again, leaping into the air. I heard a loud, lusty *whoop* from the siblings as he took off, and, apparently goaded by the attention, the Phoenix dragon only flew all the faster, beating his wings to spiral up into the air.

"Too high... Too high" Lila was saying at my side, but the dragon – now a speck – turned on an arrowhead to swoop downwards suddenly toward the land.

"Lila – they'll fall!" I gasped.

"Crux knows what he is doing," Lila said through gritted teeth. She looked fierce, angry even as the Phoenix flared his wings to pull out of the dive, just as, suddenly, he jolted in the air, temporarily losing his precise flying, turning and spinning—

"*Crux!*" Lila screamed.

I raised my hand, trying to find that quiet space inside

where the magic was. Could I do something to save them - all of them?

But before I could, Crux pulled out of the dive and flew in an erratic way, swinging side to side past us. "What is wrong with him?" I breathed, before I saw.

It was Adair and Senga. They were clinging onto his tines, not sitting down, pushing, leaping, or jumping from one side of his spine to the other as they attempted to direct his flight.

"No! Not like that – you have to think at him!" Lila shouted.

"No, Lila – it doesn't work that way. Not everyone *can* hear dragons in their minds, only those that are dragon friends, or those bonded with a dragon, like you," I pointed out.

"What?" Lila looked at me, appalled. "But, can Crux hear anyone's thoughts, or just yours and mine?"

"I don't know." I shook my head. "I think... I think that it's harder for him to reach humans who have no dragon connection, like Senga and Adair, but I don't know. I haven't read everything in the Scroll Libraries of Sebol."

"Sebol," Lila echoed, looking glum as Crux managed to turn lower, claws outstretched to catch the ground and run along it, sending up great gouts of earth behind her as he slowed down.

"What on earth were you thinking?" Lila shouted at Senga and Adair as soon as they got off the dragon, looking shaky and sick.

"He was going too fast!" Senga said from the floor. "He

wouldn't go where I wanted him to go. I wanted to fly over our house, show Mother…"

"Senga!" Lila snapped. "It was meant to be a training lesson just to get used to flying dragons, not to start directing them!"

"But what's the use of hanging on for the ride? What if we need the dragon to go and do something, like attack one of Havick's boats?" Senga frowned as Adair stumbled past to collapse on the floor.

He groaned. "That was fun, but…" He didn't need to complete the sentence, as it was obvious from the color of him what he meant.

Crux, for his part, stalked away from the two young Raiders, further up the hill to where the rocks and boulders were wilder. There, he selected a sheltered patch between the rocks and draped himself over them, flicking his tail. He, too, was clearly annoyed with how the flight had gone, and didn't want anything to do with humans right at the moment, and I for one couldn't blame him.

"Right. Great. Well – that's day one done," I heard Lila say miserably as she turned to walk back down the path. Before she got a few steps, she paused, turning to me. "Danu – If we're going to make this work, then I think that we're going to need to get to Sebol. Sooner or later."

I felt a curious mixture of elation, surprise, and distress at her words as I watched her striding away. Wasn't that what I had wanted her to offer? To come with me to the island of the witches to learn the rest of the prophecy? To accept her true destiny?

But not like this, I thought, seeing how Lila walked with her shoulders slumped down the path. It was like she was already accepting defeat, and grasping at straws.

CHAPTER 20
LILA, THE RAID

"Wake up! Wake up!" someone was shouting. "The *Ariel* has been sighted – and she's listing in the water!" I shook myself awake from where I lay against Crux's scales, looking at my little campsite in the rocks—what had become more or less my permanent home.

I had a fire pit dug and lined with stones, an awning of old sail cloth, and a stack of blankets. I still went down every morning just after dawn to Pela's house to wash and occasionally eat breakfast with her – but it wasn't my home any more. My home was up here, with Crux.

"What is it now?" The Phoenix dragon raised his head to regard the Raider who had come running up the path from the harbor. It was a couple of days after the incident with Senga and Adair, and each of the flying lessons had gone passably bad. Little Tung might make a good flier, Crux told me – if he

could get over his fear. But Senga and Adair had been banned from getting on the dragon's back again – by the dragon himself, no less.

"I don't want those two endangering their lives and mine!" Crux had said irritably to me the night of 'the incident,' and I had agreed. Danu thought that they might need to bond with their own dragon if they were ever to fly, but I just shrugged. If they wanted to travel to the dragon atoll and try to bargain with that den mother, then they were fully capable of trying– except that thought made me feel even worse. Why was I being so uncharitable? Why wasn't I inspiring more Raiders to do what I had done, to go and try to prove themselves to the dragons, to dare them to bond?

Because there were hardly any Raiders even interested in dragons. That was why. Danu had been right – I had three Raiders, two of whom were too wild even for Crux, and the other whose ability was suspect, according to Crux. I had even seen the way the Raiders looked at *me* when I went down to the harbor, as if I were some kind of witch myself. Something strange and foreign.

Why is this all so hard! I thought, childishly I knew, as the messenger Raider ran up to us.

"It's your father, Lila – out there on the *Ariel,* look!" The man pointed out to sea, where I could make out the shape of the proud *Ariel,* her swan-like hull always so recognizable to one who had grown up on her. But she was listing slightly to one side in the water, and one of her sails was down.

Oh no. "What happened?" I asked the messenger, who shook his head that he didn't know. *He's been attacked.* I started to move to Crux, intending to fly out there right away. *But he didn't want me sailing with him.* I was stopped by the thought. *He wanted to be a true Raider, not have a dragon helping him.* Would I make matters worse if I scared the crew with a dragon? Instead, I grabbed my things and ran after the messenger down the path.

⚜

The *Ariel* limped into the harbor by early morning, having had four smaller row boats working to guide her in through the reef. As she eased into harbor and was steadied with poles, it was clear to see that she had been in a fight, but she wasn't *badly* damaged.

"She's been taking in water on her port side all night, but we couldn't get enough caulk on it out there in the open drink," Kasian said as he stumbled over the plank to the dock. He looked terrible, as though he hadn't slept in over a week.

"What happened, Father?" I asked, forgetting that Pela had insisted I no longer call him Father.

"Ah, my little Lila," he said with a ghost of a smile, as around him sailors disembarked slowly, looking just as dejected as the chief was. "Get some rest and food in you, hearties!" he shouted, clapping a few on the shoulders before turning to me. "Havick," he growled, his tiredness replaced

198

with a fierce hatred. "You were right, he had three galleons out there – but he was waiting for us, I swear it. We saw smoke on the horizon and went out to investigate, only to find two war-galleons heading our way in full wind." The chief shook his head. "If I didn't think that Havick was as thick as a cow, I would have said that he had even laid a trap for us!"

"But why send three galleons out just for us?" I murmured. "All he has to do is guard his shipping lanes…"

"I don't know, but the two boats chased us, almost all the way back to the Free Isles, but I detoured through the archipelago. One of them got a lucky shot against our port side – not enough to get through the hull – but enough to spring a leak." The man looked sorrowful. "Now we're just down to two boats until the *Ariel* is fixed, and still no successful raids…" The Chief of the Raiders looked distraught. He looked up at me. "How about that great big beastie of yours? The dragon? How is it going getting the other Raiders inter-ested in your scheme?"

"Ah," I said, feeling downhearted. It wasn't going at all.

"Just get it working, Lila, I beg you," the man who had been my father said. "We need something to give the Raiders before the season's out. *Something!*"

The chief stalked away from me, his head bowed. He never begged or asked for anything in his life. It was the Raider way – for him to say that must have cost him a lot of pride.

And what did I have to give him in return? I thought.

Nothing. One Raider who was still too young and too scared to be any good on a dragon, and another two who were too wild. I *could* take those three to the dragon atoll to see if any dragons would want them – but I didn't think that would work. What if I just got them killed? The Raiders needed something now, some sign of hope.

I was the only person here who could be a Dragon Raider. Me and – as much as I didn't want to admit it – Danu.

It was all entirely up to the two of us to provide something for the Raiders; some sign that they could survive the terrors of Havick. And, if I managed to capture something valuable for the Raiders, then wouldn't they all start looking a little kindlier at Crux and the prospect of riding dragons for themselves?

That is what I would do. I would take Crux, and we would do a little bit of Raiding all on our own.

৩৯৩

"Lila?" Crux was already aware of my coming, before I had even sighted him, draped over the warm rocks of the highland. Around his makeshift home were the recent bones, as clean as ivory, of goats and sheep.

"You've been at the herds again, I see?" I said, feeling a rush of pride at my fierce dragon friend, despite the fact that I knew the Raiders must be sorely put out by his feasting. "Why don't you go fish instead?"

"I don't get to eat much lamb and mutton," Crux said philosophically. *"The wild ones usually run away – but these fat ones can't run!"* Crux snickered, licking his lips.

"Well, you're fed. Good." I reached into the awning I had erected, pulling out my cloak, my sabre and scabbard, and the hasty saddle that I had constructed.

"Not that thing again." Crux lashed his tail. *"I can carry you, Lila, no need for constricting ropes!"*

"Crux, my friend – I've told you, *I* need something just a little more comfortable, and these loops help hold my bag and any equipment I need," I said, rolling my eyes. If I had ever thought having a working relationship with a dragon would be easy, then I had been sorely mistaken. But I had to agree—I would have to get a proper saddle made of shaped leather and flat straps, one that was comfortable for the dragon as well.

"Well, I suppose you humans aren't lucky enough to have the claws and the scales that we dragons do," Crux considered. I pulled a face, and the Phoenix dragon let his thick crimson and forked tongue loll into the air as if laughing at me.

The dragon still let me affix my makeshift saddle to his back, and attach my belongings. I had only a fraction of the things that I *could* take on a Raiding mission: rope and grappling hook, armor, shield, spare provisions, star charts, bandages. My hands uncovered the scrap of cloth that Pela had found with my name and the crown upon it. I looked at it for a moment, wondering why I had it with me at all.

It's the only link I have to where I began, I thought as I stuffed it into my pack along with the spare cloak, and climbed Crux's leg.

"Where are we going, air-rider?" Crux looked up at me with his bright eyes.

"I don't know, exactly," I said. "I'll need your nose and your ears to guide me to prey."

"We're going hunting? Yes!" Crux rippled his slabs of muscles and stepped down daintily from the rocks, with me snugged at the base of his neck. I immediately felt safe, as if nothing could hurt me ever again.

"Lila!? Lila – where are you going?" someone shouted from the path down to the harbor. It was Danu, running toward us, waving one hand as the other clutched his cloak. He still wore a thin tunic and short-legged trousers.

"Not now, Danu – I have work to do," I called down, feeling a flash of superiority over him now that I was on the dragon. I didn't have to do anything for anyone else, not the adept, not my foster parents. I would show them all what I could do on my own!

"Lila, wait – take me with you!" Danu shouted, panting as he reached the top.

"No," I said. I didn't want to take Danu. *I have to prove that my scheme works to Kasian, to Pela, to all the other Raiders.* I had to do it, *me,* and I didn't want anyone looking at my achievement and say it was anything to do with witches and prophesies and magic. *That would only further alienate the dragon from the Raiders*, I thought, pushing in with my heels to spur Crux to leap into the sky – but he did not. "Crux?" I asked. "Why aren't we flying?"

"We should take that one too. He is a dragon friend, and we might need his magics," Crux said sagely.

"What? NO, Crux, we don't need him – I need to do this myself, to prove to the Raiders what I can do!"

"What WE can do, air-rider." Crux turned his sinuous neck to look back at me. *"You asked me to join you, and I will gladly – but it is not your burden alone. It is ours."* The multicolored dragon turned back his head to regard Danu, looking hopeless and frantic below. *"Yours, mine, and the adept's. We are meant to hunt together."*

There was nothing I could do to convince him, and irritatingly, the dragon stepped forward and lowered his head, neck and shoulder so that Danu could scrabble up to his spot behind him.

"Thank you, great Crux," I heard him breath, settling himself and grabbing the spine ridges as Crux took a deep breath, trotted forward, and then – *flew*.

CHAPTER 21
DANU AND THE CRIPPLED SHIP

The princess really didn't want to speak to me as we flew in the airs high above the archipelago. We flew steadily eastward until the early afternoon, before Lila asked Crux to start veering north. We were travelling in a wider and wider spiraling loop across the Western Isles, looking for *something.*

But looking for what? I wondered as my stomach grumbled. I hadn't had time to bring provisions, weapons, or even warmer clothes—I had heard the distant buzzing at the back of my head of dragon tongue and had known, instinctively, that it was Crux's voice. It had been like half-hearing a conversation on the other side of a wall; it had not been intended for me, but I could hear it anyway. I dropped everything, seizing my cloak and running for where I could feel the dragon was, to find Lila already urging him to leave the island!

I have to admit, that hurt me a little. Why hadn't she asked me to come along with her? I thought that *we* were the Dragon Riders of Malata, together, but she had said she wanted to prove herself to the Raiders.

"She is hunting prey. She is upset and will need your friendship, dragon mage," Crux suddenly broke into my mind to speak. I glanced up at Lila ahead of me, leaning over the neck of Crux – she didn't appear to notice the words. Did that mean a dragon could share minds just with whomever it wanted to? Had Crux allowed me to hear the plans Lila had been making without me?

"Ah, little magician – you have so much to learn!" Crux laughed, chittering into the sky. At this, Lila *did* look up.

"Have you seen anything, Crux?" she called.

"Yes!" This time, the voice of the male dragon was louder and resonant, and from the look of glee on Lila's face, I knew that the dragon had shared that thought with both of us.

"There is life. To the east and south. Life and blood!" He raised his wings slowly in the air, slowly spinning us toward it. We had already flown over many smaller islands on this side of the Barrens – and, although there had been smoke rising from hamlets and near flocks on the hills, they were not what Lila seemed to be looking for. Crux was carrying us towards the eastern edge of the archipelago, almost toward the Storm Seas and the Broken Coast itself. Here, battered by storm winds, the islands were little more than spires and splinters of rock, and sparsely inhabited.

"Lila? What did you have planned?" I said, more than a little nervous. Should I summon a storm again, like I had aboard the *Ariel?* How could I convince her that killing was not the way to free her people?

"She is a hunter, little magician. It is in her blood, as it is in mine and even yours," Crux said again, and Lila whooped loudly. He hadn't bothered to direct that thought solely to me, either.

But I was no hunter–what was the dragon talking about? Unless he thought fishing was hunting–no, that was more sort of waiting around and being patient, not the same as what the Raiders and dragons did. If I am a hunter, then it is a hunter after words and truth, I thought, and wondered at the thrill of savage satisfaction I felt. Were some of the dragon's emotions mingling with mine? It was hard to *not* be aware of the large fierce beast in my mind, so much so that I almost thought that *I* could breathe fire and fly…

"Not yet, little magician. But some of your ilk have taken on the powers of my kind…" Crux told me cryptically, but before I could question him further, Lila was shouting and pointing. "There! There she is!"

On the horizon, leaning crazily against a ridge of sharp Bonerock, was a fat-bellied carrack with tattered sails. This high up, I could see the shadow of the reef just below the surface that had caught her awry; it stretched like an ugly scar beneath the waters towards the headland of one of the wild islands.

"What colors is she flying?" Lila peered down at it.

I too squinted at the tattered flags and sails. Two of her three masts were broken, and there was a burn mark all along one side of her. She had been in a fight. I saw a flutter of red, a suggestion of a shape on a purple background. *Red on purple? Isn't that...*

"That's Torvald colors, isn't it?" I shouted.

"Even better," Lila grinned fiercely. "We lost that other Torvald ship in the storm, and I don't want to let one get away again!"

Crux matched her enthusiasm, diving down towards the wreck as I panicked. "But Lila – you can't attack a Torvald ship! Torvald are our allies."

"The Raiders have no allies," she returned as the ship grew larger ahead of us and the wind howled in our ears.

"Torvald are allies to *all* dragon friends!" I shouted. "That is where King Bower holds court! King Bower who restarted the Dragon Academy!" I still had one card to play, and, given the savage grin coming from my friend at the prospect of murder, I played it. "And Queen Saffron, the dragon-sister!"

Lila twitched as if struck. She frowned, and beneath us, her unease translated into a wobble for Crux. *"Saffron, dragon-sister? I have heard of that one. A great dragon-lady,"* Crux said, easing his decent into a swoop rather than a charge.

"This is nothing to do with her..." Lila said through gritted teeth, but I could see that she was troubled. Had she never realized that her raiding would directly impact on the people she thought of as her heroes?

"But still, Lila – that is how murder by the Raiders will be viewed," I pointed out. Crux circled the burned boat in a wide loop, spiraling closer. I couldn't see anyone on board, and I only hoped that the ship's boat had been undamaged, and had carried what survivors there had been to the wild islands.

"The Raiders have always raided. And here we will just be picking what the seas have already discarded," Lila said, her face stern as she directed Crux to land aboard the deck of the ship with a rush of wings and scraping claws.

۞

The deck was a mess. There were broken and smashed ship's lockers everywhere, and the bolts of arrows half stuck in the broken mast, the deck. The burn mark on the side of the ship extended through a cracked and broken gunwale and across the deck.

"There was a battle here," I said, feeling dazed at the sight of it.

"You don't say." Lila already had her sabre bared, and was stalking across the deck to the captain's quarters under the sterncastle. The door was broken open and looked to be the work of hatchets.

"Dragon fire." Crux sniffed at the burnt wood. *"This is the work of dragons."*

"But wild dragons don't usually have archers on them," Lila stated.

"And why would Torvald Riders attack their own ship?" I added, as Lila frowned, looking at the tattered remnants of the red and purple flag.

"Unless..." she said, stepping up to rip it from the edge of the railing. It was a large flag, but it was light. "Riddle me this – why isn't that flag painted or stitched onto the main sail?" She pointed to the tattered white above. I looked. She was right.

"They were sailing incognito?" I said. "Maybe they didn't want to draw attention to themselves?"

"What, and then some Dragon Riders *thought* they were an enemy and attacked them anyway?" Lila shook her head. "No. This is too strange. In fact, it reminds me of precisely the sort of tactic that we Raiders use..."

"You don't think that Kasian..." I gasped.

"No, the *Ariel* came back, remember, and went in the other direction. But he did say that he was chased by *two* Roskildean ships, and we saw *three* on our journey back to Malata, remember?" Lila said. "What if the third Roskildean ship decided to pretend to be a Torvald ship?"

"But why would they?" I asked. It made no sense. None at all. Havick already controlled the Barren Seas. He would have no reason to masquerade as the Empire of Torvald, would he?

"Lila! Danu–in the little room!" Crux suddenly snorted, turning his massive head to snarl at the shattered door of the

captain's rooms. Lila went first, crouching with sword held out in front of her. I put a hand to the center of my chest, feeling the heartbeat and the warmth, and *willing* the magic inside me to work. I didn't know what I would do or what spell I even *could* cast for this situation, but I would try...

"Yagh!" Lila jumped into the room with a swipe of her sword, and I followed, feeling something kindling in my heart. A fire. A sense of anger.

⚜

Someone cowered in the corner.

"Don't kill me! Please!" The man was thin and wearing the sort of finery that didn't belong on a sailing ship. Pale, fluttery blond hair and a small mustache pronounced him a northerner of some description, and that made him most likely to be Roskildean.

Around him, the captain's room was in tatters. The table was half smashed, papers and charts thrown about the room, heavy ax marks on the walls. I prodded one of the charts with my foot. The waters around the Broken Coast and the mainland.

"Who are you? What happened here?" Lila demanded, advancing with her sabre point until it almost touched the man's throat. He squealed and tried to look away, but Lila stayed glaring and silent until the man's terrified eyes turned back.

And then something *very* strange happened. As soon as he looked at Lila, *really* looked at her that is, his eyes grew wide and he almost choked. "By the stars. It's true. All these years, and it's true – the heir has been found!"

CHAPTER 22
LILA, THE TRUE HEIR

W*hat did he just call me?* I looked from the man to Danu, to see that my accomplice looked, if anything, excited.

"Don't say it," I hissed quickly at him, turning back to the man who swallowed hard. "As for you... Care to repeat what you just said?"

The man's eyes were wide, terrified as he made small pawing motions in the air with his hands. "It's you. We've found you!" A ghost of a nervous smile briefly lit his face. "You're the long-lost Princess of Roskilde."

"I think you must be mistaken—" I started, but the man continued.

"Please – if I may—I *know* that it is you. The poor people still have the pictures of your parents–though Havick punishes them if he finds them. You are the image of your mother, the old queen!" the man said, and, much to my embarrassment, sunk to his knees in front of me.

"Can I say it now?" Danu beamed at me. "I told you so."

"Shut up." I gestured for the man to stand. "Maybe he's wrong…"

"No, your highness – I cannot be, not only is there your looks, the cut of your jaw, the shape of your brow, but one of the West Witches themselves told Havick that the true heir had been found. I was there! In the throne room when she did it – striding in without any heed to the guards who tried to stop her, and calmly telling the Lord Havick that he was in danger!"

"What?" I glared at Danu. "The West Witches did this?"

Danu's look was one of fierce determination. "Who was it? Afar? Ohotto? What did she look like?"

"Golden hair, white robes…" the man said quickly under Danu's fierce gaze.

"Ohotto Zanna." I watched as my friend pulled a face. "This is strange tidings indeed…"

"Why? What does it mean?" I said, my confusion matched only by my anger. It would have been so much simpler if no one had been alive on the wreck. Or if this man had tried to attack us. But no – he had to start talking about the prophecy…

The fact that I was a princess.

The thought hit me. Danu had been right all along. It confirmed what my foster-mother had suspected with my name-cloth and what most of my heart had been unwilling to accept.

"So, I am this long-lost princess of the Roskildeans. Fine. What difference does that make?" I argued bitterly as I stepped back. "You want me to give up my life? Start wearing skirts, for goodness sake?"

"But, but Lila..." Danu was insistent. "This is your destiny. It's *who* you were meant to be."

"Who I was meant to be?" I pulled a face, ignoring the tremor of fear in my heart. "Give me a break."

The Raiding life was all I knew. I had grown up here, on the sea, in the islands, not in some distant court. The very thought of being simpered at by weak-kneed men like this one here in front of me only made me angrier. *I could pretend that this never happened,* I thought desperately. *I could go back to Malata and be a good chief's daughter...*

"No," Crux breathed into my heart, his mind felt steady and firm. *"We are what we are. Nothing more, nothing less, nothing else."*

He was right, but I didn't want to admit it. I couldn't go back and expect life in Malata to be just the same as before. Even the memories of my home with Pela and Kasian felt different now, thanks to everything that had happened. Like it was a dream, and I had woken up to a world for which I wasn't prepared.

But what do I do, Crux! My silent words were anguished.

"That is for you to decide. I am a dragon, so I fly. I hunt. I kill."

Life was a lot simpler if you were a gigantic fire-breathing lizard, I thought. I needed time to think this through. To work out who *I* thought I was. *I am Lila of Malata,* I tried the words in my head – but now they felt wrong somehow. Because the people I had always looked up to were not my parents who wanted me on a boat, not on a dragon as I wanted to be. Lila the Dragon Raider. That felt better... but who is that Lila? Where does she come from? And then, of course, there was Lila of Roskilde – the long-lost princess in the flouncy dresses. *No. Definitely not.*

"You are all these things, and more..." Again, Crux spoke in my mind.

But how could that be? Was it even possible to be more than one thing?

"You humans. Always putting names on things and saying this is all that they are." Crux was amused, despite my distress. *"Just because I am a dragon, it doesn't mean that I am not also a human-friend."*

That was true, I granted. Meanwhile, however, Danu appeared to be busy interrogating the man in front of me. "When did Ohotto Zanna come to you? Did anyone else travel with her? What else did she talk about?"

But the man was waving his hands in an anxious plea. "I don't know, sir!" he kept on repeating. "She has been visiting the Lord Havick for a while, I have seen her in the keep many times over the years, but always the lord and her rushes off to some private audience chamber. This time, however, the witch seemed angry enough to not care for such precautions."

"Well, that certainly sounds like Ohotto," Danu grumbled to himself. "You say that she's been to Lord Havick before? Many times?"

"Yes, certainly." The man nodded.

"Lila?" Danu turned quickly to hiss at me. "The West Witches are never meant to take sides. Never. We are guardians of the old lore, and we seek to do what we can to make that lore useful, but we shouldn't start advising lords… Chabon would never agree to it."

"But aren't *you* taking sides? Seeing as you're the guy who took it upon himself to 'find the lost Princess'!"

"Well, that's different…." Danu looked suddenly ashamed. "You had a right to know. The prophesy is your heritage. Your life."

"And what of this prophesy then, huh?" I directed my frustration at him. "What does it say?"

Between us in the cabin, the captured man's eyes were wide as he glanced from one of us to the other.

"Uh… It would be unwise to go into the details," Danu said carefully. "It is very important, and I need to be sure that I am not influencing the future if I…"

"Influencing the future?" I burst out. "What by the names of the holy waters do you *think* that you've been doing ever since I set eyes on you?" I felt angry at this young man who had sailed into my life, bringing with him his tide of problems. I wish that I had never accepted his offer of help at all!

"I, uh, you're right, I know, Lila… But…" He looked ashamed, his eyes sliding away from me to the sides of the room.

'Never trust a man who cannot hold your gaze' was one of my foster-father's small pieces of advice, born from many long seasons demanding goods from captured merchants. *'They will always be hiding something,'* he had said.

With a sudden, sinking realization, I understood just what it was that this fish-boy himself was hiding from me. "You don't know, do you?"

"What?" Danu looked up at me with worried eyes. My guess had hit true.

"You don't know what the prophecy says do you? Not all of it anyway." I made the mental leap, following my instincts. "Maybe you know a bit, or your mentors let you in on some of the secret – but that is why you are so shocked that one of your own witches is involved with Havick. You're just in the dark about all of this as me!"

"I, uh…" Danu's face blossomed with embarrassment.

"Whatever." I clicked my tongue in annoyance. "For now, we need to work out what *he* was doing here, flying under Torvald colors." I raised an eyebrow at the man, along with my sabre. "Explain."

"Ah, you see…" It was his turn to look embarrassed. "I was a courtier for the old king, your father, before Havick came. We had always been fighting the Sea Raiders, of course. They were a constant nuisance, but in that last year and that winter, their attacks had become devastating," the man said.

'They were brilliant. They seemed to know where all of our best and largest ships were going before they had even left port! Wave after wave of attacks every moon, and the Sea Raiders didn't seem happy with just plundering what they could and leaving. They *scuttled* our boats, they killed so many."

I felt uncomfortable at this tale of the courtiers. It wasn't like my foster-father to do that, was it? He had always had such a healthy respect for the ways of the sea, of taking what you needed, then a little bit extra, but at least leaving those you raided alive. Otherwise – who would there be to raid the next season? The one after that? *He was paid to attack the king's ship,* hadn't Pela told me that?

The courtier continued. "We were on the verge of entirely losing our navy *and* our fishing fleet!"

"No!" I burst out. Sea Raiders never attack just humble fishermen. Maybe some of the larger merchant vessels, but never the small skiffs and yachts of a family just making their daily food.

"It's true, princess, I am afraid. The royal family were setting out on a perilous journey to Torvald, to petition the new King Bower and Queen Saffron for aid…" The courtier stated sadly. "But they never returned. Their boat was caught by the Sea Raiders, and the royal family vanished. Lord Havick told us that they – you – must have all been pushed over into the sea..."

"They were dead when the Raiders got to them," I told him, although the courtier didn't understand how I knew. That was what Lasarn had said. Poisoned nobles on a boat, and a baby.

"It was all Havick," Danu said grimly. "It is the only explanation."

"Some of us feared so, of course," the courtier said in a mousey voice. "Especially when Havick declared himself the ruler, and his reforms were so harsh! He has nigh doubled the taxes for the Roskildeans, and the outlying islands have to pay a protection tithe on top of that! All to build his galleons and warships."

I nodded. So that was where the monstrous navy had come from. "And the Sea Raiders – their attacks slowed during Havick's reign?" I asked lightly, already knowing what the answer was but wanting to hear this man's answer.

"Oh, yes. Dramatically so. Now, the Lord Havick claims that they are almost all destroyed!"

"Not quite." I said through gritted teeth.

"But, princess, the good people of Roskilde still revere your parents," the courtier said earnestly. "They speak with such fondness for the times of peace under the true Roskildean family..."

"Good for them. But none of that explains why you were masquerading as a Torvald boat!" I said tersely.

"Ah, well…" He swallowed nervously. "I did not agree to this, but Lord Havick made me. He drew his senior advisors and courtiers aside and revealed to us that Torvald has once again started to encroach on our territory, just as they did during the bad times under the Dark King."

"What?" Danu coughed a sudden laugh. "That is crazy."

The courtier's look was owlish with confusion. "It was not such a hard lie to believe in. The Dark King ruled for so long and was so vile… Now that he has been overthrown and the new rulers are in charge, all of a sudden, they have Dragon Riders again, who patrol their borders so aggressively…" he looked fearfully around at the timbers of the lopsided ship, and I remembered the blackened scorch marks up and down its hull and across its decks.

"It is not so large a step to believe that Bower and Saffron, too, might turn towards evil…" he added.

"No," I snapped. *Not them. Not a good island girl.* "That was a lie, courtier, as well I think you know."

"Yes." The weaselly man nodded. "So we were told to disguise our boat, and drive deep into Torvald territory, past the Broken Coasts— to spy."

"But the Dragon Riders discovered you?" Danu concluded.

"Yes. When we couldn't answer their questions, they attacked us, and left us beached on the rocks here. Most of the crew managed to escape to the nearby island, but I thought that Lord Havick would at least send a rescue party to retrieve us. It was his idea, after all..."

"He will never come to save you, you know that, don't you?" I said heavily, and the courtier nodded.

"I know," he said in a sad voice. "It seems that the old wisdom is right: you cannot keep faith with someone who has a bad heart. They will never return your sacrifice."

I felt a surge of anger then at Havick – and it wasn't like the usual anger and annoyance I had felt for him before over the fact that he thwarted us Raiders, that he was always a step ahead of us. No, this was a hatred of the man himself. *He was at least meant to look after the people who worked for him! Who were loyal to him!* And yet here this thin, frightened aging man was cast to his doom by the man who had asked for his loyalty.

I had grown up thinking that the crew that I worked with – as rough and as crude, and as ill-tempered as they could be sometimes – they were my *family.* I had entrusted my life into their hands, and they had entrusted their lives into mine. It was the only way you survived out at sea.

But this Lord Havick...? I felt utter contempt, and there was an answering roar from Crux outside.

"Your dragon!" the man gasped. "I had thought that you were Dragon Riders yourselves, come to finish us off when I heard you in the airs. But you are not. You cannot be, princess?"

I can be if I want to be, I thought. "We do not come from Torvald, sir."

"But you *do* have a dragon? You are the princess who has come back to free her people?" He looked at me hopefully.

"Lila?" Danu prompted me, his eyes shining with pride —in me.

I shook my head. I didn't know what I was. "I am no princess," I said quickly. "But I *will* take you to your fellows on the nearest island. There will be a small fishing village on the far side. I'm sure that you and the survivors can barter or work for passage to Roskilde. If you want to go back."

The courtier's eyes were shadowed. "I think I might try to convince them to leave these troubled waters and head inland. They are capable sailors and soldiers. There will be work for them without one mad king or another…"

"Very wise, sir," Danu said.

I couldn't be in this room anymore, I thought as I sheathed my sword and went out onto the lopsided deck to see Crux lazing over the forecastle, rubbing the side of his snout against the bowsprit.

"Oh, what should I do, Crux?" I said wearily, climbing the stairs up to the forecastle deck where I could lean against him against the fierce wind.

"Should do?" Crux stopped his scale-scratching to look at me with what I was certain was a humored curiosity in his giant eyes. *"You are who you are, Lila wave-rider. Why do you keep on thinking that you have to be something else?"*

"I don't!" I said out loud. "It's everyone else who keeps on saying that I am this or that. I am a princess or a chief's daughter, or none of these things at all!"

"Do they?" Crux observed. *"It does not matter what people say you were, Lila. I was once an egg. Then a very naughty newt. But now I am a dragon, and I do what I am."*

"So – you are saying I should just follow my instincts?" I said in exasperation.

"It works for me," Crux commented dryly, and I was sure that he was making fun at me, until he said again into my mind. *"Listen to your gut, Lila wave-rider, air-rider. What I have seen in humans is that they spent many years trying to be something that they are not, and listening to people tell them they are this or that, without ever listening to what they feel."*

"Huh." I sniffed. "You sound pretty wise, for a wyrm."

"Sckrech!" Crux snapped out a tiny belch of flame and soot at my insult, but I could feel in the back of my mind that it was meant good-naturedly.

"And you are pretty slow, for a dragon. But for a human, I think you will do," he returned. He made me laugh, as I thumped his scales playfully. Having a dragon for a friend was proving much better than I had thought at the start.

So... Listen to my instincts? I leaned back as I saw, across the boat, that Danu was attempting to coax the courtier out towards Crux. The man looked suddenly appalled at what he had agreed to.

But what did I really feel? I felt loyal to my foster-parents,

I felt loyal to my family the Sea Raiders. But I also felt that I was different now – and that a large part of that was having Crux here. He and Danu had changed my life and my outlook fundamentally. There was more than just me and this season's loot to think about.

Like the Roskildeans, I thought in despair. Even though I didn't know them, the courtier's story had touched me. The Roskildean people had been done a terrible wrong when Havick had paid my own foster-father to traumatize them.

Havick was an evil man, of this I knew, and I felt a deep revulsion for him. He was even trying to start a war with the Kingdom of Torvald, I thought in astonishment.

"But is it really my job to stop him? Does it have to be me?" I whispered into the storm winds. In return, they only gave the lonesome, howling answers that they always gave such silly questions.

"You know there is only one place where you can find out that, don't you, Lila?" Crux answered me instead.

Yes. "Danu?" I called out.

"What?" he sounded distracted, as the courtier was clutching onto his arm for dear life.

"After we have freed this man, I will need to know what the rest of that prophesy says." I had made my decision. I would go the Haunted Isle of Sebol.

PART III

The Prophesy

CHAPTER 23
DANU, RETURNING HOME

Something had changed about the dark-haired young woman I rode with. It was in her bearing, the way she rode with her back leant low, her head peering intently to the southern horizon. I could see it in the way that her gloved hands gripped the scales of the great dragon beneath us.

"She has found who she is." The words of Crux broke into my mind, surprising me as they always did with the ease and strength that he could share his intellect with mine.

But who is that? I wondered. Lila the Dragon Mercenary? Lila the Princess of Roskilde?

"Lila," Crux said cryptically to me, leaving me none the wiser.

It had happened on that wrecked ship. Something the courtier had said about who she was, and her real parents had made her intent on finding out about the prophesy. The prophesy I had lied to her about, I thought, feeling a sudden lurch in my stomach. She knew that I didn't know all of it, and she was angry at me.

After leaving the courtier on the nearest island, Lila had asked Crux to find her father and the *Ariel*, and then told me that we were to prepare for a long journey. It took us the rest of the afternoon and well into the evening to catch up with the Chief Kasian's ship, but Crux promised to fly us over the waves straight towards it.

"Of course! I can smell the fish a hundred feet under the waves – do you think I couldn't find a boatload of unwashed humans?" Crux was enjoying this task, I could tell. He snapped and beat his wings in powerful rowing movements, catching on the slightest currents of air to swoop forward, faster and faster. Lila wasn't trying to hold him back, or to make the flight comfortable for either herself or me, I thought, and Crux delighted in that.

By the time that moon was rising into the sky, the *Ariel* was a haven of yellowing lamplight on the dark waters, slowly plowing through the waves.

"Skreyar!" Crux called a greeting to the boat, and, in return there was a shout and one of the lead lanterns on the bowsprit was dipped and lit.

"Bring us down, Crux," Lila said through clipped tones, and the dragon swept in wide circles around the boat as other Sea Raiders scrabbled to their positions. Even now, after having seen this very same dragon up close and in their home town, they still clutched bows and spears defensively. When will humans get over their fear of these great beasts? I wondered.

"Kasian! I have returned!" Lila called down in a strong voice as Crux flew lazily around the *Ariel*.

"Lila? Lila – what are you doing? I told you to stay on Malata and train the others!" The large form of the chief gripped the railings as he leaned out to shout up at his daughter. Behind him, other of the sailors watched the confrontation warily.

"Father – I do not wish to disobey you, but there is no time to talk," she shouted. "Due east of here, almost to the Broken Coasts, you will find one of Havick's ships scuttled on a reef, wearing Torvald colors. I came to tell you that it's ripe for plunder."

"My child! Did you take it? Alone?" the chief was incredulous.

But Lila had already told Crux to lift off from his swinging flight. "No! We'll talk when I return, Father!" she called.

"Lila! Come back here!" the man shouted, but Lila was not pausing for argument or debate. I felt the mighty pull of the Phoenix dragon's muscles as we turned, and Lila was waving farewell at her father.

"When I return!" she called, ignoring the chief's shouts to her.

"Why did you do that?" I said, feeling like I had missed a step somewhere. This wasn't like the Lila that I had been trying to befriend for the past few moons. She still seemed confident and stubborn, but now she seemed to have less regard for the wishes of her father.

"We fly to the Haunted Isle, Danu," she shouted back at me. "I have to know what the prophesy says about me."

Why now? I was about to say when I stopped myself. I didn't want to pour doubts into her, when she was heading down the path that I had wanted her on from the first day I had realized who she was.

Above us, the stars started to appear, and the waters became a textured silver and shadow blanket. The wind slowed, and our world was encircled by the sigh and snap of the dragon's wings. It felt like we were flying out of the normal and into a world of dreams. Up above us, the stars grew brighter, now added with silvery drifts of star-stuff, and the occasional spear of light as a shooting star winged its way past. Lila was silent, and for a while I slept on the wing.

When I awoke, it was to the change in the winds as Crux circled down to a wooded island, and a mound of rock. It was still dark, and Lila was yawning when the dragon delicately set us down.

"I am tired," the Phoenix told us. *"I will rest and wait for the dawn."*

"Thank you, you have flown far today, my friend," Lila

said tiredly, undoing the saddle and sliding from the great back to the floor below.

"Batash," I said, recognizing the shape of the hill and the sea-cliffs beyond, from which I could hear the disturbed hooting of the nesting gulls. "It's the nearest island to Sebol," I volunteered helpfully. It was also one of the lookout points the Western Witches kept an eye on – if they could see a pinpoint of fire on this very hilltop, they would know visitors were coming. I relayed the information to Lila. "Do you want me to start a fire, then?" I said as I thumped to the floor, already looking for dead twigs and leaves.

"No," Lila said quickly. "You said that one of the West Witches – this Ohotto Zanna – is working with Lord Havick. How do we know that the rest of them aren't?" Instead, she rolled out her blanket against the dragon's warm throat.

"They can't be," I said quickly. "It is against the witch's code."

"You mean it used to be. That witch told Havick about me. She is helping the lord find me, probably to kill me," Lila muttered darkly, making me pause. She was right. Something must have changed at the court of Chabon – either that, or Ohotto was working toward her own devices. *But defy the will of Chabon?* I thought that was a step too far, even for sharp-tongued Ohotto.

"Okay," I agreed, chewing a bit of the dried meat I had managed to find at the bottom of my pack, before unrolling my blanket on the other side of Crux's neck, and finding it surprisingly warm. I don't need a fire at all, was my last wakeful thought.

⚜

"So, tell me what you know about the Haunted Isle," Lila said to me the next morning, as she stretched in the grey, predawn light. Crux had already got up, diving into the cold waters to catch his breakfast as I sat on the warm flattened grass he had vacated.

"You mean Sebol. That is what we call it," I said.

"Whatever you call it. I want to know how to get in there without being detected, and how to get to this library of yours."

I thought for a moment. The Witches of Sebol lived mostly on the near eastern side of the island, with Chabon's hut and observatory on the western. The library itself was almost in the centre of the eastern "village" and connected to the council hut, the kitchens, the stores by wooden walkways that snaked throughout the woods. "Impossible," I advised, describing the layout. "You know, I am certain that my mentor Afar will listen to us. Whatever the other witches have done – she will listen to *you*."

"You think?" Lila looked at me critically. "Would she be willing to get the prophesy for us?"

I thought for a moment of my austere witch mentor. She had a much stronger interpretation of the prophesy – of *all* prophesies, as a matter of fact. That we had to be the ones to bring them into being. That we were the agents for their reality – but the thought of her directly breaking the word of the old Matriarch and head of our order, Chabon?

"Hardly." I shook my head. "The Library of the Witches is their most treasured resource, you see. It is the repository of knowledge entrusted to them by the Dragon Monks of old. They didn't even let *me* go in there!"

"Well then, we'll just have to fly in then, won't we…" Lila shrugged, buckling her leather armor about her and reaching for her sabre.

"No, wait!" I sprang up. There had to be another way than this. What would the witches do when an angry Lila descended upon then with an even angrier dragon? *And me with them.* Half of the witches had thought me a liability, a boy with magical powers. I was surely to turn to evil just as the last mage – the Dark King – had.

I had wanted to show to them all that I could prove the prophesy right. That I could use my powers for good. That they could teach me the secrets of a mage… Me riding down on the back of an angry dragon would close that path forever to me.

"The witches aren't all bad." I pleaded with Lila to consider reason. "Chabon, Afar – they know a lot. They could help us!"

Lila paused, hands on hips, looking out to the west and the bluing morning light. Behind her, the shape of Crux broke free from the surface joyously, with a giant Marlin between his teeth. Lila smiled at Crux's clear enjoyment of the hunt and of the kill.

"Okay, fish-boy," she turned back to me. "Have it your way. Can we fly to the island unseen? If we can do that, then you can approach your Afar and Chabon, and ask them what the prophesy really says, and what it means. But as soon as it looks that they are going to deny us, then I will be heading to that library, no matter who is in my way."

I felt shocked at her fierceness, and my hesitation must have been written clear across my face, as Lila frowned at me. "Havick is plotting to find me and kill me, Danu. Havick killed my real parents, and he is just a few tides away from killing my foster parents as well. I haven't got time or the eggs to create a Dragon Mercenary army – and so it seems that I have to do what you wanted all along. I have to fight Havick if I want to survive, and if I want the Sea Raiders to survive."

"Oh." I nodded, wondering why I didn't feel happier. Wasn't this what I had wanted? What Afar had wanted? For Lila to reach for the Sea Crown, her birth-right?

But she hadn't mentioned the Sea Crown at all, I realized. She hadn't said anything about taking her place as a Princess of the Western Isles. All she had said she wanted to do was to save the Sea Raiders.

"Lila, after we have defeated Havick," I began cautiously.

"*If* we defeat Havick," Lila said stubbornly. "There are still an awful lot of ships and soldiers between here and there." She turned away from me to congratulate Crux as he dropped himself onto the rocks, his breakfast having been eaten. "You still didn't answer my question, Danu. *Is* there a way to get to your Sebol by air without being spotted?"

Yes. There was.

CHAPTER 24
LILA AND AFAR

The Haunted Isle – *Sebol*, Danu kept calling it – was the farthest island to the west of the archipelago. The Sea Raiders told tales of the ghosts that surrounded it, and even now, seeing the mists that swamped it in the afternoon light gave me a creepy feeling.

"Hot springs." Danu had confided in me, revealing the island's secret. Obvious, really, I thought – and I wondered why no one had tried to raid the island before. There were plenty of islands along the Spice Coast that also had hot springs on them, meaning that they grew abundant with vegetation and were permanently surrounded by their own strange sea fogs and river mists.

Because the Sea Raiders are a superstitious bunch, I answered myself. There were generations of tales about the various ships that had gone missing past the Haunted Isle, and so naturally the island itself had gained a bit of an evil reputation.

We swooped low over the waters, keeping the dark shape ahead of us as we flew first south, and then back up towards the north to approach the island well away from its huts and villages, as Danu had suggested.

"They rarely keep watch over the south-western approach," the adept had told me. "As so few boats ever come from that direction…"

This was our plan: fly in low over the water into the mists and find some abandoned part of the wilder coast on which to land, and then sneak in on foot. Danu said that he might have a few of his 'magical tricks' to aid with that – but seeing as I had only ever seen him summon a spot of rain and wind, I didn't know how much help that would be.

Even the mid-afternoon light seemed to drain from the sky as we slid into the sea mists. The sound of Crux's wings suddenly became muted, and if anything felt like it was haunted – then this was it.

"I can't see anything!" I hissed at the dragon and person behind me.

"You don't have to. I can smell the island up ahead," Crux told me, slowing his wings, dropping closer to the waters. He flew as silent as a hunting hawk.

A dark shadow in the mists swung towards us. "What is that?" I hissed quickly, as Crux expertly flared his wings out of the way, and the shape was revealed as a spire of rock. As we flashed past, I thought for a moment that it had been shaped and carved into the likeness of a person.

"On the other side!" Danu said, as Crux once again avoided the rock-stack colossuses. This one definitely *was* carved: a man with a maw open in a shout or a scream. Then came smaller rocks, heads that had only just broken the water, a stack of rocks that looked like reaching arms…

"So these are the ghosts of Sebol, then?" I muttered as the mists darkened.

"We're here," Crux whispered into my mind, even the great Phoenix dragon subdued by the creepy surroundings. The shadows up ahead solidified into a line of broken rocks, a shattered tree-covered cliff.

"Danu?" I whispered back at him, to see his pale face nodding, and pointing a little farther to our right.

"There should be larger rocks and clearings…" he said, his voice oddly small in the murk. Crux flashed over the overgrown wood, and I had a chance to see thick vines and moss stretching between the trees, and dense foliage everywhere. There could be entire villages of people underneath that, and I would have been none the wiser, I thought. Had Danu been entirely honest with me about who lived here? He had said they were a small, isolated community – but in fact – it could be anything down there!

But in just a few wingbeats I saw what Danu had been pointing out. Large boulders as big as houses, around which the forest struggled to take purchase. Sebol must be a rocky outcrop with only a thin veneer of soil despite it lush variety of plants and life. The boulders offered as large a space as we needed, although it was difficult for Crux to swoop in and land, and instead he had to hover on quick-beating wings to lower us to the craggy surface.

"Can you wait here, my friend?" I asked the Phoenix dragon before sliding off his back.

"I would rather that than talking to witches!" the dragon said mischievously, blinking his large green and yellow eyes at me.

You and me both, I thought but didn't say aloud for Danu to hear as I followed his scramble down the side of the boulder where our dragon was now perched, and into the dense forest of Sebol.

๛

"Are you sure this is the right way?" I asked for the second time, when Danu had seemingly led us back to the small clearing where there had stood a small carved-wooden statue. It was hard to tell what it was in this green-lit murk. It could have been a statue of a bird or a dragon or something else entirely. It gave me the creeps.

"Oh, don't worry about these." Danu leaned on the thing's head, overgrown with moss, as he wiped the sweat from his brow. "The witches call these their 'Last Line of Defense' although I have never heard of anyone else trying to break

239

onto the island before…" He shook his head. "They're just scary carvings, meant to unnerve people."

"Are you sure about that?" I said. I was sure that the thing's blind gaze had followed me around the small clearing we had stopped in.

"Ha." Danu shook his head. Two paths led away from this place, as well as the third that, Danu assured me, we had walked in on. "They keep the forest wild just for this purpose, but there are paths that crisscross it, meeting other paths, looping back, crossing again. One of them will take us to Afar's hut… if I can just work out which one it is…"

"Well, just so long as you're sure, mage-boy," I said, feeling more than a little useless. It would have been much easier to swoop in on Crux. Surely even a witch wouldn't argue with a dragon?

"This way. It's definitely this way." Danu nodded, pointing down one of the paths, each one looking about as likely as any other. But I still followed on behind him, stepping over the roots that threatened to trip us up and the wet moss that wanted our feet to skid.

"You are very mean to that one," Crux surprised me by saying suddenly into my mind. I could sense a sort of amusement from him, sparked when he added, *"I am starting to think you like him."*

"What do you mean by that?" I hissed, and Danu looked around at me owlishly.

"Lila? Are you all right?" he said with concern in his eyes.

"Nothing. Just a private conversation," I muttered darkly, but when I turned my attention back to that place in my mind that connected to Crux, I found only a mirthful silence.

What does he mean – that I am mean to my friends? The thought had never crossed my mind.

What did cross my mind, however, a moment later, was a vague warning of a threat, a split second before there was a sudden crack of twigs and a shape stepped out onto the path ahead of me.

"Lila!" Crux called to me, and I fell back into a defensive crouch. I could *feel* the dragon in my mind uncurling himself from the boulder that he had sat on, pushing his strong legs up and reaching out with his snout in our direction. One word from me, and I was sure he would come winging this way with fire and fury in his maw.

"Danu Geidt," a voice said heavily. It was a woman, and behind her, other shapes were joining her.

"Master Afar." Danu raised an open hand to his brow, in what I guessed was some sort of traditional gesture of respect.

Danu's mentor was not what I had expected – although I didn't really know *what* I had expected of the West Witches. *More beads and mouse skulls, I think.* But instead, this Western Witch had skin the color of dark, almost black mahogany, and her hair hung straight down her back in thick braids. She wore a loose green cloak that stretched almost to her calves, and a simple robed dress of red that hung just a little shorter than the heavy, sensible work boots that she had on. The only obvious sign of her "witchy-ness" was a staff that looked like it was carved from bone. No beads. No feathers. No magical amulets.

I watched as the older woman's eyes slid from her charge to me, saw them widen, and a small frown appear instead. "And you must be Lila, I take it?" How does she know, I wondered.

"Lila? Do you want me to come and eat them?" Crux sounded almost eager about that prospect.

Not yet, not until I know what is going on here... I tried to comfort my friend, before raising my chin defiantly at the woman. "I am."

"Afar..." One of the women hissed behind her, a younger woman with tawny hair. Danu tensed beside me, but he didn't shout or accuse this one, and I thought that perhaps this witch *wasn't* the one he called Ohotto who was plotting against me.

"I know, Cala, I know..." Afar said, making a placating gesture with her hands. When she turned back to speak to us, her voice had taken on a more serious tone.

"Adept Danu, I cannot express how pleased I am to see you safe on Sebol again." She shared a small smile, but it was tinged with worry. "But you have broken the Conventions of the West Witches by bringing another person here. You understand that, don't you?"

"But Afar – the prophesy! This is more important than conventions!"

"Danu, please!" Afar said through gritted teeth as behind

her, the other West Witches looked appalled at what my friend had said; like it was a great insult or heresy. "Times are *strained* here at the moment, Danu," she said quickly. "And we *need to see that the letter of the law is obeyed.*" She seemed to pick her words very carefully and exactly, as she stared hard at Danu.

She was trying to send him a message, I could tell. But what?

"Master Afar, I would speak with you privately," Danu said in a loud and clear voice.

"Not now, Danu." His master's tone was quick, making a small, cutting motion with her hand. "You will both come with us to the Council Hut, where there will be a meeting…"

"A meeting to decide what?" Danu said angrily. If this was any other situation, I would almost have found this amusing. Just an hour ago *I* had been the one advocating anger and fury, and now, upon seeing the strange way that Afar was trying to send a message to her student, I wanted Danu to keep his wits about him.

"Danu," I said gently, keeping my eyes on Afar. "Perhaps we will learn *what we need to know* if we agree to go with your master."

The adept in training looked at me stubbornly, but he nodded all the same.

"Very wise, Lila," Afar gave me a perfunctory nod. *Was there a slight smile from her as well?* "Now, if you will follow me both."

243

"I would still like to know what the meeting will be about…" Danu said, unable to resist a last, desperate jab at his old tutor. But it wasn't Afar who answered him. Instead it was the one she had called Cala.

"What it will be about? You have brought another person to our shores, Danu! You have been running around the Western Isles casting your cantrips, endangering us at a time when, already, there are terrible events happening in the islands!" Cala burst out, before muttering at Afar. "We haven't got time for your apprentice's foibles, Afar. You know what is at stake: the future of Sebol itself!"

Danu looked stunned and about to shout, but I reached forward and put a hand on his shoulder. It was clear that there was more going on here than he had ever expected.

"Cala, calm yourself." Afar's tone was stern. "Danu? Lila? It is true that Sebol is in danger. We will discuss your actions Danu, *after* the meeting." With a nod, she turned to lead us to their sanctuary.

"The future of Sebol…?" Danu whispered to me. "What is wrong? Do they blame me?"

"They can't!" I said in a low voice back at him. "I won't let them."

CHAPTER 25
DANU AND THE COUNCIL

W e were led to the Council Hut, the largest hut on Sebol, right next to the library. Strange, but this place looked almost small now that I had returned. It was a struggle to think how I could have been so happy here, with its cramped and overhanging trees, its narrow wooden walkways, and the shadowy, whispering forms of the witches who could be seen clustered on the balconies outside the village's huts.

I sneaked a look at Lila, to see what she might think of this place. I felt a little embarrassed – this was nothing like her free and wild home of Malata! It was gloomy, for a start, and everyone moved in near silence as they contemplated their important tasks. The only light came from the filtered, watery sunlight that speared through the leaves of the giant trees. It was a very far cry from flying high above the world, I thought dismally.

"In here," Afar said, for Lila's benefit rather than mine, I assumed.

The Council Hut had white plaster walls over stout wooden beams, and the familiar cloying scent of incense hung heavy in the air. Twin rows of benches extended around the outside of the grand hut, with a further gallery reached by steps above. High upon us, the beams of the roof met at the chimney, and the center was a wide circle of dried rushes.

Cala, the brown-haired witch, led the way to the central circle, and we followed, first me, then Lila, and then Afar. Behind us, the room was already filling up with witches. I was shocked to see that this was to be a full council meeting – almost all of the witches I had ever seen were arriving; with some from the southern hotlands, some from the far north, and farther eastward. Most of the women wore the simple long gowns of the Sebol witches (like Afar and Cala did) but there were also some from stranger locales who wore colorful print dresses and robes, or had their hair bedecked with feathers, and still others who wore pelts and furs of strange ice creatures.

I wracked my mind for anything I might know about Cala, but all that came to me was that she was an acolyte of Ohotto's.

"Why are there so many witches here?" I whispered to my mentor Afar, who stood beside me silently. If the meeting was to be about me, how had they known I was coming, and when?

"You mean, you cannot guess?" Afar was, as ever, inscrutable. I felt mad at her, before suddenly wondering why. This was the way of the witches, to surround themselves with mysteries, and to favor caution over action.

But it made me even angrier thinking about it, now. I had been on board an actual Sea Raider ship, about to scream into combat. I had to call upon my magic to avert a slaughter. I had ridden a dragon! This life of secrecy and hesitancy seemed silly; silly when compared to the fighting and dying that was happening out there in the Western Isles every day.

"Chabon is ill," Afar said quietly to me as the room filled. "And, during her illness, there has been a change in the opinion of the West Witches. Wait... You must be patient, Danu, and then we will talk." She looked up as the outer door banged shut, and the shuffling and murmuring died down.

ᏬᏥᏮ

"Sisters!" Cala called out. "You have been summoned here today, some of you coming from many leagues far away because strange tidings have reached us!"

"Strange tidings have reached us as well!" one of the witches called out angrily. Witches love a good argument.

"You will have heard, ladies," Cala called even louder, with a bit of ice in her voice, "no doubt, that strange things have been happening in the north. There is talk of hauntings and spirit-walkers abroad once more..."

"The Darkening has returned?" someone shouted in alarm.

"No!" Afar said abruptly, striking her staff against the matted floor. "Please, do not speak such evil on this holy isle. The Darkening is a long time banished, but the reports that we have heard have enough similarity that we have called you here. Those who have been selected, speak your story!"

Cala shot a venomous look at Afar, but my mentor ignored her.

One older woman stood up, dressed in heavy white furs with hair that was almost snow-white itself. "I am a Matriarch from the Stone-Biter Clan, of what you call the Dragon Spine Mountains. Our people were the first to be attacked."

"How do you know it wasn't those wild dragons you have up there?" another witch heckled.

"Do wild dragons vanish people without a trace? Are wild dragons able to enchant entire homesteads?" the mountain witch snapped back. "No. First it came as people disappearing from their trails – which is not so strange, given where we live. Bear or lynx often venture across our paths. But the people were plagued with nightmares, entire villages dreamed of ghostly figures that strode through the night towards the west…"

"Bad dreams are the hallmark of bad magic!"

"And the Darkening!"

The witches were upset. I glanced at Lila. She looked uncomfortable, though surely, she was no stranger to heated council meetings.

"There is more!" Another witch stood up, with black skin like Afar's. "I thought nothing of it at the time, but a year ago we had scouts reach our shores in Torvald colors, searching for something. When we trapped them, and asked what it was that they dared to cross into our lands – they said that it was none of our business – but when pressured, they admitted that they were searching for weapons to stop a great darkness."

"Do you know where these people came from?" Afar asked.

"I do not think that they were true Torvald citizens," the desert witch said. "The young king and queen have been very courteous towards our people, and we do not think they would be so rude. "If they are from Torvald, then they are acting without their ruler's consent."

"There is also the possibility that they were not being honest with you," Afar mentioned.

"But why would these emissaries lie? We know that there are many great evils lying dormant in the world," Cala argued. "There are the Ghasts to the far north, there are the dragons themselves, the powers of the undead, the ancient necromancers..." As she spoke, many of the other witches were nodding in agreement with her.

"Don't forget the Ogre Brood! Everyone forgets the Ogre Brood!" a voice shouted.

"Precisely, my sisters. Which is why I and Sister Ohotto summoned you all here."

"Ohotto Zanna?" Lila hissed under her breath, her fists clenched as Cala continued.

"It is our belief that the West Witches have been dormant for too long. We have been hiding here, gathering our knowledge as Chabon directed us – at the time it was a matter of survival, we had to do so otherwise the Dark King Enric would have stretched out his evil even to us! But now…? Can we West Witches trust that the two regents of distant Torvald will be strong enough to put right all that is so very wrong with the world? It is time that the West Witches come out of the shadows and act!"

"And what does Sister Afar think?" someone shouted.

I looked at my old tutor. She was silent and still for a moment, and I remembered the way that she was could carefully sift through all of the information in front of her before she came to her conclusion.

"I think that the people who have come before the council to speak, the sisters who have travelled far and wide to get to us, have justifiable concerns," she started, and there was a shout of celebration from some quarters. Even Cala shared a smile. "If it is true that the dead walk again in the north, then the witches must do something, surely. But what my sister Cala here is advocating is for the West Witches to become a true power in the world. Rival to that of Torvald, or Roskilde, or any other. This is not Chabon's way, and I am hesitant to throw aside all of the lessons the great Matriarch has given us."

Far more shouts and loud claps agreed with her this time.

Cala shook her head. "Then what would you have us do, Afar? Sit here and wait for Chabon to wake up? We must act against this evil, and if you are too hesitant to stand proud as a witch yourself," Cala suddenly grinned victoriously, "then I think that there is a way for the West Witches to play a part in the world without endangering our way of life."

"Impossible." Afar was adamant.

"Just as the Dragon Academy supports the throne of Torvald, it is my wish and that of Ohotto – a senior sister and student of Chabon's here, I do not have to remind you – that we West Witches choose a regent to support. Lord Havick of Roskilde!"

Lila flinched like she had been struck and hissed.

"Silence," Cala said to her, and Lila's eyes narrowed. She looked murderous, but she wouldn't get far with all of these witches sitting around us, able to curse at will.

"Lila," I said warningly. *I just pray that Afar was right when she said that we would talk later…*

"No," Afar said. "Lord Havick is not a regent worthy of the support of the West Witches."

"And who are you to judge, sister Afar? Who else is strong enough to fight for us, against whatever evil is coming? We all know that Torvald is too far away. The Sea Raiders are a broken force, the islanders are weak and have no leader, and the southern desert peoples have no worthy champion!"

"Hey!" someone shouted angrily from the back of the crowd.

"I will not stand here and listen to this nonsense," Afar said abruptly, nodding to me and Lila. "These two will come with me, where I will deliver their punishment."

There was a general outcry, but Afar did not pause as she strode out, up the steps to the door, with us at her heels. As soon as we were through and the door banged shut to muffle the sounds of argument, I saw my old mentor visibly weaken in the dim light.

"It is far worse than I had feared. Cala works for Ohotto," she said, nodding towards the Library Hut. "Come, you two, we do not have much time before Cala and her agents will worm their way into the hearts of the other witches, and wrest control from Chabon."

The older woman strode fast on her long legs, her staff making thumping noises as we had to jog to keep up with her.

"Ohotto Zanna…? The witch who wants me dead? I should have cut that Cala's heart out when I had the chance," Lila said savagely.

"You didn't have the chance," Afar smirked darkly. "The sisters would have cursed you where you stood." She nodded at the library, which was a large hut with several doors leading inside. My mentor took out a large set of keys and opened it, leading the way and closing the door behind us.

I had been inside the Library Hut before, of course, but not for long periods. I always had to be supervised whilst inside, either with Afar herself or with one of the older-than-me witches. It was pure chance that I got a glimpse of the prophesy at all! The first sight that met us were the tall stacks of scrolls and books like walls.

"We need to see the prophesy," Lila said impatiently.

"Which one?" A smile ghosted across Afar's features, as she directed us down one of the avenues.

"Afar?" I asked. "What do you mean, that Cala and Ohotto want to wrest control from Chabon? That would be madness, wouldn't it? Chabon has been guiding the West Witches for…." I shook my head. Forever, it seemed.

"Precisely, Danu. Chabon is old. Very, very old. She fell into a sleep just a few moons ago, and she has not resurfaced yet." Afar looked sad. "I fear that she may slip away and not come back to us – and then we really will have a problem on our hands if we have to elect a new Matriarch."

I nodded. "Ohotto has been going there for years, apparently, and meeting with Havick."

"But why?" Afar shook her head in alarm, her eyes sparking furiously. "That is insane - to ally oneself and the witches with that brute Havick!"

"To destroy the Raiders! To find me!" Lila rolled her eyes behind us. "These witches of yours must know that I have a legitimate claim to the throne."

"If in fact you do have a legitimate claim," Afar said, her steps slowing, "it is to the *crown*, Lila. The Sea Crown of Roskilde. It is a very ancient magical artefact, forged in times when magic wasn't as rare as it is now." I could see Afar's eyes narrow. "That must be it, Lila. For whatever reason – Ohotto and Cala have decided to side with Havick to take control of the Sea Crown, and I fear that without Chabon's influence, they will use the threat of darkness and evil all around to take control of the West Witches as well."

"Then we have to stop them," I said, looking to Lila. "*You* can stop them."

"Me?" Lila asked, but I could see from the serious look in her face that she knew precisely what I meant.

"Here we are." Afar turned a corner in the shelves, reaching a section where the scrolls were overlaid with a deep rime of dust. I watched as she moved slowly halfway down the shelf, and then went the shelf down, and pulled out a scroll, which she offered to me. "It is about time that you read the entire prophesy, Danu." Afar's eyes flickered to my friend at my side. "And you, too. It is about you, after all…"

I took the scroll and carefully unrolled it, holding it so both Lila and I could read, even as I spoke the words aloud.

"A girl is born from the waters, rising from the north-east sea, under a dragon's angry call and upon her head is a crown made of leaping waves."

"The Sea Crown will be lost, and then it will be found once more, but the one who finds it will not come from the royal line. A girl will rise from the sea to seize the crown,

with a bloody sword in her hand, and in her other she holds fire."

"A boy with a forked tongue accompanies this girl. They will bring with them blood and fury, and before them and behind them, there will be the dead."

"The boy and the girl with the crown will turn the islands upside down, the girl must take her rightful throne, but the crown will still fall into dark waters. Roskilde is surrounded by dangers and dark deeds, but there is a slim chance that the throne will be restored..."

It sounds awful, I thought. 'The boy with the forked tongue' – is that me? And 'behind them there will be the dead...' What did that mean? That more people were going to die?

But the prophesy seemed unequivocal. That a boy – me – would stand at the side of the dragon-girl, and that together we would be in the center of a storm of fury and blood and battle. I was scared, I could admit that, but only about the strife and fighting that we might have to go through – not about standing at Lila's side.

"I am the girl who rose from the sea?" Lila spoke in a small voice.

"Well, you *are* a Sea Raider," I said. "And do you remember the first time that I saw you? You burst from the water with the plume of spray like a crown around you, to the north-east of here. And you have to admit that it was under the

255

dragon's call—the mother Blue dragon's when she called her warning to you."

"Well, the rest of it doesn't look very appealing." Lila pointed to the other sections. "What is this about me holding a bloody sword and fire?"

"Maybe all it means is that you are a Sea Raider?" I frowned. Even to me that sounded a bit harsh. In fact, it made it sound like Lila was the enemy, not the savior in all of this.

"And the boy with a forked tongue…" Lila tapped her lip, before pointing at me. "That's got to be you, Danu. You lied to me about knowing the prophesy, didn't you?"

"Hey!" I was hurt. "Maybe it's more to do with my ability to talk to dragons?"

"Enough of this! I have broken enough rules now." Afar shook her head. "I have still to punish you for bringing a dragon and a non-witch to the island, Danu."

I looked at my mentor in alarm. She was severe enough to consider that this wasn't a joke. "But Afar… This is important!" I started to say, before she cut me off with a sharp motion of her hand.

"Here is your punishment for breaking the customs and conventions of the West Witches, Danu Geidt – not that there will be any West Witches for long after that council meeting – I charge you with safekeeping the Prophesy of Roskilde. I charge you with keeping Lila of Roskilde safe. I charge you to keep the spirit of the West Witches alive. Do you understand me?"

None of these things were duties that I hadn't thought of fulfilling anyway, but now they took on a greater significance as I realized that this might be the last task that I could perform for the 'true' West Witches before Cala won the others over.

"I will do as charged, Master Afar." I bowed my head.

"Good." Abruptly, it was done, and Afar was gesturing for us to leave. "The stars alone know just what will happen when the council meeting is done. Cala may already have figured out who you are, Lila, and she may be coming for us. She may decide to send a contingent of fighting witches to Havick, or she may decide to try and silence Chabon, and imprison me…"

"No!" I said aghast.

"If she gets the support of the council, she can do anything. So, you two must get off the island, now. You have the prophesy. You know what you must do – you must see that the prophesy is fulfilled, you must do all that you can to beat Havick."

It was true. Since the moment Cala had proclaimed the West Witches should support Havick, I had known that somehow I must ensure that it was not Havick, but Lila who wore the Sea Crown. Havick could not wield such power, not with the care and consideration with which I knew Lila would.

Afar led us back to the door where, suspiciously, we looked at the main Council Hut where muffled, angry voices could still be heard.

"But what about you, Afar? You should come with us!" Lila offered.

"No. My place is at Chabon's side. Something that Sister Cala forgot to mention in there – was that the Matriarch Chabon had *two* acolytes that she trained. Ohotto was just one, and I was the other. There may be some of the loyal witches of Sebol who will rally to Chabon's side. Whatever Cala gets them to agree to in there, they will have a fight on their hands if they try to come to Chabon's sanctuary!"

I felt myself grinning fiercely. I didn't doubt it. "Then good luck, my teacher." *Was this the last time that I would see her?*

"You are almost ready, Adept Danu." My old tutor held my gaze as I turned to go. "If we both survive this, then I am sure that you will be ready for the final secret of the mage training…"

I was still confusedly opening and closing my mouth as Lila pulled me back along the walkways and Afar disappeared into the gloom. To be honest, since the moment in the meeting when I heard the witches voice support for Havick, I hadn't even considered my future at all. There seemed to be too many problems in the world to worry about my own training. What had changed in me so much, from the boy who was determined to receive the full mage training? *Lila and Crux happened, didn't they?* But now my dreams were back on the table. Did this mean that Afar was going to train me? *But I would have to use that power for good, not just to be the only mage in existence,* I now thought. *It wasn't about me, it was about helping the islanders, and Lila, and the dragons.* If we survived, I remembered. If I kept my promises.

CHAPTER 26
LILA, DRAGON-TRAITOR!

We rushed out of the village as night fell, racing back along the twisting paths that led through the witches' forest, but this time there was no chance of getting lost as I could feel my dragon in my mind – and he was growing impatient.

"Did you find your bits of paper?" he greeted me amusedly as he stood on the mossy boulder, shaking his scales to release the dew that had gathered there.

"I did," I said, patting the fold of paper that Danu had given in me, and I had hidden in my leather vest. It felt odd to think that Chabon could have dreamed and written about *me,* so many years ago.

"Not so strange, Lila wave-rider," Crux sagely informed me as we climbed up to take our places on his back. *"The dragons believe that all things are connected. A dragon may*

dream of its newt many decades before it is born, or remember a time when it was itself a different being entirely..."

"Really?" I said, stunned, the thought too large for my human mind. For just a moment, as the dragon surged and we leapt into the air, joy spread through me and the dragon both. *We were a part of one thing,* and larger beyond that, I thought, as Crux turned and wheeled high over the Haunted Isle of Sebol, and launched us towards the east.

"Lila?" Danu said, breaking my moment of realization as we swept high into the sky.

"Yes?" I turned to him, seeing that, even though his eyes were wide with so much recent worry, there was a small grin.

"I am glad that I am here, with you – and not still training down there in the dark," he called, and I nodded, feeling embarrassed. I wasn't quite sure how to take that, but I realized that I felt the same – this prophesy of Danu's was real, and it was about me. It was something that was too big for me to even think about alone— but I wasn't alone. I had Danu and Crux both here with me. Not that I would tell either one any of that!

৩৯৩

A girl rising from the waves, with a bloody sword in her hand... I kept on pondering the message of the prophesy as we flew back, first towards the small island where we had stopped before, and then further south and east, towards Malata. *And death follows them…*

What if that was true? What did it mean? Would someone I know die? Would someone I love, die? The words kept bothering me, waking me up in the night as we rested on one of the abandoned islands, and weakening my appetite when we ate breakfast and lunch.

"Lila – look!" Danu pointed below us. It was our second day of flying home, each of us eager to get back to Malata as quick as we could to talk with the Sea Raiders. Now that I knew that the prophesy was real – and that the West Witches were probably allied with Havick – I was even *more* aware of how I couldn't defeat Havick alone. I would need Danu and Crux; I would need the strong sailors of the Sea Raiders if I were to overthrow a king. *Someone had to stop him,* and right now, the only free peoples left in the Western Archipelago aside from the witches were us Raiders.

I had been too wrapped in my musings to see what Danu now pointed out to me: a thin line of smoke rising on the horizon.

Malata? I thought in alarm for a moment – but no, it couldn't be. We were still many hours away, by my reckoning. It was one of the Free Islands though, one of the small number of atolls and outcrops that housed people, but who were only nominally under the rule of the Roskildeans.

"Father doesn't raid there," I said. "They wouldn't have

anything worth stealing, and half of them would have brothers or cousins who seek to become Sea Raiders anyway!"

"So what could have happened?" Danu said, and, not needing any further reason, I urged Crux to take a closer look.

"I smell fire and blood," Crux informed me as we descended and a second and a third thin column of smoke appeared behind the headland of the first. The dragon's wings ate up the leagues, and soon we could see the ruins of a burnt-out fishing village. No, not a village – a hamlet, really, I thought. It was a typical sort of Free Islands village. Small, with wooden-built houses on stilt platforms, with the only scrap of shaped stone they had used to build a small quay. I knew that these places were little more than fishing hamlets really. They rarely received traders or villagers, and mostly kept themselves to themselves.

But someone had taken offense at them, clearly, I thought as we flew over demolished huts, blackened walls, and the small strips of gardens trampled to the ground. "Take us low, Crux – I want to see what caused this," I said, and ever the show off, Crux flared his wings before diving downwards in a low swoop over the devastation.

It was horrible, even to my eyes – and I had been on raids before. But what I saw below was no raid. It was a massacre.

"Who did this?" Danu said.

Arrows littered the area, stuck in the sand, and in the bodies that lay scattered– but I also saw the demolished walls as if a great weight had been kicked through them.

"Crux? Can you smell any sign of dragons here?" I asked warily, remembering the Roskilde ship that had been attacked by the Torvald Dragon Riders.

"No dragon did this!" The Phoenix was indignant. *"Why would we leave good meat?"* He indicated a cluster of bodies, each with ugly little bolts in their backs. From crossbows, I recognized. The Sea Raiders nor Torvald used crossbows as far as I knew, and the holes that had been smashed through the wooden huts appeared, instead, to look like the sorts of holes left by cannon shot.

"The Sea Raiders also don't have any cannons strong enough to bombard a village," I said sourly. There was only one force in the Western Isles that could do that.

"Havick's navy," Danu agreed. "But why? Why attack these people – totally destroying them and their way of life?"

"Maybe he was searching for something?" I said. *For me?* Although I also knew that Lord Havick probably didn't need a reason. "What was it that courtier said? That Havick was trying to push his control even onto the mainland? Maybe these poor people refused to follow his orders, or refused to pay his taxes…"

"Whatever the answer is, it doesn't help them now," Danu said through gritted teeth.

"No. Take us away from here, Crux," I said, my heart feeling heavy. This was the man that I was supposed to over-throw. This was the sort of man that the West Witches wanted to support against "the darkness"—whatever that was, and if it ever came. I wondered—was it Havick himself?

ॐ

We flew back south, skirting the edges of the Free Islands where we saw more smoke spires. If it was indeed the navies of Roskilde that had been along here, then it was clear they had done a thorough job. The sight of such destruction only leant urgency to my thoughts as we flew south, into the evening.

Please, don't let Malata be attacked as well! We soared low over the dark waters, heading for the lines of Bonerock that broke the waters of the reef. The silhouette of the hulks, black against the still purpling evening skies stood tall and alarming, just as they always had. I let out a sigh of relief, but a shiver of unease rattled the Phoenix's scales beneath me.

"What is it, Crux?" I leant forward in alarm.

"I hear shouts, and I smell fear," he said, before closing his mind off to mine.

"Fly!" I urged him, as he swept up faster and higher over Malata. I was dreading to see the plumes of smoke emerging from my hometown as well, or hear the wails and screams of dying people – but no, what I saw from the harbor instead were the many dockside torches and lanterns, and the three great ships of the Raiders snug and safe.

"Then why are people afraid?" I asked myself, seeing the

265

small shapes of the many sailors on the docks, apparently engaged in one of their large and informal discussions (which always broke out into squabbles and brawls by the end of the night, depending upon how much beer had been consumed). These dockside meetings, and their noise, was normal – but what *wasn't* was for the Raiders to be afraid during them.

"What's going on, Lila?" Danu asked me, finding the scene as worrying as Crux did, apparently.

"Dockside meeting," I called. "Father and Mother only call them when they need to consult the whole community on something." The whole community except me, I thought painfully. Why didn't my foster parents wait for me? Didn't they want me to be the First Mate of the *Ariel*?

I was still reeling from my hurt pride as Crux flared his wings into a loud flapping as he landed on the rocky headland over the harbor where he had elected to make his den while he was here. I saw the bearded faces turn to stare up at us as we landed – and I was sure that more than a few of them had grimaces and anger in their eyes as they did so.

"Uh, Lila – I'm not sure that they are happy to see us," Danu said as we slid from the back of the dragon. His suspicions were only confirmed by my mother's—foster-mother's —Pela's worried and pinched countenance as she hurried up towards us.

"Lila!" she called. "You had better come down and speak to them. The other Raiders… They're upset."

"Why?" I said, rushing over to give Pela a brief but fierce

hug. It was easy to feel the warmth and love from her as she squeezed me in her strong arms, before letting me go and sighing.

"It's the dragons. And Havick. The rest of the Raiders have got spooked, especially after the attack on Westhall."

"Westhall's being attacked?" I said in alarm. Westhall was another Free Island settlement – a village almost large enough to be a town. It was technically unallied (as all of the Free Islanders were) but it paid a tribute to Roskilde, and we traded with them. They had a mayor and a council, and even some stone buildings. In the years before, it had always been their nearness to our territory that had kept them safe – venturing too close to Westhall with an armored galleon would only mean an attack by my foster-father's ships – but it seemed that in a matter of days, the old ways had well and truly died.

"But Westhall has never raised a fist to anyone!" I said out loud, as I jogged down the path after Pela, Danu clattering behind me.

"Maybe it is time that they should," my mother said darkly.

We climbed down onto the stone docks to see that metal fire grates had been hauled out and used as impromptu firepits for the Raiders to argue and shout around. The loudest and largest such group (no surprise there) belonged to my foster-father, Chief Kasian.

"We have to respond! This is outrageous!" Kasian shouted at the Raiders as Pela drew me closer and we pushed our way through the crowd. She leaned in to me and hissed, "The Raiders don't know what to do next. Your father wants to fight, but he's a fool if he thinks that he can go up against Havick's forces. Some of the Raiders who saw the dragon damage on that boat you found for them are scared about your great big dragon now, saying that it's too much of a threat to us as well."

"But that's ridiculous!" I shouted, and my voice pierced a lull through the arguing pirates as my foster-father turned his attention to me.

"Ah, foster-daughter, I am glad that you have returned, at last." The angry scowl on his large face lightened for the briefest moment before returning to its dark expression. "While you have been away, Lord Havick has taken it upon himself to launch an unprecedented campaign against us. Attacking our allies, friends, trading partners, routing out any friend we have up and down the Free Isles."

"So I understand, Father," I nodded gravely, with Danu nodding beside me. We had both seen the destruction that Havick was wreaking out there in the islands. The rest of the crowd continued to mutter and whisper amongst themselves, but I could also tell that they were eager to hear just what the cherished daughter of the greatest chief the Sea Raiders had ever known had to say for herself.

"We have to decide what to do. As you know, it is not the Sea Raider way to go to war," my foster-father said.

"Well said!" one of the crowd bellowed. "I want to raid and to raise my family, not fight a bleedin' navy!"

"Quiet!" my foster-father barked. "But we may have little choice if Havick keeps on pressing us this hard. We need a good, strong and wealthy raid in order to secure our provisions for the winter seasons. If we do not get it, then we will have to take to the islands during the winter storms."

There was an ugly hiss from the crowd, and even I shivered. It was madness to conduct full raids in the deeps of winter. You were more likely to get blown off course or get shipwrecked yourself than to win any prize, and there were far fewer trading vessels travelling the archipelago and the Broken Coasts at that perilous time.

"We cannot fight Havick!" another sailor hollered. "We just want one more raid, that's all! That wrecked Torvald ship wasn't enough!"

"Daughter – your dragon..." I tensed as the chief gritted his teeth. "This business of dragons is keeping you from your rightful place, here at my side on the *Ariel*."

"But *you* were the one who didn't want me coming with you!" My face burned with suppressed rage. "What choice did I have, but to try and find an answer to Havick on my own?"

"Daughter..." My foster-father looked down at his feet, and I knew my blow had struck home. But he was a proud man, and he couldn't be seen to back down at a meeting – even to his own foster-daughter. "Enough is enough. I was wrong to place my trust in your dragon fantasy, and I have indulged you for too long. You must be at my side…"

"But the Dragon Raiders!" I burst out, even though the idea sounded hollow to even me, now. We didn't have enough dragons or dragon eggs, and we had run out of time to train and befriend any more – and the stakes were far higher, if the prophesy was to be believed.

"Are a dream, child," my father said heavily.

"A nightmare, more like!" one of the sailors shouted. I scowled and looked around to see if I could ascertain who it was, but all I saw was a sea of angry faces in the night.

"We must raid now. Tomorrow even. Before Havick completely closes off any shipping routes that we have access to," Kasian said.

"But, Father…!" I said indignantly. What was he saying to me? That I couldn't fly Crux anymore?

"Shhh." He held up a warning hand. "I am not saying that your idea doesn't have merit, but right now, given what has happened to Westhall and the danger right at our doorstop, we have to do what we do best. Which is raiding and fighting. Return to your dragon in the spring, when we have some breathing space…"

"If we're still alive, he means…" a sailor's voice said.

"Father! I fly a dragon." I tried to stand my ground before him. *Wave-rider, Air-rider,* that is what Crux called me. "That is what I do. I can scout, and attack from the air…"

"Foster-daughter," Kasian's voice cut through mine, and

the crowd around us fell silent. "I need you at my side." It was as close as the large man came to begging as I had ever heard him. It broke my heart. Were things really that bad?

"Daughter," Pela said to me in a mutter, holding my elbow affectionately. She pitched her voice so just I could hear. "Listen to him, for once. We fear for our way of life. We need to stand together if we are to survive…"

How could I refuse those large eyes of my mother and father – even if they were not my real parents? They were the only parents that I knew.

"Daughter?" Kasian cleared his throat and drew himself up to his full height. "Will you accept your place as First Mate to the *Ariel*, at my side?"

How could they ask me this? It didn't feel right, like they were asking me whether I was Lila Malata or Lila Roskilde. *I was both!* Could they not see that I could be the first mate *and* a Dragon Rider, if I wanted to be?

But no, as I looked into their taut faces I realized that *no*, they didn't see that at all. All that they saw was the danger that threatened them, and they did not want to face it alone.

"Of course," I mumbled, before hanging my head. I felt like my heart was breaking, and knew that I would have to go and speak to Crux as soon as I was finished here.

"You are leaving me?" the dragon burst into my mind, all fire and fury.

No, not leaving… I tried to say, but I heard a shriek of anger from the hilltop above us, and an angry jet of flame burn the night sky. The sailors around me gasped and many ducked, making the hand sign to avert evil. *Crux? Don't be mad. I have to help my father – just until the danger is passed...*

"*The danger is all around you, Lila! The man who is not your father wishes to turn you into something you do not wish to be!*" Crux almost shouted into my mind, and I heard the sudden crack of huge leather wings as the dragon took to the air. His dark shape obliterated the stars for a moment as he swept over Malata's harbor, and vanished into the night.

"No!" I couldn't help myself from calling out into the night.

"Shush, Lila – it's probably for the best." Pela patted my elbow, drawing me away from the dock meeting, and back towards the big house at the top of the village that I had grown up in.

But it didn't feel like my home anymore, not when I looked out into the night skies. Somewhere out there flew my dragon. *I belonged out there.*

CHAPTER 27
DANU, DRAGON-FRIEND

I couldn't believe it. "Why would Lila decide that?" I asked out loud, hearing nothing in response but the wind. It had been a desperate race back up the path to Crux, but I had managed to get to the Phoenix dragon as he was shaking his wings and breathing angered flames into the sky, and convinced him to let me on his back before he flew off.

I couldn't blame him for being annoyed – although not with Lila.

"She still thinks like a human," Crux burst into my mind like an angry gale. *"What those people who are not even her blood kin think of her. What she should be doing, rather than what she must…"*

"How else is she supposed to think?" I said out loud, feeling myself get angry with the dragon. Ridiculous, I know –

me, a small human angry with a dragon, and complicated by the fact that he was the only thing keeping me aloft right now!

Crux had flown high, so fast and strong that the wind caught at my clothes and made me shiver. I wished that I'd had a chance to seize my extra cloak before leaping atop him, but if I had stalled, then I would have to be stranded on Malata.

Everything was going so well – it seemed as though Lila understood just what we needed to do; together! I wondered if some of the dragon's feelings were bleeding into mine.

"Of course, you are feeling the shape of my thoughts, Danu," Crux advised me. *"That is because you know, at least, that one thing is not one thing."*

"What does that mean?" I said out loud.

"Something that I was trying to tell Lila back on that island of witches and wizards. We are a part of each other. When a dragon chooses to share his life, they become one thing. You, Lila, me – we are the same now." I could feel Crux's annoyance shiver through his muscles. *"That is why she is not just a human now. Why YOU are not just a human. A bit of you is dragon."*

"And a bit of you is human?" I pointed out.

"Hardly!" Crux roared, curling his wings to swoop down in a spearing arc that almost had me off the saddle, if I hadn't been clutching onto his back tines at the same time. *"Can a human do this?"*

We were moving too fast for me to answer as he flared out

his sail-like wings with a thunderous *snap*. We skimmed the surface of the waters, faster than a speeding hawk. It was exhilarating – and terrifying.

But I still had a moment to think about Crux's words. If what he said was true – then there *had* to be a bit of the Phoenix dragon that was becoming just that little bit more like a human, and vice versa. That would explain why he felt so jealous when Lila decided to sail with her foster family and not fly with him!

"You know that you are her closest friend," I managed to call out over the screech of the air. "Even I can see that!"

"Then why stay with those humans, and not fly with us, free?" Crux snarled in my mind.

Oh, Crux... I thought sadly. "Humans are complicated creatures, my friend," I managed to whisper as I leant low over his neck, knowing that he would hear my words. "We do things that we won't want to, and we say things that we don't even mean sometimes, because we think it will make people happy."

"Happy? Then what about making me happy? What about making herself happy?" Crux was heading north and west, far out of the reef around the Raider's islands realm by now, and heading for the wilder islands where the dragons roamed.

I didn't have an answer for him. I just wished that I knew the answer to that question as well. Still, as I closed my eyes and hugged the dragons neck, I thought that I could sense a grudging sadness from the Phoenix below me. He wasn't really angry with Lila, he just wanted to spend time with his friend.

CHAPTER 28
LILA, DECISIONS

It wasn't dark in my old room, but it still felt murky somehow. I could hear the excitable cheers and songs of my foster-father and his trusted captains through the floor-boards from somewhere below, but I had left them to it and returned to the room that I had grown up in. It was their little ritual, before a big day of raiding: poke and prod their courage with watered-down ale and songs of past victories. Most of them would be the worse for wear in the morning, but they would all be at the docks before the rest of the crew were, and my father claimed that having a headache 'gave him an edge in a fight.'

Well, I have a headache – and its name is you, Father, I thought as I kicked at a couple of my old training leather vests and a few linen shirts I'd left behind and never thought to see again. Those and my collection of small sea-wood carvings. I picked up the one that I was most proud of – a knot of wood that I had managed to carve into a snarling dragon's head.

Oh, Crux... I thought, feeling the shape of the dragon in the corner of my mind. He was annoyed with me, I could feel it. He didn't understand why I had to do this.

"My people need me." I sat heavily on the bed, whispering into the night. "These people might not be my family, but they need me."

Creak. There was a sound from outside of the room and I looked up. One of the creaky floorboards of the landing. *Just like the sound it made when Pela was walking past,* I thought, just as she used to do when I was a kid. Had she heard me mumbling in the dark?

I stood up and opened the door. "Mother?"

A light was on across the balcony, and from her room emerged Pela, my foster-mother, looking much older than she usually did. She didn't wear her heavy leather armors and gloves that she wore during her day's training exercises, and instead looked somehow a lot smaller to my eyes.

"Pela," she insisted, looking at me with sad eyes. "I'm not your mother, Lila... it's probably about time that *I* accepted that as well."

"Oh, Mother," I said, feeling my heart break as I rounded the balcony and swept her into my arms. The top of her head was at the height of my nose. How could I think that this small woman was my biological mother?

Because she had acted like one, I knew. "I will always be your daughter, Pela," I said. "You know that, don't you?"

She broke away brusquely from me embrace. "Hff. Enough of that silliness – or you'll make me cry!" She dabbed at her eyes, before composing herself and fixing me with a hard stare. "I can see that you are miserable, Lila. I saw it the moment that you agreed with Kasian, and I suddenly felt terrible."

"It's done," I said, shaking my head.

"But your dragon, and the young man – will they come back?" Pela frowned as she looked at me.

"I don't know." I shrugged, feeling my heart threaten to break all over again. "I hope so. I think so."

Pela hissed once more to herself, shaking her head. "I think that I and your foster-father were wrong. I see that now, Lila…" My foster-mother's face creased with regret. "I haven't been able to get the look on your face out of my mind when your dragon flew away. I never want any daughter of mine to feel like that. You weren't meant to captain the *Ariel*, you were meant to be out there on your dragon."

"Mother! How can you say that?" I said, feeling upset and hopeful at the same time. I couldn't put it into words. "But what about the other Raiders – how can I be one of them if I am not the First Mate of the *Ariel*?"

Pela did not answer me directly, or quickly, and from that I could tell that she did not know the answer either. But she was a brave woman. "I think, Lila, that the Raiders are going to have to change, one way or another. It is true, that they are very wary of your dragon, and they don't like the fact that you have been spending more time with it than on board the *Ariel*... But the Western Isles are changing, Lila, for good or for ill." I watched as my mother shook her head sorrowfully. "We Raiders enjoyed some good times with the Dark King Enric ruling Torvald, I will admit that. A lot of people fled to the islands, there were rich pickings to be had... But now? With Torvald a strong force protecting its resources, and with Havick as strong as he is...? The Raiders are going to have to change," she repeated. "And that means that they will have to accept *you*, not the other way around."

I felt like I was teetering on the edge of a cliff, ready either to fly or fall – and I didn't know which one that it would be.

"You should go to your dragon and your young man. Find them. Do what you were born to do." Pela nodded. "You know who you are, Lila. Who you *really* are. Stop trying to please everyone else – and become it! That would be brave." She gave me an affectionate punch on the shoulder, just as she used to do when we were training together. "And after all, didn't I always tell you that being brave was the Raider way?"

I smirked, and hugged my mother again, harder this time. "Thank you. But what about Father...?"

"Oh bah! Don't you worry about that big old lug – let me deal with him, will you?" Pela pushed me off her once more. "Go on. Go become a dragon princess or whatever it is you have planned – only don't you dare burn any of my ships!"

"I won't, Mother," I said, knowing that she liked hearing me call her that. I hurried back inside my room, changing my clothes for clean ones and refilling my pack with the supplies needed for a journey. On impulse, I shoved the carved dragon's head into the pack as well, before setting it on my shoulder. I had the sudden image of how the world *could* be: of me being a Dragon-Queen like Saffron was, only this time I would live out here in the islands. I would be able to forge some kind of peace with my family of Raiders. Perhaps we could explore instead of raid, perhaps....

"Enough, Lila," I scolded myself, imitating my mother's tone as I did so. *First I had to steal a boat, and then find my dragon and that fish-boy as well...*

I knew, all of a sudden, that I would have no trouble in either the stealing or the finding. There was a part of my heart that was forever given over to Crux, now, and all I had to do was to follow where it led.

I took the back stairs from the house two at a time before escaping into the night.

CHAPTER 29
DANU, A COUNCIL OF DRAGONS

Something woke me up – but it wasn't a noise. Crux had relaxed his angered flight and the wind had died down, making it easy for me to snooze on the great dragon's back. I was surprised at how quiet a dragon *could* be when it was flying, so long as it wasn't in a hurry!

"Where are we?" I yawned, looking at the scene ahead: a large shape of an island, dominated by a ruined, half-collapsed mountain. Its slopes disappeared into deep jungles.

"There is no name for this island in your tongue. The island dragons just call it Home Island," Crux said, his voice steady and tight in my mind. But there was something else here, something that didn't make sense. I thought that Crux was flying away because he was angry, and that he wanted to 'be happy'… But I could sense that there was no happiness in him. Instead, there was a tight ball of worry.

"Skreeeech!" A sound rose from the island below us; low and echoing like a lament.

"Skrech!" Crux stiffened, his agitation only increasing.

"Crux? What is it?"

"Something is wrong. I have been summoned." Crux flexed his wings and let out a high, mournful whistle out across the nightscape.

I felt the airs stand up on my neck as a sound answered Crux. Another hooting call, echoing strangely from the mountain itself. "Other dragons live here," I said, stupidly.

Crux didn't deign to answer, but swooped down, lower over the dark trees towards the mountain, flying in a silent, deadly curve straight into a gorge in the mountain's slopes. One that ended in a cave, and in that cave, I could see the glitter of great, shining eyes.

⚫⚫⚫

The dragon home was too large for my eyes to penetrate all of its shadows. I was brought into a great cavern, following Crux's soft tread on the sandy floor. It was a vast space, with giant chasms opening out into further caves. The slabs of the mountain's bones projected out to form ledges and overhangs, upon which lay mighty lizards of varying colors. I could see the long Sinuous Blues draping across their brethren like scarves, and the stockier Greens hunched over their front claws like cats. There was also at least two – or it could have been one, I wasn't sure – of the immense Whites, occupying the far recesses of the cavern. The largest number of the dragons here, however, were the smaller and falcon-like sea-green dragons, their scales rippling turquoise as they chirruped and whistled to each other.

"But none like me," Crux needled into my mind, and I realized he was right. There were no other multi-colored dragons like Crux the Phoenix here.

"Crux, son of Velchmar, son of Daryx, son of Sol!" a dragon voice erupted into my mind, and I looked up to see that one of the Blues had unwrapped itself from its fellows and was leaning over the space, looking down at us.

"Den-Mother Taliski," Crux said and shocked me by lowering his snout to the floor. I hadn't thought that the fierce Phoenix was willing to bow to anything! Even dragons have their own queens, I realized as I copied his example.

"I have called you here to discuss important matters with you. You know of my sister, the dragon Sym?" the blue den-mother said, her eyes flashing.

"I do. I was there at the birth of her young ones." Crux looked straight up at the queen dragon.

"Yes. She was acting as den-mother to three eggs, as is our way," Taliski intoned, earning a rattling hiss from the other dragons.

"As is our way," Crux repeated, as if this was some sort of dragon tradition.

"Of the three hatchlings, only one now remains." the Den

Mother flicked her tail, and I felt a wave of deep mourning spread through my connection with Crux and from the other dragons around me. It was clear that the hatchlings were highly revered in dragon society, and so any harm or misfortune that befell them was a loss keenly felt by all.

"I am sorry," Crux said, scratching at the ground with a claw.

"Two of them were lost not to the sea, nor the storms, nor even accident. Humans," Taliski hissed, and the rattling hisses turned sour. I shook where I stood, my knees going weak. These dragons were angry, terribly so.

"Fiends!" Crux roared his displeasure. *"Who did this?"*

"We were hoping that you, as the only bonded dragon in the isles at the moment – and not even an island dragon yourself – might have an answer, Crux!" Taliski stated with obvious displeasure. I was beginning to sense that there was an entire world of politics on the other side of the human-dragon relationship, one that I didn't understand at all. Was Crux in trouble for being the first to bond with a human since Queen Zenema's island dragon did, decades ago? Was it not an honor to bond with a human?

Crux stared back at the queen. His answer was clear, even before his mind-voice spoke through all of us. *"The human I have bonded with, Lila wave-rider, sought to bond with dragons, but she is the only one that I know of capable and brave enough to do so."*

"Skrech!" Taliski hissed, pulling herself closer over the ledge, this time, I was aware, to look at me.

"I had thought as much. The young ones were too small to bond, and Sym has sensed magic around her den ever since..." The great den-mother's eyes settled on me alone, and I felt her presence suddenly in my mind, as close as my own skin.

"Tell me what you know, Danu Geidt."

"You know of me?" I stammered in panic.

"I can read you, Danu. I can read your heart, but not your memories. I can smell that you bear a great love for our kind, which I acknowledge... But what of those witches you have lived with? Sym is certain that it is only by magic that the young ones could have been taken from her..."

I shook my head, my knees growing weak. Afar would have said something, wouldn't she? If she had heard of some vile plan to steal young newts then she would have been against it, surely?

Ohotto. As soon as I thought it, I became certain.

"It is not the first time in the history of the world that dragons have been sought after, or that we have had our young ones stolen from us. We believed this evil practice stopped many centuries ago..." Taliski continued. *"But, if any is to revive it – it would be those who dabble in the magic arts!"*

"I...I know nothing, your highness..." I stammered, my eyes tearing up at the mere idea that those young creatures could have come to harm. Dragons were noble and powerful creatures – any harm to them was like silencing a part of the world itself.

"Hmm… Your heart is true, of that I am certain… But who could it have been? Old Chabon has always been a friend to us – but humans have such short memories…"

"There is one witch, great den-mother, by the name of Ohotto Zanna. I do not know if she has anything to do with this great evil, but she is the one who seeks to undermine the ways of the West Witches. She seeks to use our traditions and power for evil in the world!" I was certain of my words, and yet I had no proof. It felt as though the old den-mother could sense that in me, as she shook her head irritably.

"Then Danu Geidt, and Crux-Phoenix, as you are dragon-friends, and as you, Crux, have bonded with a human, I am asking you to get to the bottom of this mystery." She looked at me directly. *"If you humans seek to know of our ways, then you must also share in our burdens."*

Find out who killed the dragon newts. Help Lila defeat Havick. For a moment I felt overwhelmed by all of these tasks

I was just Danu Geidt, an acolyte, not even fully trained! But even as I felt worried, I could also see how these tasks were two sides of the same coin. *Havick and Ohotto aren't just a problem for the Sea Raiders, or Roskilde,* I knew. They were an evil that would spread across the islands. Everyone would be affects, and would be in danger. I had to get back to Malata and convince Lila somehow to give up her father's rules…

"It would be an honor, Den-Mother Taliski." I bowed once more. "And I know that Lila wave-rider will be honored by this task as well."

"Good." Taliski withdrew her head on her long neck, and at that, I knew our council was done. I was left feeling shaken and disturbed by the troubling news, if what Taliski said was true—and I had no reason to doubt her— then Ohotto was trying to revive a practice that was evil and centuries old. The butchery of baby dragons, and use of their bodies for magic. This was not what the West Witches were built on. Not what we stood for, and even Crux beside me seemed troubled by this news as he lashed his tail against the cavern walls.

"Come, Danu. We will fish, and I will rest for a few hours before we return to find Lila." I could sense a new sense of purpose radiating from the drake now. He carried his snout higher, he walked more forcefully. It must be the defenseless newts being harmed, I thought. He is willing to overlook his hurt feelings with Lila in order to put a stop to this evil.

CHAPTER 30
LILA, OUTNUMBERED

T he small schooner skipped over the night waves easily and eagerly, and for just a brief moment in that early morning dark, my troubles faded as I gave myself to the rhythms and patterns of sailing. Some people believe it to be hard work, which I guess it is, in its way; there is the constant playing out of the rope, one hand on the tiller, another on the guide line to the sail – the constant searching for wind and currents around you. But in actual fact, when everything worked well and accordingly—as it did now – it almost felt like flying.

Almost, I grimaced. Nothing really even came close to flying, actually, but skipping along the tops of the waves in a brisk breeze was as good as I was going to get at the moment —maybe ever. I tried to focus on the task in front of me, and the pull of my heart towards my dragon.

Crux. I am so sorry, I thought towards my friend, wondering if he could even hear me over this great distance. I should never have agreed to stay with the Raiders… I had hurt Crux's feelings, and not only that – I could see now that what my foster-mother and Danu and Crux had been telling me all along was right. I *wasn't* just Lila the Sea Raider, I was also Lila the Dragon Rider, and, although I hated to admit it to myself, Lila of Roskilde. I *was* all of these things, and I had been trying to force myself to be just one!

"Lila."

I startled, not expecting to hear him – but it was unmistakable. There he was, the dragon in my mind – but he was faint, a long way away.

"Crux?" I stood up in the boat. "I am coming to you! I am sorry!" I shouted over the waves.

"I know." The voice of the dragon against my mind was faint. *"I should not have been so annoyed with you,"* he stated, much to my shock. Who had ever heard of a dragon apologizing?

With every passing meter that the boat clipped, I could feel the connection growing stronger in my mind. As the morning sky started to grey with the dawn, I thought that I could even sense a bit more of the dragon hurtling towards me. There was the feel of his urgency, the distant shadow of Danu on the other side of his mind.

And upset. Loss. I rocked on my heels.

"Crux, my friend? What is it? You are upset!" I called.

"Wait." The Phoenix dragon did not spend time talking to me over such great distances, but I could feel how he put his power into his wing muscles to fly faster, and nearer. Soon, my heart led me to find a speck low on the north-western horizon, growing larger by the second. With the sight of him, my heart flipped over into relief, but also our bond grew stronger. I could feel the Phoenix dragon's worry and his fury over something, and I also knew that it was not directed at me.

Something has happened. Something very bad indeed...

I waved my arm up at him – although he of course knew where I was as he soared across the sky like a shooting star. The sun had just broken the eastern horizon, and I could see his deep black, green, and purple scales in all their glory. Crux was magnificent, and he greeted me with a loud, deafening roar.

"Skreayah!" I watched as he flared his wings to rise above me, before swooping around, bringing up his feet to catch the waves and throw the water to either side of him in massive plumes as he settled on the ocean like a great seabird. My little boat rocked, and I was fairly drenched by the time that he paddled towards me, bearing Danu on his back.

"Lila! Thank the stars we have found you!" Danu called, looking exhausted but grinning, and I felt that my own face was grinning too as Crux leaned his massive head over the side of the boat and I swept my arms around him.

"I will never choose another over you again," I whispered fiercely to the wyrm.

"Good." Crux's mind was warm against mine. *"Now scratch my ears, will you. Your human hands must be good for something."* I smirked, and did as I was asked.

⚜

As happy as our reunion was, however, I was still very much aware of the thread of anxiety and upset that was thrumming through Crux as I worked to seize my pack and clamber from the boat over to his broad slab of shoulder. I had decided to leave the schooner–perhaps it would wash back up on one of the islands, and someone could make use of it. *I would only be riding dragons from now on!*

"What is wrong?" I asked Danu as I settled.

"Sym's hatchlings. The newts that you tried to bond with on her island?" Danu's face was worried.

"I remember," I said, smiling as I thought of the way that they had gamboled and pounced, completely ignoring my efforts to bond with them.

"Two are missing." Danu's face was grim. "Presumed dead."

"What?" I burst out, gripping onto Crux's scales in shock.

"Sym sensed magic, so my best guess is—"

I beat him to it. "Ohotto," I snarled.

"We must find out what happened to the little ones," Crux said as the waters around us started to ripple. I could sense him kicking his great, tree-trunk like legs to power us through

the water, faster and faster. I sat down quickly on the saddle, and attached my feet into the hoops.

"But where is Ohotto? How will we find her?" I asked the dragon and Danu at the same time. All thought of the navy and of my father's raiding party fled my mind when I thought of those innocent newts endangered.

It was Danu who answered me. "There is only one place that I think she can be at the moment, Lila," he whispered in a serious voice. "She wasn't at Sebol, and she has been spending a lot of time at the court of your uncle, on Roskilde."

Roskilde. It looked like I was going to get a chance to see just what my uncle had done with my island country first hand.

꧁꧂

We had flown deep into the region known as the Free Islands and it was just past mid-morning when I told Danu about my foster-mother's kind words, the words that had sent me into the sea toward Crux and Danu.

"They must be so worried about Havick," Danu said.

"But there is only one way for the Raiders to be free – and that is to change," I echoed Pela's words to me.

"Which might be a lot sooner than you think…" Danu said, nodding to the shapes amassing on the horizon ahead of us.

They were Havick's ships.

We hurtled towards them, the shock of what I was seeing ahead of me stilling my mind. The navies of Roskilde had never travelled this far south before; crossing the doldrums of the Barren Seas to the far Free Islands of the southern end of the archipelago. Sure, there had been the lone patrol boat – even a galleon heading to patrol the lawless south – but my foster-father had once explained it to me thus; that it took so much effort to cross the Barren Seas (mostly oars, as the currents were so poor) that it wasn't worth their while to transport a large fleet so far south. That was why us Sea Raiders lived there, after all, in a corner of the world where we could breathe a little free air.

But what I was looking at now wasn't just a fleet. It was an *armada*.

"They must have been travelling for days. Weeks!" I said in stunned awe. What sort of a captain does that? I almost felt a sort of begrudging respect for the man, whether Lord Havick or an admiral under his command. The long hours of cajoling his sailors back to their oars, tiring themselves to the point of exhaustion every day... what reward did he promise was waiting for them, all the way down here?

I could see at least twelve full-size galleons, each of which could easily dwarf our smaller *Ariel*. The Roskildean galleons were some five or six decks tall, with at least four or five masts sprouting an assortment of square and lateen sails. On their wooden-hulled bodies were the thick nests of gun ports, gaping like dark mouths.

How many guns has each one of those got? I thought in alarm. Ten? Twenty each side of each galleon?

But then came the smaller support vessels: the brigantines, the clippers, the caravels, and the carracks. There were enough to invade an entire country, let alone restore 'low and order' to the scattered southern islands. I knew that the *Ariel* could probably match any of the smaller vessels, and she would be faster than the cumbersome and slow-going galleons for sure – but against so many?

"That doesn't look good," Danu said.

"Isn't that a bit obvious!?" I said irritably, my anxiety getting to me.

"I smell magic," Crux growled from the recesses of my mind, and from Danu's flushing face, I could see that *he* had heard it too. Yet another dragon mystery I had yet to fathom, that dragons could sense magic.

"Yes – I can feel it too…" Danu said from behind me. He pointed at the dark cloud that hung low over the fleet, just above the masts of the tallest ships. I had first assumed was a stormfront, until I realized that it was lower than the towering pillars of clouds of the skies.

"Is that a fog?" I said uncertainly. But I already knew what Danu's answer would be, and his pale and pinched face confirmed it. These clouds were darker than a sea fog, slate grey at their fronts, descending to pitch black in their bodies. It almost looked like lamp smoke, but I could see no burning anywhere.

"That is no natural sea fog," Danu said. "It's a magical smoke. An *ether*, it is called. I was taught on Sebol that only the dark magicians used it, and that the original Darkening, hundreds of years ago, was made up of the same foul magic…"

"Great," I said, curling my lip in disgust. "And what does this magical *ether* do? Will it hurt us?"

"Ohotto must have made it… Although I have no idea why," Danu stated, before confessing, "I have no idea what she can make the ether do, or what dangers it hides."

"This Ohotto—she is the one who has stolen our young ones?" Crux's voice was full of fire and fury in my mind, as he pulled at the currents of air, every tendon in his body eager to swoop down on the fleet to hunt out the witch who had so gruesomely attacked his kind.

"Steady, Crux, I know… I share your pain." I set my hands to his scales, letting him feel my own horror and anger. As soon as I touched him, it was like feeling a furnace – but one that was in my mind and heart, not under my hands. "We need to be careful, Crux, we need to wait for our chance to strike…"

But that chance was taken from us, as I heard the harsh, braying call of a horn from the fleet below.

"They've spotted us!" I shouted, as the lead galleon turned its nose in our direction, and its brother and sister ships followed suit. Up ahead, one of the smaller clippers of the fleet sped ahead, skipping along the waves towards us.

But we were flying, many hundreds of feet high above the ocean, and with barely a flick of his wings, the mighty Crux sped up further into the skies, so that the entire armada was blanketed in the darkened smoke, only punctured by the odd crow's nest. This high up, and we could see clear behind them where the ragged tails of the ether dissipated in their wake, and the sea plumes of their passage fragmented into widening ripples.

Not only that–we could see the burning ruins of the Free Islands behind, as well.

"Oh!" I gasped, knowing what I was looking at but even still feeling the horror. The Free Islands were an agglomeration of large and small islets, some which were barely shelves of rock and trees to others that had their own villages, even towns. They formed the southern end of the archipelago and they were usually a green and verdant place. But not any longer. A great swathe of destruction had been levied against them by the Roskildean fleet, which reminded me of the destroyed villages that we had seen earlier – but this tumult was near-total. Towers of smoke rose from the villages – and not one of the coastal villages stood standing. Those in the interiors of their islands, or those that were fortunate to be sheltered by cliff and peak, had been spared, but not so for any of the harbors or ports.

"The monster – why?" I burst out. "I mean, he's only ruining his own taxes and tithes with all of this…"

"They'll rebuild, they have to," Danu commented sadly. "But he's also destroying *your* livelihood as well."

I struck a palm to my face. *Of course!* Havick was making sure that the Sea Raiders would have no friendly port or village to visit or trade with.

Pheet! Pheet! In our soaring, we had taken our eyes off of the cloud below, and now I heard the whistling and then saw the outlying black bolts rising from the etheric cloud towards us.

"Skreak!" Crux almost laughed at the gesture. We were still far too high to be hit by such paltry projectiles, and, one by one I saw them lose their speed and power, and fall harmlessly back towards the grey seas.

"They dare attack us?" But just as quickly as the arrows were gone, Crux's mirth gave way, as anger got the better of him. He tucked his head and neck downwards into a dive.

"No – Crux!" I shouted, but it was already too late. "There are too many!"

Heedless of my warnings, Crux dove like an angry falcon – straight towards the dark clouds, and the ships it sheltered.

CHAPTER 31
DANU, BATTLE MAGICS

We screamed downward, the wind shrieking as we accelerated into the murk. "Crux!" I shouted, but the Phoenix dragon wasn't going to listen to me – especially as he had also just disobeyed Lila, his bonded partner!

I had a moment to gather my thoughts, reaching for that space inside of me where the magic dwelled – but then all of that was thrust aside as we vanished into the ether cloud.

"The evilest of things always prefer the dark," Afar had once told me, at the time that she had introduced me to the concept of the ether. "They say that, in the beginning, the fire and the light were one thing – and they drove away the evil darkness – but now darkness seeps back into our world, seeking to always extinguish the light." The notion had terrified me as a younger adept, and I had lost many nights to wondering what it meant. Now, I thought I knew.

All magicians and witches could summon that darkness – just as we could reach out to summon the weather, and light. But I knew instinctively that to do so would be to be inviting more of that darkness into the world; a sin, a heresy, a crime.

It is no wonder, then, that the cloud that Ohotto had summoned was also laced with dark and evil magics.

"Lost…"

"So, hungry…"

We were surrounded by voices, although they also sounded like the creaking and sighing of the wind. Crux roared in a muffled and distant way, as if the cloud itself was snatching at his voice.

"Danu! Can you hear that?" I heard Lila shout in alarm.

"Yes! Don't listen!" I called back, but even this close to her, I had no idea if she could hear me or not. The murk was near total. It surrounded us, and I felt immediately cold, despite the fact that heat had been radiating from the dragon underneath me just a moment earlier. With the cold came not only the voices, but also the fear. An icy terror clutched at my heart, one I knew wasn't natural, and yet I was almost power-less to stop myself from crying out.

"Lila!" I put my hand out to her shoulder dimly visible as a deeper shadow ahead of me, not sure if I wanted to reassure her or myself – to find that she was hunched, her muscles tense.

"Hold on," she turned to say through gritted teeth, her face grown pale, but still courageous.

"So very hungry…" the words rose around us, and I thought that I could even *see* forms in the dark – but what were they? We were hundreds of feet above the sea!

They were phantasms, or apparitions. Ghostly forms just slightly paler than the frothing cloud that Crux was screaming his anger through. They appeared to be ragged and tearing, their edges indistinct, and yet I thought that I could see suggestions of heads, arms – even ghoulish dark spaces for eyes…

"No!" I shouted, just a fraction of a second before Crux burst out of the bottom of the cloud, and into a volley of crossbow bolts.

※

The galleons were thick around us as Crux flashed his leathery wings – but still I could hear the distinct *thock* noise of the many barbs hitting home on his belly. Most, I hoped and believed, would break harmlessly, unable to puncture his young and strong hide.

"Skreyar!" Crux bellowed in pain and rage, bucking his neck to release a jet of his dragon fire out into the air as he wheeled around a crow's nest. Everywhere I looked below, I could see the top decks and sails of the ships – it seemed to me like there was hardly any water at all, there were so many of them! And clustered on their decks were crossbowmen and spearmen, and half of them readying weapons at us.

Thew! A much heavier, tearing sound came from off to my right as Crux once again grunted in pain.

"Crux!" Lila shouted in alarm as I turned to see that something had punched a hole clean *through* his leathery wings! *But they are as tough as armor!* I thought, until I saw another of the culprits arching across the air towards us.

"Arbalest!" Lila shouted, indicating the harpoon-sized bolt, fired from one of the heavy weapons on the decks of one of the galleons. The bolt alone was almost as tall as me, and probably thicker than one of my legs. Lila threw her weight to one side as, in tandem, Crux curled his lower wing underneath him and we cornered downwards, and the arbalest's bolt passed meters over Crux's back tines.

"Ready cannons!" I heard one of the Roskildean captains shouting, and saw small gun shutters bang open on the nearest vessel.

"Lila – we have to get out of here!" I called, knowing that she knew, but perhaps could not control the angered dragon beneath us. With a mighty tail swipe, Crux demolished one of the smaller masts of the nearest galleon, but every moment spent in the air only invited more crossbow bolts, and more time for the cannons and arbalests to reload their murderous weapons.

Only use magic if you have no other choice. Wasn't that what Afar and Chabon had taught me? Well, if there were any time in which I had no other choice – then it had to be now, right? Despite the rushing in my ears and the pounding of my heart, I closed my eyes and tried to find that space where the magic came from.

"Hiyah!" I could hear snarls as Lila let loose arrows from her short bow down onto the decks of those below, and I was thrown first to one side and then another by Crux's desperate aerial maneuvers – but I could feel the magic, there, waiting like a dark well.

I dipped my mind into it, and came back glittering with power.

"Light. Light to dispel the darkness!" I called, not knowing what I was saying or why, but the magic itself was strong and had taken a hold of me, pitching me forward in my seat and forcing me to place me hands on the dragon below.

"*SKRECH!*" Crux roared in defiant joy, another shake of his head and this time the fire that belched from his mouth was an incandescent blue and green. It was much stronger than the previous dragon flame, and it engulfed the forecastle of the nearest galleon, making the entire boat rock and shake like it had been hit not only by fire, but by a great weight.

I slumped back as the shouts and screams rose up amidst the storm of bolts, feeling exhausted. In front of me, Lila was still firing her bow, but Crux had now flared his wings to catch the breeze, and – with a crack, we were swooping low between the ships, flashing first one way and then another in our desperate race to get out from their murderous assaults.

"*Danu!*" I heard a screech that chilled the blood, and, just as a patch of clearer blue skies opened up in front of us, I turned back to see a form emerging onto one of the decks behind us. It was too far away to be sure, but I could swear that it was a woman, dressed in white and with golden hair. I saw her raise her hands and spit, and I tried to remember the protection magics that I had been taught – but then we were skipping across the grey waters, out from the cloud and ahead of the boats, but the seas appeared to be boiling and frothing at our feet. Plumes of super-heated water were blasting their way into the sky, hitting Crux's wings and legs, and making him snarl and try to lift himself higher.

Ohotto. How could I face such a powerful witch? She was older than me, she had trained for far longer than me, and now she had the power of whatever dark magic she had summoned as well.

But I was a dragon-friend. I had a power that she didn't, I thought. My powers were stronger when around Crux – would it be enough?

"Fly, Crux, fly!" Lila yelled, and the dragon snapped his burnt and searing wings in a rapid drumbeat, lifting us up into higher and higher into the blue, and away from our enemy.

We had survived – but only just.

"We have to get to Malata." Lila was gasping for breath as Crux turned south. "My father is due to take to the waves in the last, biggest raid of the season – or so he wanted to do last night – but the Raiders cannot stand against a fleet of so many, with such strangeness. We have to get to them, and we have to warn them."

I nodded, too weary from my spell casting to even say anything in return. I didn't know how the Sea Raiders would survive such a force, just as I didn't know how I could resist the magical ether and the trained witch Ohotto Zanna either.

CHAPTER 32
LILA'S PLAN

We flew southwards at the head of the enemy fleet, moving faster and faster until they had become a dark shape on the horizon, and then a dot, and then were gone from view entirely. *But not gone from the oceans,* I knew.

I felt my heart lift a little as I saw the old, wrecked galleon and the darker circlet of the Bonerock reef around Malata grow in our sight. There, already gliding ahead of them sat the three larger carracks of the Sea Raider fleet, and a host of smaller sailboats. My foster-father had been serious when he had wanted to go on a grand raid – and it looked like he had managed to roust out every ship that could be fought with to go and plunder.

But now you will need every ship in order to keep your lives, I thought grimly, waving an arm at the *Ariel* as Crux swooped towards it.

"It's Lila!" someone was calling, but even so, the crew of the *Ariel* were still gathering bows and spears as we approached.

"Lila!" It was my father, storming onto the deck in his high boots, gauntlets and armor. He looked serious as he called to us. "We have no time for any more of your adventures!"

He's angry at me choosing the dragon over him, he thinks I am just that same girl I was, dreaming of dragon adventures. But I wasn't.

"You're right, you don't!" I said angrily as Crux swept his wings back and forth in an uneven hovering motion. "Havick is coming – and he has the biggest fleet with him that the Western Isles have ever seen!"

My father was, if anything, a pragmatist. He immediately waved his guards off from the decks, and ordered them to make space for us to land.

"Skreych!" Crux barked his annoyance as he had to fit his large body onto the smaller ship, making it bob up and down on the water. Several of my father's sailors gasped, hurriedly jumping out of the way as the large Phoenix dragon settled himself.

"Your dragon is hurt," my father said, and the exhaustion that had distracted my mind vanished in an instant as I slid from the saddle.

"Crux? Why didn't you say?"

"No point," Crux admitted practically. *"We couldn't stop. Nothing good can be done for it."*

"Of course, there is something good to be done!" I burst out. "Where does it hurt?" I started stalking back and forth up the length of the dragon.

"There." My father pointed to where one of Crux's front legs was dripping with green ichor. I could make out the shapes of the stubby bolts that still sat there, having found their way on either side of the hardened scales.

"We have to get them out!" I gasped, reaching for my knife as my father put a restraining hand on my shoulder.

"I'll get Kemper here. He is better at this kind of thing," he grunted, before bellowing for the ship's medic to bring his work equipment to the deck.

"Okay. Thank you." I nodded, feeling relieved but also worried as I set a hand against Crux's side. "Kemper is a good man. A skilled healer," I said to Crux, who had already turned his head to start sniffing at the barrels of salted fish.

Danu thumped to the deck beside me, washing his hands before offering to assist the old, white haired man in the procedure, saying, "I have some skill with herbs and healing and the like." Kemper grumbled and clicked his teeth as he always did, but he worked methodically and with great care on this, his largest of patients. I tried to keep an eye on what was going on, but my father was drawing me away from the scene as Crux hissed painfully, and casually crunched open one of the fish barrels and helped himself to its contents instead.

"Lila… I still find it strange how you share *minds* with that creature," my father muttered. I glared at him sharply, but I could see that he meant it when he raised his large hands defensively and said, "No harm is meant by it. I just find it…*odd*, that is all." He frowned, before clearing his throat noisily. "Your mother talked to me last night. When she was sure that you were already many leagues away…"

"Uh-huh," I said noncommittally. I was half expecting him to say that the trouble that we had run into was something that he would have expected when I had 'run off after a dragon' but instead he shrugged his large shoulders and sighed deeply.

"I am sorry, Lila. I have tried to make you into something you are not, which is very poor of me. That is not the Raider way," he said through a strained voice.

"Oh, Father." All of my feelings of resentment towards him melted away in an instant as I saw the effort it was for him to admit his mistake. I threw my arms around his big form. I couldn't keep on calling him Kasian anymore. It had always been awkward on my tongue; and now I wouldn't say it. He was the only father I knew, anyway.

"Shush, you…" he said gruffly, hugging me in a bear hug before gently pushing himself back from me. "Lila, I need to tell you this. After we lost our firstborn babe… I think that both I and your mother both went a little mad. Sad, and angry at the world. That is why I agreed to go on those raids to Roskilde. It was a very deep hurt."

"I know, Father," I said grimly, seeking to spare his feelings.

"No. Let me say this out loud," he continued. "The Raiders are meant to be free. That is what we love most in life – not bowing to any tyrant or king, and I see now that I was trying to mold you into what *I* wanted. But you are Lila Roskilde, *and* Lila Malata. You should find out for yourself what your freedom holds." He breathed out once again, patting his belly, with a look of relief.

"Thank you again, Father," I said to him, tears starting in my eyes, even when I knew that we had no time for such emotions.

"Now, Lila whatever-we're-going-to-call-you," my father and Chief of the Sea Raiders said, straightening himself up. "What are you talking about – this fleet of yours?"

I retold our experiences to my father, and watched as his face turned from shock to horror at the enormity of what we were facing. I explained the burned-out villages we had seen, and then the total devastation of the nearby Free Island ports and harbors. He nodded at that, as if he had been waiting for this to happen.

"It has only been a matter of time before that Lord Havick tried to choke off our supplies and provisions..." my father growled.

"Yes." I nodded, before launching into the rest—a description of the fleet that faced us, their weapons and their numbers.

"By the sacred waters and the stars," my father said, as reality hit him. "They mean to destroy us totally."

"I fear so – but there is more." I didn't go into exact detail, but I explained a little of the dark magical fog that had hovered over them, and how Danu believed that some of the renegade witches had swept to Havick's side. As sailors and Raiders are ever a superstitious bunch, I was expecting my father to pale or quail under this strangeness – but instead I saw his jaw clench in determination and in anger.

"Then I see that we have no choice but to fight, and to fight well at that!" He snarled defiantly. "Lord Havick has allied himself with the worst and darkest of magics, and it would be an honor to free the Western Isles of his menace!"

I might have whooped for joy, were it not such a patently foolish emotion. "I agree, Father – but we have only three large ships. Three against what, twelve? Fifteen galleons?"

"We have the fishing fleet, and the smaller yachts. They can sail rings around any larger boat, and you know that!" my father said fiercely.

"I know – but I still fear whether it will truly be enough," I said, biting my lip with worry.

৩ঃ৩

"We make our attack here." My father prodded a section of the parchment map spread before us. Danu and I stood at the edge of the table with the others clustered around his 'war office' –

actually the largest room in the mansion, with Captain Lasarn of the *Fang*, Captain Helda of the *Storm*, and a dozen other Raiders of the smaller yachts. All in all, I thought that there must be twenty or so able-bodied men and women representing their crews here.

"They don't look happy," Danu whispered at my side.

"I'm not surprised," I muttered back. They had just been told of the fleet that was coming for them, and although we had spared them the details of the magical fog that surrounded the galleons, the threat of so many cannons and crossbows alone was enough to frighten any heart.

"Not at the mouth of the reef?" Lasarn countered, his old grizzled face frowning with determination.

They were scared, I thought – but I also felt a swirl of pride for each man and woman who had risen to the challenge. They knew what was at stake: everything.

"No." The Captain shook his head savagely. "The inlet is for the *Ariel* alone. She's the fastest, and she is the only boat that can do this."

"Aye, you have a point." One by one, the other captains and ship's officers agreed. Not that they didn't have a choice. My father had asked for all opinions, and whether they were outlandish or farfetched, all knew he would listen to their ideas if it meant a chance to save Malata.

"Then are we agreed?" he said, looking primarily at Lasarn and Helda. "You know what you have to do?"

"I don't like it," Helda grumbled, but she thumped a

gauntleted fist on the table with the others. "But it's the best we can do." She finished with a reckless grin. "We'll send 'em to the ocean floor. Chief – don't you worry!"

"I know you will," my father agreed, straightening up as he sighed heavily. "And may the stars and waters help us, is all I can add."

A moment of dark reflection settled over the crowd, before my father clapped his hands together. "Right! You have your orders – jump to it!"

The room emptied, leaving me, Danu, and the captains in it as the others ran down to their docks, shouting orders to their crews as they did so.

"Lila – are you sure about this?" my father turned to say to me. "You'll be taking the brunt of it…"

"We can do it," I said, nodding.

🙢🙠

It had been my idea to use our bodies—Danu, mine, and Crux's— as bait, but now, as we circled high above the harbor of Malata, watching as the boats scrambled to their positions, even I had a moment of worry. Crux's right wing still had the hole in it, and that made his flying less controlled – but he was still fast.

"I can fly faster than your boats!" Crux assured me.

"I know you can, my friend, but still… I would not

313

endanger you so easily, not when there might be another way."
I agonized over what we were about to do.

"You are not endangering me!" Crux's tone was certain in my mind. *"You think you can stop me fighting? From wreaking vengeance against these fiends who have stolen our brood?"*

There was no answer to that. Of course, I couldn't stop the feisty and hot-hearted Crux. I hoped that at least this way we might have a chance.

"There they go," Danu said, pointing out to where the expanding ripples of the smaller boats fanned out around the reef, and the shapes of the larger *Storm* and *Fang* started turning away in opposite directions, one to the east, and the other to the west. It left the *Ariel* alone in the wide inlet that led through the Bone Reef to Malata's harbor. We didn't have long to lay our trap, but the Raiders had grown up in and out of these waters. They knew them well.

"Then it's time," I said, and, with a challenging roar, I spurred Crux into swooping forward, to find our enemy.

CHAPTER 33
DANU, CUMULUS DRACONIS

We flew north at breakneck speed, passing the protecting reef around the island and moving towards the north and the west, following Crux's fine nose.

"It smells ugly," he informed me, and I thought for the briefest of moments I could sense a little what he did, through his strange dragon-senses. There was fear, anger, mistrust and jealousy, all curled up into a taut ball.

"Ugh!" I shook my head. "That is what the magic smells like to you?"

"It is the magic of the darkness. Bad feelings. Bad thoughts. Small minds." Crux needled the thought into my mind as we beat ever forward, straight into the teeth of our enemy.

"What is it?" Lila, blissfully unaware of what we had sensed, asked.

"They are close," I told her, taking a deep breath as I tried to ready my own hesitant magics.

"Are you ready? What do you need?" she asked me, her face tight with worry. I shrugged.

"I don't know. But I'll be okay." I told her, wishing that I could believe my words. *Could I really do this? I hadn't even completed my training yet!*

"Think not of what might happen; only what must happen," Crux told me, with words that sounded shockingly like Afar or Chabon for a moment. He was right, though. I took a deep breath, cleared my mind and reached for my magic....

It was there, like a raging torrent. I was shocked at how strong it was, and in my mind, I could feel the heat of the dragon radiating up and out through me. It was as if just having the dragon near increased my magic. Is that why the ancients used to believe what they did about dragon blood and bones? The magic wobbled and withdrew from me as my stomach turned over at the thought, before I calmed my heart and settled once more into the trance. No more dark thoughts. I had a living, breathing, healthy dragon to lend me power.

"Danu – they are up ahead!" Lila was saying, and I opened my eyes to see our enemy with a different vision.

There, spreading over the northern horizon, was the vast group of Havick's ships. They were covered with the same dark fog, and to my magical eyes the fog was made up of ghostly faces and bodies. I watched in a state of transfixed horror as I saw the suggestions of helmets and armor on some of the larger faces, as some of the spirits had grown large.

They are the dead? Is that what the magic was telling me – that the etheric darkness made by Ohotto Zanna was made up of unquiet spirits?

Whatever the answer– it still did not change my purpose. I reached for the river of magic inside of me and the dragon, just as the cloud *convulsed* ahead of us.

"Danu? Whatever you are going to do – can you do it quickly?" Lila called out as she hunched over Crux's neck ahead of me. The dark witch's fog rose from the ships and scudded towards us. Left behind, in its absence, we could see the fleet in much sharper detail now. There seemed to be so many ships against the Raider's forces. How could we ever beat so many?

The magic. Just think about what you have to do, I berated myself, once again plunging my mind down into that current of power, before I raised my hands once again into the sky…

"Cumulus Draconis!" I shouted.

Nothing happened.

"Cumulus Draconis!" I shouted again and again. The dark fog started racing towards us, and I could see angered, ferocious faces with fingers of cloud like claws stretching across the sky…

"Cumulus Draconis!" I begged, threatened, and entreated with the power as the dark spirit-ether was almost upon us. I could *feel* the rise of the ensorcelled fear against me, as the

brush of terror from the cloud threatened to tear our courage away…

And then a breath of fresh wind from the east.

Come on, come on. I threw my hands out to the clouds as the ships grew larger underneath us, and now I could see masts and sails, and rows upon rows of gun ports.

Hsssss! With a scream, the spirit-ether was all around us, and I felt instantly terrified.

"Danu!" Lila shouted through chattering teeth.

"It's the magic. It's not real!" I told her, although the fear threatened to turn my guts to ice and make tears fall from my eyes. *Please work, by all that is holy, please work!* I begged, as the breeze from the east grew a little stronger, and stronger still….

"Hiyah!" Lila said through clenched teeth as we were diving in and amongst the racing ships.

Pheet! Pheet! Small and dark bolts flew up towards us, but Crux's speed was unrivalled, as he buffeted one cloud of crossbows with a violent snap of his great wings before lashing out at a sail –

"Get them! Bring them down!" a male voice jeered from below – but the power of the fog was so strong that it was all that I could do to hold onto Crux's tines and pray.

THABOOM! I heard the first cannon go off, as Crux briefly touched claws on the deck of one of the ships, pushing off and out into the air again, and making the galleon beneath us shake in the murk. The fog didn't seem to affect the sailors of Havick's navy, I thought, until I realized that the fog was hanging around *us* and above the ships – Ohotto was too wily to let it settle for long on any of her own troops.

THABOOM! Another cannonball fired, missing us by meters as Crux lashed out his tail at a smaller brigantine, rupturing a hole in its stern before swooping out low over the waters – just as the magic that I had cast finally came into effect.

The winds from the east blew and howled over the water towards the fleet of Roskilde. Sails that had previously been limp suddenly filled as the captains and quartermasters barked orders to turn their ships across the gales. A ship can survive heavy winds, and the sailors could even use it to their advantage if they were quick enough. But the gale from the east was not intended for the ships. It was intended for another enemy entirely.

The spirit-ether held for a long moment, as the tendrils of its outliers dissipated. But the magical winds I had summoned grew only stronger, and pummeled the ether fog, driving it back and away, lifting it from the seas and from our minds at the same time.

"By the waters!" Lila gasped, as she must have felt what I did too… A new sense of determination and confidence as the magical frights were lifted. I didn't know for how long my magic would last, especially against such a powerful witch as Ohotto – but we had a little time.

"Urk…" my head suddenly pounded with a vicious headache and my body flooded with exhaustion.

"You have given too much! Stop!" Crux forced his way into my mind, and in my imagination, it *felt* like he was lowering his wings over me, shielding me from the magic that I had summoned.

"No, Crux – I need to be able to counter Ohotto," I murmured, earning a worried glance from Lila ahead of me as we flew south and west, back towards Malata.

"You did! Now onto the next step of the plan," Lila cried back at me, as we flew at the head of the fleet.

Havick and his captains, angered by our attack and our display of both flying skill, bravery, and magic, bore down on us with full speed.

Just as we had hoped they would.

CHAPTER 34
LILA, THE BATTLE FOR MALATA

I knew that Danu was flagging, but Crux told me that he had him safe, and once again I felt relieved, thankful, and worried—all in equal measures. That Crux could do all of this — flying, advising, avoiding being shot, as well as lending his strength to the adept behind me— was a wonder.

Thank you, great friend... I reached out to him as the islands of Malata swam closer towards us.

"Don't thank me yet." Crux cut off our mental communication and I knew he was trying to concentrate. Behind us the fleet was fast-moving, and ahead of us Malata and its reef looked pathetically small in comparison. Shapes bobbed out there in the ocean – the smaller forms of the schooners and ships—but of the *Fang* and the *Storm*, there was no sign at all.

Only the *Ariel* was left. My father's ship waited just in

front of the inlet, all flags raised high and daring those that swept after us.

"Ready!" I shouted, although I knew that my father couldn't hear me. I unfurled the red scarf and waved it high above my head, and my father's plan rolled into motion. The smaller sailing yachts and schooners tacked away, leaving an undisputed challenge from the *Ariel*.

"Easy now, slow..." I purred at Crux, who slowed his flight a little to allow Havick and his ships to catch up just a little.

THOOM! The *Ariel* didn't wait for negotiations or a declaration of war, but fired its cannon straight at us.

"Dive!" I shouted, and Crux tipped on his side to swoop down, down, down, his claws skimming the surface of the water as my father's cannonade flew over us to meet the first brigantines and fast patrol boats of Havick.

THOOM! THOOM! My father's flagship fired all that it had as we curved around the battle, Crux lifting his belly and his legs as we swooped over the Bone Reef. I saw the almost mechanical, well-ordered way that my father's crew moved, setting firing torches to cannons as the metal guns rocked back and the next Raiders moved in, heavy canvas gloves carrying the iron shot and stuffing it down the still hot gun barrels as the next packed the black powder, and off again it was fired.

But the barrage was like a toddler skipping stones against a galleon when I saw the enormity of Havick's fleet bearing down on my father's boat. There were plumes and sprays of water as some of my father's shot missed, as well as the screams and crashes as some found their homes in the faster and smaller ships that outpaced the main body of the Roskildean fleet.

"Yes!" I punched the air in fierce celebration as we swung around the rear of the *Ariel,* with the entire might of Havick's fleet bearing down towards us.

But none of the galleons were damaged, I saw. Not from the *Ariel's* attacks at least, although a couple limped from the attacks that Crux had performed – and now they answered the singular ship with all the thunder of their own guns.

THABBA-BOOM! At first there were little movements as shutters opened along the galleon's high walls, and then small puffs and plumes of smoke rose, just before the wave of sound hit us. A clash of a hundred thunderstorms sounded all at once as the galleons returned fire.

My mind raced. How much shot was in the air? Fifteen galleons' worth, with how many guns on the foredecks of each one? Any boat's true firepower lay in its broadside, as most of the guns sat along the sides of the boat, but there would still be anywhere between four and eight cannons at the front of each vessel as well.

At least forty cannon, all heading for my father... I growled in useless frustration as I watched the *Ariel* turn a tight circle. She was the fastest of our larger ships, and the flagship. She leaned out into the winds as she spun, cutting a wide plume of white water as she turned back, seeking the relative safety of the harbor behind.

THOOM! THOOM! Like murderous rain, the cannon shot fell all around her.

"No!" One of the deadly missiles tore straight through her main sail and plunged deep into the top-deck. We could only hope that it didn't puncture a hole all the way through or she would start taking on water.

White plumes of water were thrown up on either side and behind the *Ariel* as it fled, and bits of the reef exploded as the shot fell amongst them.

CRACK! Another cannon hit the deck of the *Ariel,* and another crashed through her aft gunwale. I heard screams.

"Father – no!" I felt the answering surge of fury from the dragon. "Now Crux – now!" I called, as we swept towards the old hulk of the galleon on the reef. We couldn't fight the entire armada of Roskilde, but we could do this….

"Skreyar!" Crux hit the edge of the galleon with all four legs, grappling it and his weight shoving it off of the Bone Reef and into the deeper waters towards the fleet. The smell of pitch and lamp oil filled our nostrils as Crux kicked out at the old, festering hulk that had been my father's trophy for years.

The Raiders had followed my plan to the letter. They had doused the old hulk in whatever spare oils and gunpowder that we could spare, and, as Crux pushed himself back, he let out a mighty roar and hit the side of the boat with his dragon flame.

WOOOSH! The flames pushed the hulk toward the

Roskilde fleet, chewing up the meters and yards as the flames caught and leapt from rotten timber to rotten timber. The hulk wobbled and shook as the flames suddenly blossomed through it in a ball of fiery light, as it ploughed into the nearest galleons of the enemy.

"Yes! It's working!" Danu called weakly as we flew around our floating missile, and Crux once again laid a sheet of dragon fire down on the smaller vessels that dared turn towards us. The burning hulk wedged into the heart of Havick's fleet, crashing past one and entangling itself with another galleon as it broke apart and its burning timbers went everywhere. Enemy sailors leapt overboard, whilst others with more grit seized buckets to scoop up water to douse the flames....

"*Hyargh!*" There was a dim and faint roar as two shapes emerged from the smokes of war – the *Storm* and the *Fang*, each one firing its own cannons at the muddle of Havick's ships as they cut quickly across the battle site. The Raider ships were fast, firing their broadsides and continuing on to beat around the enemy. These two were followed by even faster schooners, darting like small arrow-fish to fire their arrows up onto the decks. It was like watching gulls or sharks attack a shoal of fish – quick, darting movements in before flying out of there.

But, even with this harassment, I was aware that we were still facing an armada, and we only had a tenth of the ships that Havick did.

THOOM! THA-BOOM! The galleons returned fire, the mighty fleet breaking apart into smaller battlegroups, three to five galleons a piece, with a cloud of smaller armored brigantines to give chase to the Raiders. My ears whined with the thunder of the guns, and the rattle of their reports reverberated deep in my belly.

"Lila! Beneath us!" Crux roared, lashing his tail out at a mast as a small torrent of crossbow bolts peppered into the sky all around us. I screamed, shielding my face as Crux bellowed in hurt from the many cruel barbs.

"Aurelis Lumin!" Danu yelled, as something flashed behind me. For a moment I thought that the stocky-little fisherman's boy had caught a lightning bolt, until I saw that there were enemy sailors' underneath us stumbling back, holding their eyes. He had used his magic to blind the nearest of them, but as he slumped against my back, I realized he had worn himself too thin.

"Danu? Are you still with me!" I said, to hear a mumble behind me. The magic was taking its toll on him – and I didn't know if we could afford to not have it in this fight! "Danu – breathe. Relax for a bit!" I said, as Crux lifted us high over the battle, high above the flights of the bolts and the cannons.

As we spiraled higher, I could see the expanse of the battle in its entirety. Havick's armada was separated into four distinct groups, with the largest being right here at the mouth of the harbor. The burning hulk had taken two of the enemy galleons with it, and an additional one had been seemingly disabled by Raider ships – but, aside from a host of smaller injuries and damage, the armada was still shipshape.

"The *Ariel?*" I scanned Malata's harbor, hoping beyond hope that my father had somehow managed to slip the trap and sail away – but no.

There was my father's flagship, half sunk in the harbor, and sinking fast. Men were leaping from the prows and the bowsprit into the water, as Havick's cannons fell around them, and even, hit some of the harbor wall itself; splitting stone and making sharp, cracking noises.

"Father!" I shouted into the murk, but it was no good. He might have made it safely ashore, or he might be fighting for his life even now in that wreckage. The thought that I couldn't stop this from happening speared through me. There are too many of them. They have too many guns...

"If we cannot win – we fight anyway," Crux snarled in an anger that mirrored my own. *"I cannot save the young dragons – but we can take our vengeance!"*

Vengeance. I thought as I gripped my short bow, and searched for the largest and biggest of the armada. Its flagship. "Yes!" I shouted my own challenge as Crux roared out a long, ululating call that echoed strangely over the battlefield.

"Skreeayayayar!"

CHAPTER 35
LILA'S CROWN

W e swung around the burning seascape, and I felt like there was a red line of anger connecting me to the lead flagship. I could see the wreckage of the Raider ships all around. *Where was the Fang?* I couldn't see it – did that mean Captain Lasarn had fled the battle? Or had the ship already gone under?

The screams of our own and the Roskilde forces rose to reach me. It was hard to even *see* any Raiders' flags or colors, as the smoke of the guns and the burning ships cast a dreadful pall over the entire, grisly scene.

But there was one galleon that drew me downward. The largest, the most well-defended with two smaller galleons on either side. "That has to be Havick's ship – it has to be!" I shouted, and heard a mumble from Danu behind me. "Can you do this?" I asked, suddenly scared for my friend when he did not answer.

Vengeance. We had to try. We had to try to stop him.

"Skreyar!" Crux plummeted, from almost directly above them. Their flagship rose larger in my view as I took aim with my bow.

Maybe if I could kill him, it would all be over...

A storm of bolts soared from the decks below to meet us, heading straight for Crux's face.

"No!" Crux roared, turning in mid-flight at the last moment so that the bolts struck his side and legs, and not us. *"I will not have you injured, Lila – I cannot!"* He called out in my mind even as I felt the pain of many small bolts finding the small gaps in his hide.

"No – Crux!" I called as he swept up and out of the danger, a cannon shot narrowly missing his wings. We swooped around the battlegroup, high over the waters that were now churned and murky with soot.

Another cloud of bolts, this time peppered with the harpoons of the arbalest arced ahead of us, and Crux had to turn in his flight once again. The two accompanying galleons moved at pace with their larger parent, always circling in between us and the flagship.

"Damn you, Havick!" I shouted out across the waters, lifting my head amidst the fire and shot. Was it a trick of the eyes, or did I see a man on the deck, and beside him a woman with golden hair? A shock of recognition ran through me as I saw, for just the briefest of moments, that the man wore a golden crown of leaping waves. I cannot explain it, but I knew then, in that instant, that all of the prophesies had been true, and the Witches of the Haunted Isle had been right. Havick wore the Sea Crown, and he had turned it to evil. *"That crown has magic. I smell it,"* Crux confirmed my suspicions as I gritted my teeth.

The Sea Crown will be lost, and then it will be found once more, but the one who finds it will not come from the royal line. The prophecy was all true. Havick wore the Sea Crown, but he did not deserve to.

If only there was a way to get to him! I raised my bow, but Crux had to veer again as a second of the battle groups – this time four galleons and a host of attending ships, came to intercept us, and protect their lord.

I screamed in frustration. Malata would be destroyed. The Sea Raiders would all be destroyed – and for what? For nothing. For the power-hungry greed of that one man.

"SKRECH!" A booming voice called as a shadow passed over the battle. Crux lifted his snout and chirruped, as another roar joined the first.

"Skrear!" Another shadow darted across the water, and then another – dragons!

"I summoned my brothers and sisters. They have come to deliver justice!" Crux was jubilant, flaring in his wings to take us out of that death trap and up towards the others. In moments, we were soaring amongst a flight of dragons – not

330

as many as I had seen at Sym's island, but still more than I had ever seen in the air, and all of them vengeful.

With roars, they descended in ones and twos to strafe the edges of the fleet with great sheets of flame. One brigantine, caught in the crossfire between two dragons, exploded when its own powder rooms ignited.

"Brothers! Sisters! Bring fire down on those who would hurt us!" Crux roared his excitement, but even I could tell that he was flagging in his assault, his wings dipping lower and the pain of his many crossbow bolt wounds starting to weaken him. He moved to join the next attacking flight, but I felt that I had to stop him.

"Crux, my heart – please no more. The dragons are here, do not endanger yourself anymore."

"Lila wave-rider is right," shouted a voice in my mind—Sym, the Sinuous Blue brood mother. She was flagged by other Blues as she rode high on the thermals. *"You have fought bravely and well, little-brother. Now take care of your humans, and let us continue our work!"*

"Skreyar!" Crux snapped his disagreement, but still turned in a slow, protesting circle back around the battle, high above the seeking missiles.

I could not take my eyes from what was happening around and beneath me. The dragons were merciless, but they also attacked with all the intelligence and wile of a top predator. They singled out the stragglers, they assaulted those that were the easiest to kill, and they sought to drive wedges between the bigger groups. Many, many of the brigantines of Roskilde went down in fire and flames. I just hoped that the smaller Raider's schooners had managed to get out of there as soon as they saw the dragons in the air.

"What about Havick? Ohotto?" I heard a mumbling from behind me, as Danu's cold hands gripped my shoulders as he peered around.

"They are trying," I said, nodding to where the fiercest and largest of the dragons – Sym and a host of stocky Greens— were attacking the largest knot of galleons. I heard a strangled roar of pain, as one of the Greens went down into the ocean in a plume of water that jumped higher even than the crow's nest of the largest of the galleons.

Danu's hands suddenly pinched my shoulder and I heard a low groan of worry.

"I know!" I called out in dismay. Several of the dragons were injured now, and still the armada was afloat.

"It's not just that…" Danu was saying, pointing to the north where the dark cloud that he had shredded apart was returning, faster than ever.

"*Cumulo…Cumulous Dracon…*" Danu tried, but I could tell that his power was spent. The darkness enveloped the last remaining ships of the armada, and floated up to snatch at the dragons.

"SSskreych!" The calls of the dragons were alarmed, their mind-talk filled with complaints of bad and evil magics.

"*Fly out of it, my brethren!*" Sym shouted, breaking the

head of the dark fog like a cormorant bursting through a storm-wave. One by one, the other dragons broke free from the clawing grasps of the evil magic, and then the cloud, and the ships, grew fainter as they sailed into the fog and away.

"We can harry them! Follow them!" Crux was saying, but even I knew that was a false hope. Crux the Phoenix was at his last ebbs of strength, as was Danu, as were many other of the dragons ahead of us that day.

"We have done enough, for now," Sym screeched to the others, leading them back to us in the safety of the upper airs. Looking down, I could see (much to my dismay) that she was right. The Bone Reef around Malata was littered with the burning wreckage of ships from both sides, and the seas were a wasteland of floating debris.

"But we didn't finish Havick and Ohotto," Danu gasped.

"Not yet," I said, my voice low and grim.

EPILOGUE
LILA'S VICTORY

It was a strange victory – if that is indeed what I could call this feeling. The seas around Malata had become a grave-yard, and not just for the ships that were both our own and our enemies'. There were at least two dragon bodies in the waters by the time we'd tallied the numbers and counted the losses.

For days and weeks afterwards, the Bone Reef was picked through by Raiders on row boats for salvage, although most of the burnt spars and bits of wood were left where they had snagged, so now we had a low wall of ruinous ships almost entirely encircling our island home. This salvage fleet had managed to haul a lot of useful things out of the wreckage as well – something that made the Raiders a little happier. Weapons and trinkets washed up daily on the reef from the shattered boats, and teams of swimmers dismantled anything they could find and sell to make the winter season easier. The Sea Raiders would survive until spring, just.

"It will make defending it easier the next time," my father said as we looked down from the boulders of the headland above Malata's stone harbor. He had survived, but only just. He had used the *Ariel,* his pride and joy, as a decoy to draw Havick's navy deeper toward the reef after I, Danu, and Crux had led them here. I would never forget the fact that, at the end of the day, my father had decided to sacrifice everything he had worked for to implement my plan.

Not that it was only my father who had sacrificed his dreams for me. On the fourth day from the battle, I found Danu in the docks, greeting a strange new visitor to our shores. Not the dragons, no – but a messenger of the Western Witches. The messenger was a woman just a few years older than us, but shorter by a hand.

The acolyte Sheng had arrived on the moonlit tide the previous night, and her boat was the color of deep green, about the size of our rowboats, with a crew of just three younger training witches (as she herself was).

"Danu, what is it?" I asked him. He still wore his rough canvas work clothes, as he had been helping to reclaim the salvage with all able-bodied sailors like the rest of us.

"It's Afar, and Sebol." Danu looked distraught. "She has lost the vote, and the witches have split into factions—many side with Cala and Ohotto – but some still side with Afar and

Chabon. My mentor writes to me to say that, sadly, she cannot complete my training until safety is restored to the island."

"Oh Danu…" I had tried to cheer him up, but he was already shrugging off my concern.

"It's not the training that I'm worried about – it's Afar and Chabon!" he said bravely, although I wondered if I saw a hint of regret somewhere in there as well. Instead, after provisioning the messenger Sheng and sending her with wishes of luck and strength, Danu threw himself into life on the island. *He is an able hand,* I thought wryly, remembering my father's original challenge to him. But more than that, he spent time with Crux and me, as we endeavored to understand more of this mysterious bond that drew us three together.

My father walked now with a stick and a limp, and he coughed, as he had been trying to free some trapped sailors after the *Ariel* had been hit by thirty or more cannon shots. He had saved the sailors as the rooms had filled with water, but had to swim out as wooden beams crashed into his legs and arms. If he wasn't as strong as an ox, he would never have made it out alive at all.

"The next time," I agreed. We both knew that Havick and Ohotto were still out there, gathering followers, and we both knew that they would probably still regard me, as Lila Roskilde, child of the prophesy and a friend to dragons, a threat.

I knew that was who I was now, really. As much as I had

fought against it; I knew from the prophesy and the crown and a hundred other things that this was who I really was.

But my name wasn't all that I was. Just as Crux had said – I could be many things in one. I didn't have to 'just' be a princess, just like I wasn't 'just' a Sea Raider. I was everything that my parents – my real parents who had raised me, Chief Kasian and Pela – had taught me to be, but I was also a friend to dragons. I rode dragons. I had the blood of royalty in my veins.

I don't have to be just one thing. I can be all of them.

"You will have to go after Havick, you know," my father said severely.

"And Ohotto," Danu added grimly.

"I know." I sighed wearily. But for now, we had bought for ourselves and the entire Western Isles a little breathing space. Our own Raiding fleet was sorely depleted – but so, too, was Havick's armada. The heavy storms of these islands' winter would soon assail us, and that meant there would be few opportunities either for raiding or for our enemy to send his navies south after us.

We had a little time to recoup, and to rebuild.

"But we have a lot to keep us occupied now," I said, and turned to look back over the island of Malata, where Crux and several of the young dragons that had followed the Blue Sym into battle flew above the headland. Most of the dragons had returned to their atolls and home island, swearing to seek out vengeance when they were rested. But some of the youngest of dragons had been so entranced by the bravery and skill of the human Raiders that they had stayed, inquisitive of us.

It seemed that I would have my Dragon Raiders after all — only we wouldn't be mercenaries any more. With the Sea Raiders at my back, and with Crux and Danu at my side, we would be engaged in a war for the freedom of the Western Archipelago itself.

END OF DRAGON RAIDER

SEA DRAGONS TRILOGY BOOK ONE

Sea Dragons Series

Book One: Dragon Raider
(Published: March 28, 2018)

Book Two: Dragon Crown
(Published: May 30, 2018)

Book Three: Dragons Prophesy
(Published: July 25, 2018)

PS: Keep reading for an exclusive extract from **Dragons of Wild** and the next book in the Sea Dragons Trilogy, **Dragon Crown.**

THANK YOU!

I hope you enjoyed **Dragon Raider**. Please don't forget to leave a review.

Receive free books, exclusive excerpts and be kept up to date on all of my new releases, when you sign up to my mailing list at AvaRichardsonBooks.com/mailing-list

Stay in touch! I'd also love to connect with you on:

Facebook: www.facebook.com/AvaRichardsonBooks

Goodreads:
www.goodreads.com/author/show/8167514.Ava_Richardson

BLURB

In order to embrace her true nature, a young Dragon Rider must accept who she is—and where she came from.

Lila knows her people's way of life is dying, but trying to get Raiders to become Dragon Mercenaries is no easy task. Although the world around them is changing, many among the Raiders still cling to the old ways of piracy. When a desperate message arrives from the West Witches, Lila and her new friend, the eccentric, unseasoned monk Danu, must risk a mission to the island of Sebol to learn what they can of the new danger they face, a threat that menaces all the Western Isles.

To face it, Lila must leave her Raider past behind and become the leader Danu knows she was born to be. Knowing the crown of Roskilde holds the key to her destiny, and perhaps the key to defeating the deadly threat that is upon them, Lila must seize it. But to do so, Raiders and dragons will have to learn to trust each other—and Lila—as she leads the charge. Can Lila let go of fear and doubt and face the future, or will the only life she's known be destroyed?

Pre-order **Dragon Crown** at
AvaRichardsonBooks.com

EXCERPT

"Senga! Adair - Pull up!" I shouted, as the two Raiders clutched onto Kim, their sinewy Blue dragon, as she hurtled towards the sea. "What is wrong with them?"

The Blue that they were riding awkwardly flared its wings, shrieked, and tried to slow its descent. It was embarrassing all round, as Kim scraped her toes along the choppy blues, the small form of Senga was thrown forward, and Adair was flung from the blue's back, plunging into the Malata bay like a cannonball.

"Sweet Waters," I swore, turning to look at Danu at my side. We stood on the rocks above Malata harbour, trying our best to coordinate what few Dragon Raiders we had. Just learning how to talk to a group of dragons all at once was also a learning curve. Danu could hear them and talk to them with his innate dragon ability, and, through their excellent hearing, the dragons could hear my voice. Or I could convey our instructions to Crux, and hope that he would get the right message across. But these techniques were taking time to simplify. Some situations called for Danu to mentally 'shout' at all of them, and sometimes it was easier to just holler at the dragon that we wanted to listen – if they did! Del and Vaya were on Thiel, another blue and Kim's brood-brother, whilst older Martov was on the stocky Green Porax, and half a dozen other younger Raiders were still waiting on the shore for their turns on Retax, Holstag and Grithor, Ixyl, Viricalia and Lucalia.

"It's not going well, is it?" Danu said, blinking his eyes as if he had been dozing, and not paying attention. Great, I thought irritably.

"What's wrong – are we keeping you up?" I sniped at him. I knew it was unfair, but I was in a foul mood, and Senga's and Adair's antics weren't helping improve it at all. Danu had been complaining of bad dreams recently, and he was always awake and looking pale when I encountered him in the mornings. I put it down to his highly-strung nature.

All through the long, storm-lashed winter I had been encouraging the Raiders to take to the dragons that now regularly visited our skies. I hoped that their appearance meant that the dragons were willing to bond with our Raiders – or at very least that our Raiders wouldn't reach for their spears every time they saw them! Ever since the battle against Havick's forces in the fall, Malata had been locked down by the fierce winter storms that swept around the Western Archipelago; There was no raiding, and only a little fishing near the inshore waters, but that hadn't stopped some of the dragons of the Western Isles from taking an interest in us. *I spent years dreaming of this day, and got into a lot of trouble sailing to Sym's island just to be brushed off by her hatchlings,* I thought a little ruefully, *when all I needed to do was to get into a fight with Havick!*

Of course, I knew that wasn't entirely true – there was a

whole lot more going on that had made the dragons come to our aid. But when I was in a bad mood, it at least felt good to have something to grumble about.

Thank goodness someone was taking an interest, I thought, frowning as Danu's eyes glazed over once again.

"Danu! Come on – we need to get them ready before…" my anger failed me as my words trailed off into silence. Danu's eyes snapped into focus once more, shadowed and worried as he nodded. He knew as well as I what was coming. With spring would come not just fairer weather – but Havick's return to terrorize the southern half of the Western Archipelago – the Free Islands of which Malata was but one.

"I'm sorry," Danu shook his head. "I don't know what is wrong with me today…"

You're spending too long out on the harbor with all the other of my dad's sailors, I thought but didn't say. But it was true. Over the winter we'd all had our fair share of work to do – there was the wreckage on the Bone Reef that needed sorting and clearing from the battle (we'd had a lot of good bits of salvage from that!) as well as general defenses that needed replacing after the fury of the winter's waves, and before the Roskildean fleet returned. Father had his dock teams working from break of dawn until after dark, rebuilding the walls, re-caulking the hulls of the boats, and making a thousand other minor repairs – all of which Danu threw himself into, often staying for the harbor-side bonfires afterwards.

If I didn't know better, I would have said that he liked this life.

"Incoming!" Senga shouted from above, howling with laughter as Kim swooped low across the bay and extended her back legs just like a fishing eagle, to snatch Senga's spluttering idiot brother from the wave tops.

"You have to admit, that was a good move," Danu grinned.

It was. But I wasn't going to let a chance maneuver spoil my bad mood. "They're doing this on purpose. They're just playing about!" I said, incredulously. Even Kim appeared to be enjoying herself as she whistled and called to her brother Thiel to join them.

"No, wait!" I waved my hands at the other Blue, but it was already too late. He roared in his young, bullish voice, letting out a puff of flame as he and the two humans on his back dipped even closer to the bay. Thiel trailed his foreclaws along the waves, sending up huge plumes of white water over his sister.

"Bah! Right, that's it!" Senga laughed indignantly, pointing for the blue dragon underneath her to do the same.

"Not with Adair underneath you, for heaven's sake!" I groaned, watching as Kim dropped Adair in the harbour waters with a *plop* and circled back to antagonize her own brother.

"This is ridiculous." I growled at the spectacle. "I'm supposed to turn them into fighting fit Dragon Raiders, not children messing around on the backs of dragons!"

It wasn't as if we even had enough Raiders or dragons wanting to fly together. Although Sym's brood visited our skies, only the younger dragons took an interest in the day-to-day life of the Raiders, despite my cajoling. And of the Raiders? Only those around my and Danu's age showed any interest in dragons, ever since the battle for Malata when they had seen just how devastating an angry dragon could be.

But it wasn't enough, I thought. We couldn't always rely on Sym to decide to fight our battles for us, the Raider part of me thought.

"Why claim that tomorrow it will rain?" Crux's reptilian voice breathed soot into my mind.

"Huh?" I said.

"You humans. Always borrowing trouble from tomorrow, when you have enough today!" I could feel the mirth in his words. *"For now, sister-Sym fights with you, until we can find the witch that attacked the dragon newts. You have the same goals as her."*

Almost, I thought, not wanting to disagree outright with Crux, the Phoenix dragon I had bonded with and that Danu and I rode. (Who *does* ever want to argue with a dragon?) But still – I knew it wasn't enough.

"Lots of my people lost their lives during the Battle for Malata," I murmured, my eyes wavering towards where the shell of my father's flagship, the *Ariel*, was still shackled to the harbor wall, undergoing repairs from the barrages of cannon shot that had rained down on it.

"And many dragons were injured!" Crux replied indignantly. He, too, still had a ragged hole in the leather of his wings that had only closed-up a little, and still gave him trouble in strong winds.

"I know that, my dragon-brother," I sat down on the boulder feeling frustrated and useless. Danu still stood in front of me, starring glassy-eyed at the horizon as if he was asleep standing up. *Maybe I'm not the only one who is being useless,* I grumbled to myself, turning instead to Crux. "And believe me, I never want to see any of your kind hurt for us – not you, not anyone. But I'll be asking the Raiders to fight Havick's fleet – maybe not just his fleet, but also his armies as well. I don't want to ask that of any who aren't bonded."

There was a moment of silent regard from Crux, which could have meant anything. Finally he spoke. *"You are wise to want to rely on yourself, Lila Wave-Rider, and not just the good wishes of sister-Sym. But you should let the dragons of the Western Isles come to their own decisions about when and with whom they will fight. They might surprise you."*

And with that rebuke, he was gone from my mind, leaving me feeling even more stupid than before.

Just great. I really *had* annoyed a dragon.

"Woohooo!"

My grumbling thoughts were broken by another plume of water thrown up by the antics of the young dragons and few brave human Raiders on their backs. I scowled.

"Don't be so harsh on them, Lila." Danu said lightly,

rubbing his eyes as if they hurt. *Oh great, I forgot about that,* Danu can hear and speak to all dragons, and only when Crux has chosen to speak to me alone are our conversations private. But Crux didn't have the same notions of privacy that I had. Where I might have a private word with a crewmate if I wanted to tell them off – Crux would just blare it out to every dragon (and Danu) that could hear it. "At least humans and dragons are having fun together?". Danu said. "That's, uh… more than you could say four months ago."

"Four months ago we were fighting for our lives, Danu," I muttered back, wondering how to get through to them all that this was serious – it wasn't a game!

"Urk." The sound that Danu gave was very slight, and for a split second I thought he was just going to yawn – until his body thumped to the grass at my side, out cold.

Pre-order **Dragon Crown** at
AvaRichardsonBooks.com

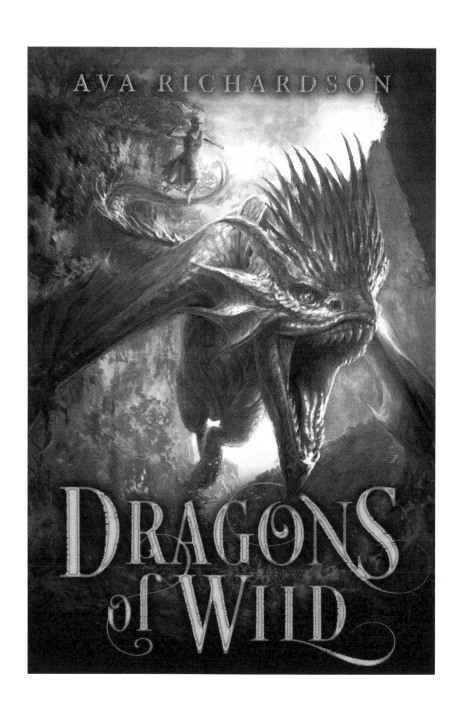

AVA RICHARDSON

DRAGONS of WILD

BLURB

The once-peaceful kingdom of Torvald has been ravaged by evil magic, forcing Riders to forget their dragons and their noble beasts to flee to the wilds. Now, anyone who dares to speak of dragons is deemed insane and put to death. Into this dark and twisted land, Saffron was born sixteen years ago. Cursed with the ability to see and talk to dragons, she's been forced into a life of exile and raised by wild dragons—secretly dreaming of a normal life and the family she lost. But as her powers become more uncontrollable, Saffron knows she must find her family before she hurts herself—or worse, her dragon clan.

Scholarly and reclusive, Bower prefers to spend his days reading about the legends of the Dragon Riders—even if being caught means death. But as the son of a noble house on the brink of destruction, it falls to him to fulfill a mysterious prophecy that promises to save his kingdom from the rule of the evil King Enric. When fate brings him into contact with Saffron, Bower gains a powerful ally—but one whose wild, volatile magic threatens their very lives.

Their friendship might just have the power to change the course of history, but when King Enric makes Saffron a tempting offer, their alliance will be shaken to the core.

Get your copy of **Dragons of Wild** at

EXCERPT

The Salamander Prophecy:

'Old and young will unite to rule the land from above. Upon the dragon's breath comes the return of the True King. It will be his to rebuild the glory of Torvald.'

(date and author unknown)

Vance Maddox

The city is in uproar. I have never seen the like—even in the old days when the wild dragons would raid from the north. Never has there been so much terror, so much bloodshed and so much anguish. Screams fill the air as people are thrown from their homes. The ringing of bells, the call of the Dragon Horns, and above it all the fire and shriek of the agonized, enraged dragons.

Another beam from the roof splinters and explodes in a shower of sparks on the flagstones at my feet. I dodge to one side. Through the gap in the tiles above I see the red and orange scales of something vast and threatening. The dragon tries once more to get at us inside—to get at me!

"Protect the prince!" I call to the guards, all of them Maddox men and women like myself: tall, light-haired and pale-skinned. They have that rangy look those of the Maddox line never seem to quite outgrow.

"Captain!" The guard chief gives me a quick, stern nod. Gone are the smiles and the fine tunics that marked this small group of bodyguards as ambassadors. We've all thrown aside finery, replacing it with the hardened steel and iron armor of my family.

A hissing roar comes from above. The red-orange dragon once again throws its weight onto the roof. We can all hear the intake of its breath like a giant bellows.

"Flame shields," I call, falling to one knee and holding up the specially-treated oval shield over my head, and not a moment too soon as a firestorm bursts into the hall from the dragon.

One of my guards is not so lucky. He screams and the stink of burning hair and flesh choke the hall. The dragon's fire is fast, incinerating him in seconds, leaving ash floating on the air.

The flames last only a brief second, but already my arm aches from the force of the dragon's breath. Maybe my brother and late father were right—how can any human live near such dangerous beasts, let alone build a city underneath their nests? This is the day that my brother, Prince Hacon Maddox, has decided to overthrow the rulers of Torvald and seize it for himself. May the storms guide me; I have sworn to help him.

"Up! Up and to the prince!" Lowering my shield, I stand and leap forward, knowing we have only a little time before the orange and red dragon will be able to breathe fire down on us again. I catch a glimpse of the charred armor of the soldier who has died, melted now into slag. I don't even know his first name.

No time for misery or cold feet now. We run through the long hall, feet pounding and armor rattling. Above us, dragons pound at the roof and walls and roar. Luckily for us, but not so lucky for Torvald royalty, this palace has been designed to withstand rogue dragon attacks. Its many halls are reinforced stone, shot through with metal bars. The king and queen's best protection will become their prison.

Turning a corner, we face the next phalanx of Torvald guards, all wearing the imperial red and purple of the Flamma-Torvald household. Scars show how many battles they have fought, and their stance is that of fighting men and women.

But Flamma-Torvald, for all of its might, for all of its fame throughout the Three Kingdoms, has grown soft. The Maddox clan hails from the furthest east some generations ago. We've fought every tribe, every bandit and every upstart warlord between here and the ends of creation. The people of the Middle Kingdom have no idea what we can do—or what strange and terrible things we have already done.

"Death to the traitors!" shouts one of Flamma-Torvald guards, throwing his longsword forward in a jab that would have skewered me were it not for my reflexes. I catch and turn the blow, spinning to step inside the man's guard.

A kick to his solar plexus sends him back. He falls,

sprawling onto the floor. My second-in-command dispatches him with a solid thrust of his blade. The battle is fast and hard. I spin and parry. I hack until my sword no longer connects with armor and tissue and bone. Half my guard has been slain by the time we're done, but all the Flamma-Torvald troops have fallen under our blades. My men and women look as though they have been drenched in red by the time that we finish, and I lean on my sword, panting.

"Sir?"

Looking up, I see one of the women of my guard pointing to the brick dust and mortar raining down from above us. She is right. We don't have time for even a breath.

Ahead of us is our goal—what looks to be the ornate, wooden double-doors of the throne room. All this carnage has been planned months in advance by Hacon, my brother by our late father—and by me as well. Hacon and the Iron Guard are to be inside the throne room, seizing the king and queen, while I lead a group of soldiers through the palace halls to deal with any Dragon Riders we might meet.

Hacon has said the people of Torvald have no chance against us. I'd thought that mostly bravado. It is only now, standing outside the doors of the throne room with blood dripping down my blades that I start to believe. How long have I heard him and father rail about the day we would take the city? I never truly believed it possible.

Even now, I can hear Hacon's shouts. 'They are abominations! Dragons are evil, vile creatures—and they have enslaved the entire Middle Kingdom through their control of House Flamma-Torvald!' Our father never tired of repeating those same rants.

Why should I feel uneasy now?

The twin doors of the throne room open. Two of the Iron Guards step out, their full-plate suits looking like the scales of dragons and gleaming in the torch light. Behind them, I see the opulent throne room of House Flamma-Torvald. A ring of the Iron Guard surrounding King Mason and Queen Druella Roule.

The carpets of the throne room seem washed in blood. Bodies of the royal guards lay hacked apart. The stench is almost unbearable. Looking at the blood, my stomach clenches and turns. It wasn't meant to be like this. It wasn't meant that so many should die. What have we done?

From behind his prison of blades, King Mason shouts, "How could you? We welcomed you to the citadel! We gave you a home!" I hear tears in his voice as well as anger.

My brother, his black hair revealed with his helmet off, walks to the window. Outside, dragons swoop through the sky as the city burns. Just a scant few years ago, we came to this citadel with our Iron Guard as a fine gift for the 'glory of the dragon-king.' King Mason had been pleased then, giving us high places at court, installing our Iron Guard at every city gate and guard house. Little did he know this day would come, when our gifts would spring into action under our orders, seizing power and delivering the city to us.

Turning away from the window, Hacon smiles. His face seems sharper than ever, narrow and long. "Call off your dragons." Hacon points his sword at the queen. "Or she will be the first to die."

"Cowards!" King Mason snarls the word. "Try me first, man to man!"

He is brave, I'll give him that. I stride to my brother's side. "Hacon, let them live. We have seized the city, and with a word from this man, the dragons will retreat. There is no need to wallow in blood."

"Silence, brother!" He slashes the air with his sword and turns to Mason again. "Call your beasts off, or your wife and child both die."

"Hacon, this wasn't part of the plan." This is a holy mission—or so I'd thought. I knew it would be ugly, but I also thought this is the right thing. "We are here to liberate the city, not kill innocent babes. Imprison these two or exile them. We have broken their power. It is enough!"

"It is never enough," Hacon hisses. "Exiles have a habit of returning, and babes grow up, brother!" With a motion and a thought, he orders the Iron Guard seize Roule, a queen no more. I knew my brother hid a cruel streak. I knew he sometimes used our family magic without wisdom or thought. But I had hoped he'd grown up over these past few months. That he had learned a little from our late father.

With a mournful call like the herons in autumn, the dragons call out. Glancing out the window, I see them disperse into the thunderclouds above the city, circling ever farther and farther. Sweat breaks out on Mason's forehead. I know he is using his unholy connection to these beasts to send them far away. Every now and then, a dragon swoops to pick up a rider —another unhappy alliance. Those that can flee are doing so, snatching handfuls of humans in their claws. But the Iron Guard raise long spears to show them never to return.

"There. It is done." Mason hangs his head and reaches out to take his wife's hand. "Leave my child and my Roule. Let us flee. You have the citadel. Take our riches, the crown, but let my family live!" He looks up, his eyes red, but his voice is firm.

Hacon's smile widens. "You really are all fools." Hacon nods. The Iron Guards lift their blades and strike down the royal couple. I turn away, sickened by the waste of it. A battle is one thing—to bring down an enemy who will take your life if you do not take his is a glorious thing. But to slaughter a man and a woman as if they were pigs meant for a feast brings no honor and tests no skill.

Hacon's voice calls me back to my duty. "The rest of you go find the babe and destroy it." The Iron Guard lacks the intelligence to question orders. They are things, soulless and mindless, made of magic and metal. They storm out, clanking, to find the royal chambers.

I turn and slam a fist into my brother's shoulder, making him stagger. "A child? You mean murder. I don't know what you have become, Hacon, but I want no part in slaughter."

Turning, I stride from the throne room. Hacon's plans and maps are in my head and I know some backstairs the servants use. I can reach the babe ahead of the Iron Guard.

The door stands open. Bursting in, I find two Dragon Riders—man and a woman—standing between me and a crib that contains the royal babe. The man draws his sword. The woman bends over the babe.

I close and bar the door behind me. A shadow dims the light from the window. Then a flash of orange and red brightens the light. Storms protect us. Is that the same red and orange beast that attacked before? Has it bonded to the child? My throat dries, but the baby gives a gurgling laugh, and I know that allowing it to be murdered is something I cannot stomach.

Glancing at the riders, I tell them, "If you seek a glorious end, it follows just behind me! But if you seek to keep the baby alive, you must flee now! Forget the child's true name! Never speak of the parents, and you may spare its life! But go–go now!" I must look—and smell—hideous, covered as I am with blood. I can only hope they will listen.

"But the king and queen?" The man's voice shakes slightly. The woman seems to size me up with a look and seizes the baby to wrap it in her cloak. The man lifts his sword and his voice firms. "Where are they? We leave together."

The heavy clank of iron boots is muffled by the door—the Iron Guards are coming. "There is no time! Just get that child somewhere safe and never, never come back, please!"

The woman nods to the other Dragon Rider.

My brother's angry words echo outside. "Break open the door! Kill my brother if he stands in your way!"

The man glances at me, eyes side. "You are Vance Maddox?"

The door at my back shudders. A powerful fist rattles it again, shaking the hinges. It won't take much for them to get through. "Does it matter? Now please. Go. Save what you can. I will hold them as long as possible."

"Come on, this one is right. The flame must live on." The woman gives me one final look and pulls on her friend's sleeve, tugging him to the window. They flee to the waiting dragon. Its lands on the rock tower, clings there as they jump for its back. For an instant, I wonder at this horrible alliance—for an instant it almost seems an amazing thing. But I cannot think that—dragons are beasts and meant to live far from all humans.

Behind me, wood splinters. Just one more blow and they will be through. Metal hinges shriek. Turning, I step back and lift my blade. Outside, the rising mournful calls of the dragons that circled the citadel reverberate, unsure, and I wonder if they understand what is going on, or do they cry just to cry.

The door shatters, and Hacon steps through the splinters. He glances once around the room. "So, my brother—you would seek to undermine my rule?"

"It is done. You have won."

"Done?" My brother swears and shakes his head. "It will

never be done until these half-humans, half-dragons never walk the land again. I will work a magic so deep and so powerful no dragon will ever remember having a human rider, and no child will ever think of dragons as anything but nightmares."

I give a shrug. "Fine. Work the magic. But the killing is done this day."

The Iron Guard step into the room. I summon the tendrils of magic within me—the ancient Maddox storm-magic that speaks to us of wolves and thunder, of the wild and forgotten places.

My brother's eyes narrow. He glances at the empty crib and back to me. "You were to be my right-hand man, my trusted adviser, my own blood who is all I can trust. Instead, you stab me in the back. You make your own plans instead of heeding mind. For this, I strip you of your name. I strip you of your family. No one shall befriend you wherever in my whole realm you go. I forbid any to feed you, to clothe you, or to shelter you. You shall be the scourge of all, and a curse I place upon your soul!"

He lifts a hand. The dark wave of his magic washes toward me. He is going to curse me into the grave, but I also have some power. I throw myself forward, the old storm magic clean and pure against his darkness. It may do me some good. But next to me, one of the Iron Guard swings a fist larger than my head. I have no time to duck the blow.

As I fall to pain and blackness, I know I have bought

myself—and the Dragon Riders some time. The child survives. The flame still burns. And I can only mutter a prayer that the flame will one day purge Hacon's black heart.

Get your copy of **Dragons of Wild** at
AvaRichardsonBooks.com